Many Arrows slept restlessly that night. An hour before dawn, he dreamed of the light. In his dream he was standing beside the horses, and the light came down the side of the hill. It passed under the horses, dancing beneath one horse's belly, then another, and finally it leaped to the back of Many Arrows' horse, the one he had taken from the white man, Cole Sykes. . . .

As soon as the light became still, it began to swell until it was the size of a man, and Many Arrows could see an old person in the middle.

"Napi!" Many Arrows cried aloud in his sleep. Red Beads stirred at his side. "Napi!" he cried again.

The old man reached out and pointed his finger at Many Arrows. "There will be war," he intoned. "Only those who prepare will be saved. Tell your young men to paint their faces and their horses and pray. There will be war!" As soon as the old man finished speaking, he disappeared, leaving only the bluish-white light, which shrank smaller and smaller.

"Napi!" called Many Arrows, bolting upright in the robe, fully awake. He repeated the name softly again, three more times until he had spoken it seven times. At the end of the seventh repetition, he threw back his head and gave the wolf howl. . . .

THE AMERICAN INDIANS SERIES

Ask your bookseller for these other titles:

COMANCHE REVENGE
CROW WARRIORS
CHIPPEWA DAUGHTER
CREEK RIFLES
CHEYENNE RAIDERS
CHEROKEE MISSION
APACHE WAR CRY

CATHERINE WEBER

A Dell/Standish Book

Published by
Miles Standish Press, Inc.
37 West Avenue
Wayne, Pennsylvania 19087

ISBN: 0-440-00590-6

Printed in the United States of America

First printing—October 1981
Third printing—November 1982

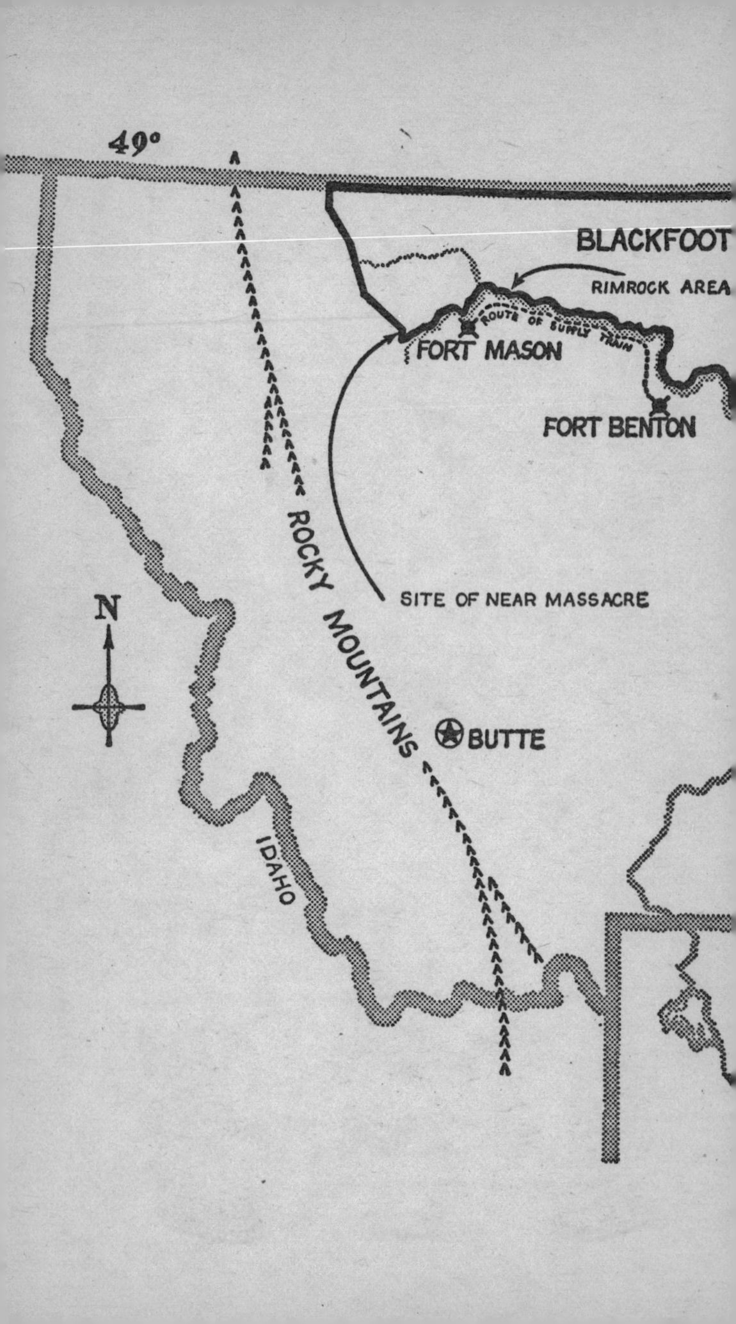
49°
BLACKFOOT
RIMROCK AREA
ROUTE OF SUPPLY TRAIN
FORT MASON
FORT BENTON
ROCKY MOUNTAINS
SITE OF NEAR MASSACRE
N
BUTTE
IDAHO

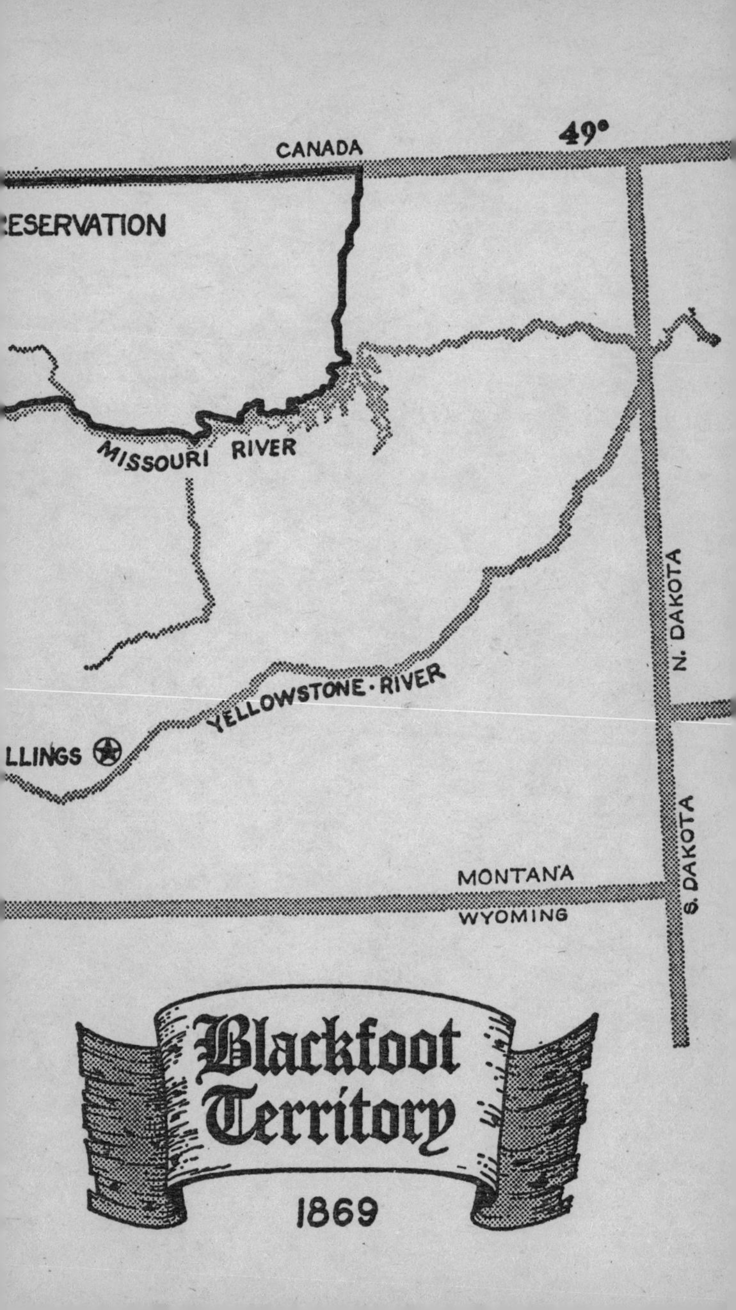
49°
CANADA
ESERVATION
MISSOURI RIVER
YELLOWSTONE·RIVER
LLINGS
N. DAKOTA
S. DAKOTA
MONTANA
WYOMING
Blackfoot
Territory
1869

You must go forward, young man—though the cost may be high—You must not sorrow for what you leave behind—for the Spirit of that which is meant to be Yours will never leave you—

ADOLF HUNGRY WOLF

Chapter 1

He stood at the window and frowned down at the street below his office, one hand on the cigar in his mouth. His other hand, doubled into a fist on his hip, held his coat away from his side so that the entire length of the heavy gold chain stretched across his vest could be seen. The air above his head was filled with smoke from the cigar.

When he looked up from the street, his eyes went to the dome of the Capitol building. An office in the Department of the Interior, Office of Indian Affairs, was not as close to the Capitol as the commissioner wanted to get. As he stared at the dome his eyes narrowed. And then he turned abruptly, strode across the room and slammed his fist down on top of his desk.

"I'll tell you how I'm going to handle it this time. The next agent I send out there is going to be the damndest, son of a bitch I can find!"

The chief clerk sat back in his chair, crossed his legs, and laced his fingers over his upraised knee. "Right now, a fighter instead of a peacemaker might not be a good idea," he said quietly.

"A fighter's all those hostiles can understand."

"That may be, Tarking, but—"

"Don't give me any reasons why it won't work.

Eight arrows in Silvers' back was murder—nothing else—and now there's a goddamned savage out there someplace with another white scalp. Well, he isn't going to have it for long. Not if I have anything to say about it."

"What you're talking about is a job for the army, not one of our agents."

"You're not thinking about this right, Madden. Think about that election coming up for a minute instead. If Grant is elected, that'll be our chance to have some real influence, won't it?"

"Yes."

"And it'll be my chance for the appointment I want, won't it?"

"Yes."

"But if this office can't handle the Indians the way it's expected to, then I'm a failure, correct? And failures don't get higher appointments, do they?"

"I can't argue with that, but so far the Blackfoot haven't given the government as much trouble as some of the others. I think the whole thing needs investigating first. Give it some time before you do anything that might stir things up more than ever."

The commissioner stalked back to the window, then turned to face his chief clerk. "I don't want an investigation. I don't want anything like that. No publicity at all. Just a new agent tough enough to handle things out there, at least until the election." He put the cigar back in his mouth. "Then, Madden, I hope to God you're in a position to take care of those Indians any way you want." He turned and stared at the Capitol again, expelling a new cloud of cigar smoke into the air above his head.

Andrew Madden crossed his legs over the other way. His face was impassive as he studied the commissioner's back. Madden was a quiet, almost laconic man. Now middle-aged, he had been chief clerk for several years. His uncle, Charles Madden, had held that position for twenty-five years, and he had brought his nephew into the department. Like his uncle, Andrew Madden held a deep-felt concern for the Indians and their future. He had been West many times and knew about reservation life firsthand. But he realized he had little chance of persuading the commissioner to take a conciliatory approach to this latest incident on the Blackfoot reservation.

He sighed. "Who are you thinking about for the job?" Madden asked, his voice as expressionless as his face.

"I don't know anything about that part of the country. You're the one that's spent time out there. Who is the meanest bastard you know about? I want the best."

"The worst is what I'd call it."

"Call it what you like. Who is it?"

"Well, I guess Cole Sykes first comes to my mind. I heard a lot about him the last time I was out there. But he's not available, and if he were, he wouldn't work for agent's wages. His kind gets top pay."

The commissioner turned to face the clerk. "Why isn't he available?"

"He's in prison—where he belongs."

"What's he in for?"

"The story I heard was he shot three men because of a card game argument in some saloon."

"He shot three men!" Tarking exclaimed.

"That's right," Madden replied, his voice tinged with disgust. "He's fast as lightning with a gun. Those men didn't have a chance."

"Sounds like just what I want. Where's he in prison?"

"Rawlins in Wyoming."

"How long is he in for?"

"I don't know. I've only heard about it by word of mouth, and I haven't paid it that much attention. But if he got out, he still wouldn't work for $1500 a year."

"What's his background?"

"It's hard to tell what the truth is and what's exaggeration about somebody like that."

"You mean he's already a legendary character?"

"I wouldn't give him that much credit."

"All right, you don't have to. What have you heard?"

"He was supposed to have gotten into the Texas Rangers when he was underage—"

"Ahhh!"

"He was big for his age. He's a big man, that's all."

"Go on."

"Well, he had no trouble holding his own in that outfit, I guess. They're all billy-be-damneds, so I've heard."

"So have I."

"After that he helped bring the longhorns up from Texas. There he got into some trouble that he couldn't fight his way out of. He drifted from Abilene into the Wyoming Territory, got into this card game I told you about, and was convicted for the killings. Makes me think Wyoming's got a future."

"So, maybe he'd like a little vacation from prison about now. Send someone to see him. Tell him I'll use my influence to gain him a furlough for as long as he can last as agent to the Blackfoot."

Madden stood up. "You can't be serious, Tarking!"

The commissioner turned and studied the ridges in the dome of the Capitol. "The hell I can't," he retorted.

Cole Sykes walked through the barred door and then stopped, staring at the man across the room while the door clanged shut behind him and a key turned in the lock. Although Andrew Madden stood up, he remained at the far side of the table and held out his hand.

The prisoner's hands were shackled together in front of him. He was as big a man as Madden had expected, broad through the shoulders, and heavily muscled from hard labor on the work gang. As he walked forward, he kept his weight on his toes, balanced and ready. His deep-set eyes were cold and hard. After one look, the chief clerk was certain Cole Sykes had earned every bit of his reputation.

Madden could tell that Sykes hadn't stopped fighting in prison. A two-inch red line ran down his cheek in front of his left ear, the kind made by the point of a knife, and one eye was swollen and bruised. What surprised Madden was that Cole Sykes was a much younger man than he had expected.

"I am Chief Clerk Andrew Madden of the Office of Indian Affairs." Madden formally introduced himself as the convict stopped across the table from him. He glanced down at Madden's extended hand without moving his own.

When Madden saw that Sykes was not going to shake his hand, he sat down and folded his arms over his chest. "I have a paper in my pocket authorizing a furlough for you." He found it hard to conceal his dislike for this man.

"You mean a pardon?"

"No, I mean a furlough."

"For how long?"

"That depends on you."

"What does that mean?"

"The Office of Indian Affairs needs a new Indian agent, and Commissioner Tarking thinks you're the kind we need."

"Why the hell me? You think I'm some kind of Indian lover?"

"Hardly."

"All right, what's the story?"

"The Blackfoot are restricted to a reservation in the Montana Territory. Thousands of square miles, almost all of the northern part of the Territory east of the Rockies, is Blackfoot land."

"I know, I know," Sykes cut him short. "You mean there's no agent up there for that whole damn reservation?"

Andrew Madden frowned. He took a deep breath and let it out slowly. "Considering the fearful reputation the Blackfoot have always had among the other Indians, as well as whites, they've accepted the idea of a reservation exceedingly well. However, last month the agent appointed by the territorial governor was killed."

"Who killed him?"

"As far as we know, the Indians. He was found beside his horse with eight arrows in his back and his scalp gone."

"Christ! Now I can figure it. Somebody thinks that's a good way to get rid of me, too." Cole Sykes turned toward the barred door.

"No, that's not the reason." Madden stood up. "Commissioner Tarking asked me who was the toughest fighter around, and I told him you were as far as I've heard."

Sykes stopped and looked across his shoulder at Madden. "So it was your idea?"

"No. I disagree with Tarking. I don't think we need someone like you up there. I'm carrying out orders, that's all."

"What's wrong with someone like me?"

"I only know your reputation, of course, but I'm sure you know what that is. A troublemaker. And a troublemaker isn't my idea of a good agent."

Cole Sykes turned to face Madden again. "Let's see that agreement," he said.

Chapter 2

Miss Patricia Ashley walked out of the colonel's house and down the steps to the side of the buckboard. She put her hands firmly on her hips while her wide green eyes traveled disdainfully over the weatherbeaten rig. From beneath her broad-brimmed straw hat her thick chestnut hair tumbled about her shoulders. A half smile played across her well molded face. The single seat on the rig, fastened across an open row of slats that substituted for springs, appeared anything but comfortable, and no cover of any kind went over the seat. A man climbed down from the buckboard and walked around the back to where she stood. She sighed as she thought of the different carriages they had at home, all the best of their kind.

"Well, Mr. Ross, and where did you find this?" she smiled. It would be good to get away from the fort for a short time, no matter how hard the ride.

"Gaines had it down at the livery stable in town," replied Ross. Somewhere in his middle years, Sam Ross served as Fort Mason's scout and interpreter since the fort had been built. He dressed in the fringed buckskins of a trapper and wore moccasins that made no sound as he walked.

"He had to dust it off good, too. Doesn't get much use around here."

"No, I suppose not." Tricia accepted the scout's help into the buckboard. She settled her skirts into place around her and turned her head so that her hat shaded her face from the sun. Ross walked to the far side again and climbed up beside her.

"You don't know how hard I had to talk to persuade Uncle John to let me do this," she remarked, looking ahead at the fort's gate as the scout picked up the reins and let out the brake.

He glanced at her without speaking.

"I do think that the danger out here has been greatly exaggerated in the East. Don't you agree?"

"Well, I guess that'd be likely. Seems like the farther a story goes, the bigger it gets."

"There's certainly been no trouble since I've been here."

"Most people are resting easier now that they got the Blackfoot agreeing to stay on the reservations."

"Most people? What are the others worried about? All the Indians I've seen since I've been here are quite peaceful. They certainly don't go running about with—what is it called? War paint?" At the scout's nod she continued. "With war paint on their faces, brandishing their bows and arrows. The ones I see look quite dull, in fact. There's no expression on their faces at all."

Sam Ross glanced at her once more. He remained silent, staring ahead as they drove out between the two guard towers beside the gate.

The road outside the fort led directly to the bridge that spanned the river separating the fort from the town. Before he started across the bridge, Ross pulled aside and waited for a wagon already on the bridge and coming in their direction to finish crossing. Then he turned back into the road and urged the horses onto the planks. At the same time a horse and rider appeared at the other side of the bridge and again the scout pulled aside and waited.

The rider was an Indian, a tall man who sat erect in the saddle. His eyes looked straight ahead, appearing not to notice anyone else, least of all the two waiting for him to cross the bridge. He rode slowly forward, his bronzed shoulders and chest gleaming in the hot afternoon sun. His shining black hair, long and loose around his shoulders, was smoothed around his face, and the leather cord around it had a number of objects hanging from the back that Tricia was unable to name. They seemed like pieces of feathers and skins. Although his chest was bare, he wore full-length leggings fringed down the sides and decorated with wide bands of colored beads. He carried a rifle across the saddle in front of him, and his bay horse was as large and powerful-looking as its rider.

As the Indian passed the wagon, Ross raised his hand and said a few words in a language that Tricia could not understand. The Indian also raised his hand and rode past them without a word.

Tricia turned and looked questioningly at the scout as he started the team ahead. "Why on earth did you stop and wait for him? He's only an Indian."

Sam Ross turned away from her and spit at a white rock in the road, and then he stared ahead over the horses' ears. "That was Many Arrows," he replied in way of explanation.

"Am I supposed to know what difference that makes?" she inquired as she glanced behind her at the Indian's back. Then she looked at her companion again.

"He's Flying Hawk's son," Ross continued. "Flying Hawk is the head chief of all the Blackfoot around here, and Many Arrows is the war chief in Flying Hawk's band."

"Well, how do you know? I don't see how you can tell them apart."

When Ross remained silent, she looked behind her one more time. Suddenly she laughed and turned in the seat to face the direction of the fort. "Do you see what Uncle John has done? He's sent a patrol with us. So that's why he finally decided to let me see the town."

A detail of a half-dozen soldiers was following them, and the young corporal in the lead smiled and waved as soon as he saw Tricia's eyes on him. After a moment, still laughing, she turned in the seat and looked ahead at the town.

Mason City had only one main street, and as the buckboard jounced onto it, Ross leaned forward and put his hand down to his rifle behind his feet. Then he straightened up and glanced around them. A moment later a gun fired somewhere in the distance. Ross started and looked toward the sound as though waiting for something.

Beside him, Tricia shivered slightly. She gripped the seat of the buckboard and tried to stifle her apprehension. After all, the army detail was not far away. But she could not help thinking of the stories she had heard of the untamed West. The tales of men who settled their differences with gunfights in the streets and saloons of lawless towns.

She turned to Ross. "Have you ever seen a gunfight?" she asked tentatively.

"Not too many times."

"But you have?"

"Do you see that man standing over there in front of the blacksmith's shop?"

Tricia leaned forward to see where he was pointing. "The tall one with the leather vest?"

"That's the one."

"Yes, I see him. What about him?"

"You could learn all you want to know about gunfights from him."

"Why?" She turned to stare behind Ross as the buckboard rattled by. For a long moment, she looked into the iciest blue eyes she had ever seen, eyes that met hers and held them, startling her so that she gazed over her shoulder for longer than was proper. In that time, she saw that the man's face was gaunt and clean-shaven, and pale as if he had not been in the sun recently. His dusty black hat was set firmly forward to shade his face. His clothes looked worn and his boots were scuffed. A leather holster, the butt of a gun protruding from its top, hung from his belt and was tied to his right thigh by a leather thong. But it was his unblinking eyes that riveted her gaze as they seemed to bore into her very being.

"Oh!" She drew in her breath as she turned abruptly and stared at the street in front of her without seeing it. "Who is he?"

"You were looking at Cole Sykes. He's a gunfighter, and most people figure he's the best there is with that Colt revolver he's got strapped to his leg."

She glanced over her shoulder again and gasped when she saw that his eyes were still on her. "I don't think he needs a gun," she said, putting one hand up to her throat as she straightened in the seat. "He could stare you to death!"

Sam Ross did not respond. He suddenly swerved

the team to one side and headed for the edge of the street.

"Where are you going?" cried Tricia.

"I'm going to turn around as soon as I can," he told her, his eyes on a group of men lounging in front of the Trapper's Last Chance Saloon.

"But we haven't gone all the way through town. I want to see all of it," she protested.

"There's going to be trouble."

"How can you tell?"

"By the way those men are looking at Sykes."

Tricia frowned as the rig jerked to a stop and opened her mouth to protest again. At the same time one of the men stepped out in front of the others and started down the sidewalk, looking across the street at the blacksmith's shop while he walked. The other men stepped into the street and followed a few steps behind. The man in the lead had a gun at his side, but there was no thong tying it down like the one around Sykes' thigh.

As soon as the man began walking, Sam Ross snapped the reins along the backs of the horses and hustled the team into the open space between the two nearest buildings. When they came out behind the buildings, he started whipping the horses through an empty lot in the direction of the bridge.

"Wait!" Tricia exclaimed, "I—" As they jolted across the rough ground, she grabbed for the handrail beside her. It was all she could do to stay on the seat.

Ross kept the rig bouncing along until there was a large building between them and the gunfighter. Then he slowed and glanced behind him, listening again.

It was sweltering in Hugh Gaines' blacksmith shop. While Cole Sykes waited for his horse to be shod, he stepped to the doorway and looked slowly along the street in both directions. It wasn't much of a town, he thought. It had a long way to go to live up to a name like Mason City. One thing was sure, they had built a good bridge so they could get to the fort fast enough when they needed protection. He assumed that the buckboard had come from the fort. He smiled to himself when he thought of the handsome young woman who had stared so boldly at him. "Who the hell is she, anyway?" he muttered.

Standing there, he reached down and caressed the gun at his hip, lifted it slightly and then let it settle back into place, ready. Sykes spotted the group of men standing in the street, two doors from him. There were five of them, and all five faced his way.

As soon as Sykes turned toward them, the man in the middle of the group stepped out ahead of the others, looking arrogantly in Sykes' direction. The man stood with his hands on his hips until Sykes looked past him. Quickly, he turned and said something over his shoulder to the others as he started walking along the other side of the street. The others followed.

"Christ," Sykes blurted out as he stepped onto the sidewalk to face the man. Here it was, coming already. The last killings had put him in prison, and he could go back there fast enough, too.

Cole Sykes' usual expression was cold and hard, but as he set his jaw, waiting for the trouble he knew was coming, the lines in his face deepened and his face went bleak. He stood without moving. His eyes, deep in the shadow of his hat, narrowed and held steady on the man swaggering ahead of the group.

A moment later the man veered and headed across the street, while the men behind him quickly separated and spread out along the road.

"I'll be damned if that ain't a fancy way to wear a gun," called the man derisively as he sauntered close enough to Sykes to be in easy range for a handgun. "Where'd a cowboy like you learn to do that?" The man's eyes, filled with contempt, traveled slowly up and down Sykes' frame. Sykes wore the clothes of the long cattle drive, a sun-faded blue shirt, worn denim pants, high-heeled boots with spurs and a broad-brimmed hat. Over his shirt he wore a leather vest, short enough to stay clear of his gun in case he needed to make a fast draw.

The man facing him was dressed in a dark suit, new looking and expensive.

Sykes could tell from the man's expression that there was time yet, and he looked at each of the other men in turn, deliberately meeting their stares. Then he turned back in the direction of the blacksmith's shop.

"Hold it, cowboy! I'm not through talking to you yet." The man spit the words out in a bold challenge.

Cole Sykes turned slowly to face him. "Yes, you are," he said, watching the man's eyes. His voice was steady and as icy as the expression on his face. "Either draw that gun or go back to your drinking until you're brave enough. I've got better things to do than stand out here in the sun waiting for you to make up your mind."

"Watch out, stranger," called one of the other men as he moved farther out of line from the challenger. "You don't know who you're talking to, do you?"

Sykes had his eyes on the man in the street and did not answer the question. The man confronting Sykes took another step closer. Then suddenly the man crouched, holding both hands ready at his sides, glaring at Sykes.

"What are you waiting for?" asked Sykes contemptuously.

In a flash, the man grabbed for his gun. But before he had it halfway out, Sykes' bullet slammed into his shoulder and the gun dropped into its holster as the man staggered backwards and slapped his hand to his shoulder.

Sykes aimed his gun across the street until he was sure that none of the other men intended to take up the fight. He lowered the Colt to his side and slid it into his holster.

When Sykes' hand was away from his gun, a man with a full, black beard stepped cautiously toward the injured man. His narrow eyes glinted. "Come on, Littan," he called, stretching out an arm, "you can walk, can't you?"

The man in the street cursed as he turned away and staggered toward the others, blood seeping from his shoulder wound.

Chapter 3

A half-hour after the buckboard returned to the fort, Cole Sykes rode in through the gate. He reined in his horse and looked around. This fort had no outside walls, and was several times larger in area than Mason City. In the center of the fort was a large, grassy area, probably the parade ground. A two-story stone building extended along one side of the open space. From the number of men on the wooden porch and the full-length balcony above the porch, Sykes could tell it was the main barracks for the troops. At the far side he made out several smaller buildings and a row of tents, and at the far end stood several single-family houses.

Sykes reined his horse to the right and trotted past the trader's store and several other support buildings until he reached the large one at the end with a flagpole in front of it. Pulling up at the hitching rail in front of the building Sykes swung down, tied his horse and stepped onto the porch that ran the length of the building.

Sykes asked a passing soldier where he could find Colonel Forbes. The soldier pointed to a door at one end of the porch, and Sykes walked toward it. The door was open and he stepped through it into a hallway leading to the back of the building.

As he made his way along the hall, a young woman opened a door at its far end.

I was right, she does live here, Sykes thought, as he recognized the same open face and large clear eyes that had looked so long at him. Her shining hair was caught behind her head with a ribbon and her white muslin dress gracefully fell around her slim figure.

As soon as Tricia saw him, she stepped back, her eyes wide. "Oh," she exclaimed, "then you weren't—"

Sykes continued toward her. He removed his hat, ignoring the startled expression on her face. "Is that Forbes' office?"

She stepped all the way through the doorway before she motioned behind her. "Uncle John is in here," she indicated. At the same time a young man in uniform appeared in the doorway.

"You want to see Colonel Forbes?" he asked.

"Yes, tell him the new Indian agent wants to see him."

"Yes, sir."

As the soldier turned around, Sykes glanced over his shoulder at the woman still standing behind him. As soon as he looked at her, she walked quickly down the hallway to the front door, holding her skirts off the floor with both hands as she went out the door.

"The colonel will see you, sir," the soldier announced.

Colonel Forbes rose and walked around his desk as Sykes entered the room. He extended his hand. "I'm Colonel Forbes. We've been waiting for you, although we didn't know . . ." his eyes appraised Sykes' clothes before he went on, "who it would be. You got here as fast as the mail with the notification of your appointment."

As the colonel turned from Sykes, he motioned in

the direction of the man sitting in front of the one window in the room. At the same time, the man stood up and walked toward Sykes, offering his hand.

"This is Sam Ross, one of our scouts," introduced Forbes. "Don't know how we'd deal with these savages if we didn't have him. Sam speaks their language in more ways than one. You're free to make use of him if you need him. We're all after peace out here, if we can get it." The colonel tucked in his chin and swallowed before he went on. "And if not, we're damned ready to do our job."

"This is a different kind of fort," Sykes began as the colonel gestured to a chair facing his large, polished desk and then seated himself. Sykes glanced at the window and shifted his chair so that his side was to the door and he faced the window.

Forbes noticed the precaution and laughed, "You have no one to be afraid of here." Turning to the scout, he nodded, "Isn't that right, Ross? We've made this the safest place in a thousand miles, haven't we? And without any walls to hide behind."

The scout exchanged looks with Sykes and said nothing.

"Well, Sykes," continued the colonel, seeming not to notice the silence of both men. "I suppose you want to get to work right away. Where do you plan to set up your agency?"

"Where was the last one?"

"Right here in the fort, of course. Safest place, like I just said."

Sam Ross cleared his throat. "Didn't do Silvers all that much good."

The colonel frowned at the scout. "Sykes, I'm sure you know Silvers was the previous agent. What happened to him was his own fault. I told him not to go out there alone." Colonel Forbes continued to face Ross. "How many times did you hear me tell him that, Sam?"

"Plenty," affirmed Ross as he got up, walked to the window, and stood there with his back to the room.

The colonel laughed as he looked at Sykes. "Sam and I don't agree on everything, especially about the Blackfoot. But then he has his own reasons, and his reasons are different from mine, that's all. Now Sykes, I'm prepared to offer you Silvers' old quarters here, and you might as well get moved in this afternoon and then plan to have dinner with me tonight. We want to welcome the new agent here properly."

Sykes stared at Ross' back. "It won't take me all afternoon to unload my horse."

"You travel light, do you?" asked Forbes.

"I can use Ross for the afternoon, if you can spare him. I'd like to have him show me around."

"Around where? Now don't you start off on your own, too. We lose too many Indian agents that way." The colonel stood up as Sam Ross turned away from the window. "Listen, Sykes, I don't want you going any place without at least a dozen men with you. I can spare them. They're just getting lazy sitting around here all the time."

Sykes met the scout's eyes, and Ross nodded.

"We're not going that far," replied Sykes. "I'll let you know when I need an escort."

"Sykes, don't be a fool," demanded the colonel, starting around the end of his desk.

"What time is that dinner?" asked Sykes. "I said I wasn't going that far."

"How'd that shooting come out over there?" Ross

nodded in the direction of the town as their horses trotted out through the gate of the fort.

Sykes looked steadily ahead of him. "You figure I'd try for a killing first thing?"

"No, just curious, that's all."

"He gave me plenty of time."

"None of that bunch would have been missed."

"You know them?"

"Sure. They've been hanging around here off and on since the vigilantes got busy down at Virginia City. If I had a choice, I'd take my chances with the Indians any day."

"They don't look like miners. What do they do?"

"Hard to say. I've never seen them working."

As the two men approached the bridge, they rode by Many Arrows, sitting atop his horse beside the road. Silent, unmoving, the Indian did not look directly at them, and the scout gave no indication that he recognized him as they passed.

Sykes turned and stared at the Indian for a moment. "That one of the Blackfoot?"

"Yes, that's Many Arrows. He's Flying Hawk's son."

"You know him?"

"Sure."

"You didn't say anything to him."

"He showed me he didn't want me to."

"How?"

Ross glanced at the other man. "You haven't spent a hell of a lot of time around Indians, have you?"

"No."

"How'd you get picked for the job then, if you don't mind my asking?"

Sykes eased himself forward in the saddle and then settled back again before he reached to the pocket under his vest and pulled out a sack of tobacco and a book of papers. He made a trough out of one of the papers and tapped tobacco into it, watching his hands in silence as he worked.

While Ross waited for an answer, he spit over the far side of his horse and shifted the wad of tobacco in his mouth.

Tucking the sack and papers back in his shirt pocket, Sykes licked along one side of the paper and rolled it into a tube. Then he withdrew a match from his vest pocket and snapped it into flame with his thumbnail. When he had the cigarette going, he left it in the corner of his mouth, squinting around the smoke as he broke the match in two and flipped it away. "I guess the commissioner wanted someone that wasn't going to turn his back and get it full of arrows," he replied finally, the cigarette dangling from his lips.

Sam Ross studied Sykes' profile for a moment. "If you get shot first like Silvers did, it won't make a hell of a lot of difference about the arrows."

Sykes pulled the cigarette from his mouth and blew out the smoke. "I hadn't heard he was shot first," he said, turning toward the scout.

Ross spit again and wiped the back of his hand across his mouth. "I saw the body." He looked straight ahead, his eyes slightly narrowed, until they entered the main street of the town. Then he turned and met the gunfighter's eyes. "He wasn't killed by a Blackfoot."

Sykes shoved the cigarette into his mouth and left it there while he moved his eyes over both sides of the street ahead of him. He twisted in the saddle and glanced behind him. "You must be a damned Indian yourself, if you think you know that much about them."

"My wife was a Blackfoot," Ross revealed in an even tone. "She and my children died from the smallpox that wiped out half of the tribe back in the fifties."

"Sorry," said Sykes, without emotion.

They rode in silence after that. Sykes continued to look around him as they cantered through the town. He sat easy in the saddle, moving in harmony with the motion of his horse, his jaw set, his mouth in a straight line, his eyes watchful, giving no sign of what he was thinking.

When he and Ross reached the far side of town, they headed north along the road beside the river. "How do you know it wasn't a Blackfoot that killed Silvers. That one we saw had a damned good gun. It looked like a Henry to me."

"Because whoever shot him left Silvers' gun and his horse. All they took was his scalp, and they did a clumsy job of that."

"Go on."

"A Blackfoot doesn't go on the warpath for the same reasons you or I do. He goes for the honors it can bring him, personal honors, that he'll have for the rest of his life. The highest honors come from the most dangerous kind of fighting, close to the enemy, hand-to-hand. Getting the enemy's weapon is the number-one honor of all. Getting a scalp ranks second-rate because someone else could have made the kill. Taking a horse is even lower, although it's usually what they're after. Taking horses is war to them, not stealing. Anyway, Silvers' horse was left ground-reined beside him, and his rifle was still in the saddle boot on his horse. Just killing a man is a pretty minor honor, Sykes. That's because it can be done from a distance. And why the hell would an Indian waste eight arrows, all of them close together like it was done standing over the body, on a dead man? There'd be no honor to that at all."

"With a name like Many Arrows . . ."

"Yeah, sounds suspicious, doesn't it? But just think about that one a minute."

Sykes glanced behind them. "He isn't following us anymore." He had known for some time that Many Arrows was riding behind them, even though he couldn't see the Indian.

"He probably took the shortcut now that he can see the way we're headed."

"Where are we headed?"

"This road will turn into a trail on the other side of the river, and then it'll take us to where Flying Hawk's band is camped. I figured that was where you wanted to go."

"It'd be a good idea, wouldn't it, to go there first thing?"

"Sure. He's the head chief of all the bands here. He can call a council, and the other chiefs will come from all over the reservation. Saves you from having to go to them."

They stayed on the road until it turned down to a shallow place in the river where they could ford it. Ross led the way as they splashed into the water and urged their horses across.

As they emerged on the far side, the road that had been wide enough for wheeled vehicles had become little more than a trail with branch trails radiating from both sides.

Ross turned his horse sharply into a narrow trail nearest the water and Sykes followed. He reckoned they had ridden about a mile when he saw the haze of smoke drifting over the rise before them. Sykes spurred his horse up the incline and pulled up short. Scores of tepees were clustered in the shallow valley below, the smoke from the open tops of the buffalo-hide lodges curling upward. In the stillness of the late summer day, Sykes could hear dogs barking and children playing.

"Move in slow," Ross called, as he signaled Sykes to follow him down the hill. As they came in full sight of the encampment, the sound of the voices gradually died out and only the dogs continued barking.

"Looks like Many Arrows got here first," Sykes remarked. He eased forward in the saddle a few inches and dropped his right hand over his gun. His impassive face resembled those of the Indian braves ahead of him at the edge of the encampment. When they made no greeting, neither did he. The ranks of the silent braves parted slowly to let the riders pass. Sykes noted the quivers of arrows slung over their shoulders and the short, sturdy bow each man held.

"That's Flying Hawk's tepee there in the middle," Ross pointed to a huge lodge. Several poles poked from its top, and the hide around the smoke hole was dark from the smudge of many fires. The figure of a large hawk, its wings spread, was painted on one side. A wide bank of black circled the bottom of the dwelling. Its opening, like all the others, faced east.

"How much of what I say will they understand?" inquired Sykes as the two dismounted.

"More than they'll let you know," Ross answered.

They walked in silence toward the chief's lodge. Suddenly, a man stepped through the opening and stood to one side of it, facing them. Ross raised his hand in greeting and Sykes followed his example. Without speaking, the Indian turned and ducked inside the tepee. Ross stepped aside to let Sykes enter first.

Once inside, Sykes paused a moment, letting his eyes get used to the sudden dimness. On one side of the fire that glowed in the center of the lodge, a half dozen braves sat cross-legged. Their naked chests, painted with symbols and designs, gleamed in the firelight. Some wore eagle feathers, others had beads and quills and tufts of fur in their long, loose hair. One powerfully built man wore a headdress of buffalo horns and ermine skins that dangled to his broad shoulders. Opposite the half circle of braves sat two women, their legs tucked up under their doeskin dresses. Many Arrows was not in sight.

Sykes waited, standing with Ross near the women. His eyes roamed over the round buffalo-hide shields and the long lances with their fur and feather decorations that were stacked against the walls of the lodge. He guessed that once the scalps of Indian and white foe alike had dangled from their shafts.

Suddenly, the Indian with the buffalo-horn headdress raised his hand and motioned to Sykes to sit beside him. Chief Flying Hawk looked straight at Sykes, his broad face with its large, curved nose betrayed no sign of welcome or friendship. Ross nudged Sykes forward, and the agent stepped to the left around the fire, passing directly between the fire and Flying Hawk. The chief stiffened and his deep-set black eyes narrowed. The braves stirred slightly.

Sykes eased himself down, crossing his legs. As he settled into place, he felt a tension in the lodge. Something was wrong. He had done something wrong. He felt it, even though the faces around him remained impassive.

At once he looked to Ross, standing inside the opening. The scout waited there until the chief beckoned to him. Ross circled around behind the Indians, even though they had to lean forward to let him pass.

As Ross sat down at his side, Sykes swore silently,

staring at the scout until Ross turned to meet his eyes. "After this you take the lead," growled Sykes, keeping his voice as low as he could.

The scout nodded almost imperceptibly. A look of approval entered his eyes as he looked past Sykes to Chief Flying Hawk, who gazed into the fire in front of him.

After his initial blunder, Sykes kept his eyes on Ross and imitated his actions. Even if he did not know the reasons for the rituals, he was determined to follow the etiquette.

Flying Hawk filled a long-stemmed pipe with tobacco and lit the bowl with a stick from the fire. He took several puffs before he passed the pipe to Sykes. A pungent odor drifted into Sykes' nostrils. As Sykes reached for the pipe, he looked at Ross.

"Do the same and then give it to me," whispered the scout.

The pipe went to each of the men in turn until it reached the man nearest the opening to the tepee. It was then passed back from hand to hand to the chief. Flying Hawk took another puff and then, to Sykes' surprise, handed it to the older of the two women sitting opposite him. She was about the age of the chief. Her hair fell in two long braids down her back. To Sykes, she looked rather squat and thickset. But her shapeless dress was elegantly beaded and fringed. The woman puffed on the pipe as the men had done, but she handed it directly back to the chief, ignoring the younger woman beside her.

Sykes studied the young woman. He hadn't paid any attention to her before, but when she lifted her head to watch the pipe, he could see the even outline of her features. When she turned toward him, her eyes, dark and luminous from the fire, met his for an instant.

The pipe passed around the circle twice again, each man and the woman solemnly puffing in turn. After the second round, Flying Hawk turned to Ross and spoke in low tones for several moments. Ross responded quietly as the chief carefully refilled the pipe. Sykes was growing restless and somewhat irritable. His legs were cramped and his throat burned from the acrid smoke. He had come here to talk to Flying Hawk, to sound him out, and here they all sat, passing a foul pipe back and forth. The chief took a last puff and exchanged a few more words with the scout. Then abruptly, Flying Hawk began to clean the pipe, signaling that the meeting had ended.

Ross touched Sykes' arm and the two men stood. Outside the lodge their horses waited where they had left them, their reins dropped on the ground. As they mounted up, Sykes became aware of the bustling camp life. Where before there had been silence as they rode in, now the children shouted and played. The women gathered in front of their lodges, preparing the evening meal. Bending over what looked like skin pouches suspended from poles, some were stirring the contents, while others dropped hot stones from a nearby fire into the pouches. A savory steam rose from the cooking and wafted through the camp.

As soon as the riders started up the hill, Sykes turned to the scout and glared. "All right. I should have waited inside the door, but what did I do wrong when I was sitting down?"

"You walked between the chief and the fire."

"Christ, if that's so important, couldn't you have told me about it before we got there?"

Ross ran one hand down his thigh and back again, and then he turned and grinned at Sykes. "Now how would I have figured Cole Sykes wanted advice from me?"

Sykes glanced behind him at the Indian camp still in sight. "Well, I do," he claimed.

"All right, then. Quit looking back as though you don't trust them."

Sykes straightened in his saddle and frowned at the hillside ahead of him. After a moment he jabbed his spurs into his horse and loped the rest of the way up the hill, his back square to the encampment.

When he was over the top and out of sight of the camp, he slowed and waited for Ross to catch up to him.

"Is that the same advice you gave Silvers?" he accused, reaching to his pocket for his tobacco sack as he cast a long look over his shoulder.

"No," Ross chuckled softly. "Silvers never asked advice from me."

Cole Sykes rolled a cigarette and smoked in silence. His eyes continually searched the landscape as he rode. It was one habit he didn't intend to give up. Ross might trust these savages, but he, Sykes, didn't. He was angry about the blunder he had made with Flying Hawk and annoyed because the chief had virtually ignored his presence at the meeting. He had no intention of being pushed aside again.

He turned to Ross. "What did Flying Hawk say about a council of the chiefs?"

"He agreed to it finally. At first he said it was too late, the summer's over. That's when they usually have their councils. Now everyone's finding a place to camp for the winter. And it's my guess he doesn't want the others using up the grazing land he wants to use for his own band this winter. But he said he'd call them in and see how many would come."

"When?"

"Be a couple of weeks before all of them can get here."

Sykes nodded. The two rode silently until they reached the river. The trail had worn down the river bank above the ford so that the bank was nearly level with the water. Trotting through the cut to the edge of the water, Sykes scanned the banks above and behind him.

They reached the water before he saw them. A dozen yards away, silhouetted against the setting sun like huge dark statues, posed six mounted braves. Many Arrows had placed himself at the highest point on the bank, with the five others strung out in a line behind him. Unmoving, erect, the braves sat on their horses, their gaze turned partly away, as if not deigning to acknowledge the two men below them.

The braves were young men, broad-shouldered and sinewy. Each held the rawhide reins of his horse tautly in one hand. Cradled in the other arm was a bow and arrow, the arrow pointed directly toward the river.

Sykes jerked his horse around and faced squarely into the arrows. The hair on the back of his neck rose involuntarily. Moving slowly, his eyes on Many Arrows, Sykes reached to his hip and pulled his revolver. Holding it in front of him in both hands, he glanced down as he rubbed one hand over it. Then he looked up at the warriors again and leaned his arms across his saddlehorn, the gun pointed at the ground, ready.

"Ross," he ordered sharply, "you tell those bastards up there—"

"Careful, Sykes!" warned Ross, as he pulled his horse up beside his companion.

"You tell that son of a—chief up there that this

gun has six bullets in it, enough for all of them, and I'll sure as hell get a few shots off before they can get me."

"Ease off, I say!"

Sykes gazed steadily at Many Arrows. "Let's hear you tell them," he barked at Ross.

"Goddamn it!" cursed Ross. He looked up at Many Arrows and began speaking, slowly and clearly. At one point he gestured in Sykes' direction.

Many Arrows did not appear to be listening. He did not respond when the scout finished speaking, even when one of the other warriors said something to the war chief.

"Let's go," advised Ross, turning his horse into the water without looking again at either Sykes or the Indians.

Cole Sykes stared for another minute at the Indians still motionless above him. His face a harsh mask, he shoved his revolver back into its holster, picked up his reins and spurred his horse into the water. He gazed stonily ahead while he crossed the river.

They rode without speaking until they were nearly to the town, and then Ross turned to face him. "You made an enemy there," he stated. "Why did you have to pull your gun? They weren't painted for war. They wouldn't have started anything."

Sykes replied grimly, "He was already an enemy, Ross. I can tell that much about any man."

Chapter 4

Many Arrows picketed his horse and left it to graze outside the encampment. Striding between the tepees to his father's lodge in the center of the circle, he ran his fingers through his flowing hair and pushed it back over his shoulders. As he passed his own lodge, a small boy ran out, calling to him. Many Arrows scooped up the child and hoisted him above his head, holding him at arm's length. He smiled broadly at the squeals of his son as he tossed the boy into the air, caught him and lowered him suddenly.

The child cried out as his feet hit the ground. "Do it again!" he begged, holding both arms upward.

"No. Go and play. I have work to do."

"Do it again!"

"No, I said. Go on now."

"Do it—"

"Go on, I said." He shoved First Moon in the direction of his own tepee and continued toward Flying Hawk's lodge.

Many Arrows stepped through the opening and saw several men seated inside. When Flying Hawk saw the scowl on Many Arrows' face, he tapped the tobacco out of his pipe, and the men stood up and filed out one at a time past Many Arrows.

Flying Hawk carefully laid the pipe aside and motioned for his son to approach. The young war chief stepped forward and waited until he was asked to join his father at the fire. Flying Hawk nodded, and Many Arrows sat down beside him.

"What troubles you, my son?" he asked quietly.

"That new agent—he is an enemy. He will cause trouble for all of us." Many Arrows hissed the words.

"How do you know? When he was here he showed us that even though he did not know our ways, he was willing to learn them."

"I took the warriors, Runs-at-Night and the others, to see him. We stopped at the river bank. We said nothing, we were only watching, but he took the short gun from his side and threatened us with it."

"How did he threaten you? Did he point the gun at you?"

"No," he hesitated, "the man did not point the gun, but he told Sam Ross to say to us that there were six bullets in the gun, one for each of us."

"Why did he do that? He is not a man to toy with a gun for no reason. Anyone can see that. What were you doing with your weapon, Many Arrows?"

"We were on the bank above where the river is shallow and the Under Water Persons let us ride through. We did nothing, we said nothing to provoke him."

"Where were your arrows?"

"We held them as always in front of us."

"Where were they pointed?"

"Down at the river."

"Could he have mistaken them as aimed at him?"

"Anyone could see that we were not prepared for war. Our faces were not painted," he added angrily, "as they will be the next time we see him."

Many Arrows was taller than his father, but he never felt above him, especially when Flying Hawk looked at him with the expression that shone in his eyes at Many Arrows' last words.

"We will seek more wisdom before you do that." His voice neither commanded nor questioned.

"Yes," agreed Many Arrows, "I will go with you to talk to Walks-on-Crooked-Leg. Did he see the white man?"

"He was in the lodge with the others."

Flying Hawk led the way to the tepee of the medicine-pipe man, who was standing outside, talking to Runs-at-Night and Kills Bear. From the sound of the young warriors' voices, Many Arrows knew what they were discussing.

The younger men stepped aside as Flying Hawk approached, and arranged themselves on either side of Many Arrows while Flying Hawk spoke to the medicine man.

"You have heard of the insult to my son and the others?" the chief asked.

"Yes." The medicine-pipe man nodded his head in reply. The knot of hair coiled over his forehead, the symbol of his position, bobbed up and down. He was an old man, his face deeply lined with the years. The rest of his hair fell in three braids, one in front of each ear, and the other down his back. A bear-claw necklace hung around his neck, and when he moved, the bells tied to his shirt tinkled in harmony with his motion.

"But I do not know yet what was meant by it," he cautioned, watching Flying Hawk's face.

"You will find out?" asked Many Arrows.

"Yes, but it is nearly time to eat. First I will tell my wife to prepare more food so that you may feast with me, and after that we will sing and pray together until we have the answer."

"Good," agreed Many Arrows. "I will lead the warriors as I am told by the Spirit."

As Many Arrows walked back to his own lodge, he heard Walks-on-Crooked-Leg calling out the names of those invited to the feast that night. He felt the anger drain from him at the sound of it. It was right that he had waited.

Red Beads was kneeling beside the fire, and she looked up as Many Arrows entered. Her glossy hair shone in the firelight. She had only recently dressed it again with the fat of an eagle. She had removed her soft doeskin dress, and now she wore a long, loose robe of wolf skin, its paws dangling from her shoulders.

"That new agent has caused trouble already," he commented as his wife stood up and walked toward him.

She stopped, studying the expression on his face for a moment, then returned to the fire, kneeling beside it without speaking.

Many Arrows went past her to the rear of the tepee and took down a doeskin pouch hanging from a pole. He opened the pouch, and paused silently with it in his hands. Placing the bundle back on the pole, he sat down below it, and for the next few minutes pulled a porcupine-tail brush through his hair. Then he parted his hair into three sections, pulled one third of it over his right ear and began to braid it.

As soon as Red Beads saw what he was doing, she moved to his side and sat down. When he had finished the three braids, she reached up and touched the braid nearest her.

"What are you going to do?"

"You do not like this?"

"It is time," she replied firmly.

"You did not like my hair the other way?"

"You will soon be a father again, so you should not look like such a young man."

He put his hand down to the swell of her stomach. "It has been many seasons since First Moon was born."

"Yes," she whispered, "but it is time again for another son."

"Red Beads, I have braided my hair because I must be seen as one of the wise men. There will be trouble with the kind of man they have sent as our agent, but I will act as one who cares only for the good of his people. I do not like this new agent. And I have never liked the idea of limited hunting grounds, of trusting an agent from the outside to take care of our needs. From the first that I saw him, I have felt that I will be the one to lead us all as my fathers have done in the past."

"The Spirit has told you this?"

"I must listen to the Spirit now, more than ever before. The long cold is coming, and our people are not ready for it if anything happens to the gifts the treaty promises us."

"I know. We could not eat all winter on the amount of food we have now."

"And we cannot trust that man."

"You were not there, but I was in your father's lodge when he visited. He does not know the customs of our people, but when he knew he had made a mistake, he—"

"Hush! Do not excuse him. I saw him today, too, and he threatened me."

"How did he do that?"

"You saw him. His very appearance threatens,

but he also took out the short gun he wears at his side and threatened me with it. I had not threatened him first. I was only watching."

"And you told your father?"

"Yes, and Walks-on-Crooked-Leg. That is why he is calling a feast for tonight. Afterwards we will pray until we are told what to do."

Red Beads reached up and touched the braid again. "Then there is no hurry for the meat I am cooking, is there?"

Many Arrows was frowning into the fire, but as he thought about the possible meaning of her words, he glanced at her. He turned and smiled, and he put out his hand in her direction. When she moved closer to him, meeting his eyes steadily at the same time, he slid his arm around her shoulders and pulled her gently down onto the soft beaver-skin robe.

She laughed and ran her hands over his braided hair as he leaned over her.

Walks-on-Crooked-Leg did not eat with the others. After he had placed a bowl of meat in front of each man, he went to the back of the fire and prepared the tobacco for a pipe. When all had finished eating, he filled a pipe and lit it. There was little talk in the tepee while the first pipe was being smoked. When a man did speak, however, the others listened without interrupting.

At first Many Arrows was disappointed when he saw that the medicine man was not going to unroll the sacred medicine pipe. The young warrior believed he had felt the insult from Sykes strongly enough for the pipe to be used, but he did not question the wisdom of Walks-on-Crooked-Leg, and he said nothing.

After the first pipe was finished, the medicine man

moved near the fire and raked a burning coal out of it to the ground in front of him. Placing a handful of dried sweet grass on the hot coal, he waited until a thin column of smoke started to rise and then passed his hands several times through the smudge. Next he opened the finely tanned and beaded pouch in front of him and scooped out enough red paint to cover his hands and face.

His ritual decorations completed, the old man stood. Throwing back his head, he fastened his eyes on the smoke curling upward to the tepee opening and began his medicine song. Low and guttural at first, the chant increased in intensity and pitch as his voice rose and fell. Abruptly, the medicine man crouched, and still chanting, now softly, began a slow, rhythmic step. He danced in a tight circle, bringing up one foot and then the other in cadence with his song. The others in the lodge took up the chant and repeated it with him.

Chapter 5

A half-hour before his dinner appointment with Colonel Forbes, Cole Sykes left his quarters and walked around the inside of the fort, studying the lay-out and the buildings. Then he stopped in the bar at the commissary and watched some troopers play bil-liards while he sipped a glass of beer.

He thought about the fort and wondered how it could be defended if the Indians turned hostile. What was this place anyway? An open fort near a one-horse town, a vast wilderness beyond it. True, there was a garrison of soldiers, but he hadn't decided what he thought of Colonel Forbes yet, and he hadn't even met the junior officers.

In describing this assignment, Madden had told Sykes that the Indian agent represented the govern-ment out here and was the final authority. He would get some instructions from Washington, but what help would that be when he was surrounded by thousands of Indians, many resentful and angry—angry enough to kill an agent? He had to police thousands of Indians, keep them on the reservation, and try to prevent them from killing him or the soldiers, or each other for that matter. If he wanted to, he could tell the Indians where to camp and where to hunt. He was in charge of dispensing supplies to them. He could hand out justice as he saw fit. In theory, he was the king of his land. Hell, he thought as he drained his beer, I can probably do as well as any of those political types Madden said they usually send out here. They don't know much more about Indians or running this place than I do.

Leaving the commissary, Sykes strolled toward the colonel's quarters in the row of single-family houses. It was already late enough in the fall to be dark by seven o'clock, and as he went up the steps to the porch he could see the colonel's niece through the parlor window, lighting the candles on the dining room table.

As soon as he knocked, she turned from the table and disappeared from view. The front door opened. "Mr. Sykes," Tricia bowed her head slightly, "you are exactly on time."

She seemed composed. There was no surprise in her manner as she smiled at him, and her motions were those of a woman in a well-practiced role, a woman who knew exactly what she should say, and enjoyed it. She wore a deep-red dress, wide at the neck and baring nearly all of her shoulders. The bodice clung so tightly that he could see exactly how slender and trim she was. The skirt, flaring from her waist, ended in a deep ruffle that swept the floor as she turned and motioned in the direction of the parlor.

"Uncle John will be here in a moment," she told him, still smiling as she turned her profile to him. "And since I am the only woman here to take care of him, I will have to do as your hostess for this evening. Follow me, please." She closed the door and led the way into the parlor.

Across the room, beside the fireplace, a wooden table held eight goblets and a decanter filled with an amber liquid. "Uncle John thought that perhaps we'd enjoy a little sherry before dinner," she explained, gliding ahead of him to the table. "There are several others coming. You're the first to arrive."

Following her, Sykes observed the motion of her hips, and it seemed to him that they moved more than necessary from side to side.

"There are cigars in the box on the mantel," she added as she filled two glasses. Extending one glass to him, she picked up the other. He took the glass carefully so that his hand did not touch hers. He raised the glass for a moment.

"Are you going to make a toast?" she questioned, holding her glass a little higher.

"Yes." Staring steadily at his glass for a moment longer, he toasted, "Here's to your recovery from this afternoon. Then he touched his glass to hers and downed the sherry in a single swallow.

"What do you mean?" she said sharply, for the first time looking directly at him.

While he met her eyes, the pink in her cheeks deepened, but before he could say anything more, Colonel Forbes walked into the room. At the same time a knock sounded at the front door, and Tricia hurried away to answer it, her hips no longer swinging quite so obviously.

It was twenty minutes before all the guests arrived, and during that time Sykes stood in front of the fireplace, smoking a cigar and sipping another glass of sherry. He talked with each of the officers that Forbes introduced to him and paid attention to what he said.

Major Campbell and Captain Olin had brought their wives, but the three lieutenants were unmarried and had come alone. When they all entered the dining room, the officers knew their places and went directly to their chairs.

"Mr. Sykes," Tricia paused, as she stopped at the end of the table opposite her uncle. "Please sit here." She pointed to the chair at her right. Sykes held her chair for her and then sat down.

As soon as he was seated, Tricia turned to him with a hostess' smile and took a breath as though she intended to say something. But when she met his eyes, she looked away again, wrinkling her brow. A moment later she turned back, leaned toward him, and spoke in a low voice. "Are you deliberately being difficult?" Then without waiting for an answer, she smiled at the officer on her other side. "I hope you'll enjoy a roast again, Major Campbell. I'm afraid we can't vary our fare here as much as at home." He nodded genially, his beefy face flushed from several glasses of sherry.

She chatted with the officer until after the first course was served. Sykes was trapped with Captain Olin's wife. A large woman, Mrs. Olin seemed stuffed into her clothes, and she carried on an endless monologue about nothing at all.

Damn boring, he thought, when he was able to turn away from her chatter a few minutes later to look at Tricia. At least she knows how to shut up, he mused. He continued to watch the younger woman as she picked up her fork and put it to the food on her plate. Her eyelashes were long and dark against her cheeks when she lowered her eyes to her plate, and her features were like a cameo against the darkness outside the light from the candles.

As Sykes reached for his own fork, she looked at him again, and for an instant there was no pretense, no fear, only her eyes, wide and searching. When he met the look without mocking her, her eyes continued to question him.

"Miss Ashley," interrupted the lieutenant sitting beside Major Campbell.

Tricia turned away at once and smiled at the young officer. "How are you this evening, Lieutenant Barkley? I'm sorry I haven't had a minute before this to speak with you."

Lieutenant William Barkley glanced briefly at Sykes before he returned Tricia's smile, his heavy-lidded eyes perusing her face. He was a slim man in his early twenties, young for an officer, but he had the air of assurance that came from his success at nearly everything he did. From the way he looked at Tricia, Sykes could tell success with women had been one of those things.

"I am always in high spirits when I have the opportunity to attend one of your dinners," he complimented. "But I spoke to you just now because I wanted to ask you how you enjoyed your little drive into Mason City today. I trust Corporal Eddy and his men did not intrude." He laughed softly when she set her face into a mock frown.

"Lieutenant! Was that your idea?" she chided.

"You saw how full the town was of—" Barkley glanced arrogantly at Sykes as he hesitated. "—of ruffians."

Major Campbell put his napkin to his mouth and cleared his throat audibly. The awkward silence that followed was broken by Colonel Forbes' loud laugh. "I've been telling Tricia that for a long time. But she had to go anyway. I guess you believe me now, don't you, my dear?"

"I had very little time to see anything, as you well know," replied Tricia. "However, Mr. Ross seemed quite capable of taking care of me. We were safely back inside the fort before Corporal Eddy managed to find us."

Lieutenant Barkley smirked when he looked away from the colonel's end of the table, as though the two of them completely agreed. "I heard there was a shooting of some kind while you were there. Next time, Miss Ashley, I'd like the pleasure of seeing to your safety myself."

Tricia scowled. "Thank you, but that will not be necessary." She moved defiantly in her chair, facing away from the lieutenant in a manner that ended the conversation.

"Mrs. Olin," she said, leaning forward and ignoring the agent squeezed between her and the other woman. "I heard you talking about Timmy. Is he any better? Do you suppose it could have been the cooler nights that gave him the croup?"

The remainder of the meal passed with relative ease. Sykes made one or two further attempts to engage Tricia in conversation. She was polite now, but distant. "If that's the way she wants it," he shrugged and decided to concentrate on his food. The roast, elk he learned, was savory and tender. Prairie turnips and greens, and plenty of freshly baked bread rounded off the meal. The guests emptied three bottles of good red wine, and the meal ended with coffee.

The last of the coffee had been drained when Tricia excused the women and led them into the parlor. The men stayed at the table, smoking and talking.

The officers spoke in generalities, about the weather, and the "hostiles," as they characterized the Indians, barely including Sykes in their talk. Madden had warned him that the army and its officers still seethed because Indian affairs had been taken away from the War Department and given to the Department of the Interior. Sykes knew Forbes was responsible to the War Department and not to him. But, as agent, he had to control this garrison somehow if he was going to have any authority on the reservation. It seemed clear he wouldn't get much help from these officers. He would have to rely on Sam Ross and his own good sense.

Abruptly, Sykes excused himself and made his way back to his quarters.

Colonel Forbes looked up from his breakfast coffee as Tricia sat down across the table from him. "Well," he tilted his head to one side and smiled, "and what did you think of our distinguished guest last night?"

She lowered her eyes as she picked up her napkin and spread it over her lap. "Oh," she asked, feeling the warmth come into her cheeks, "in what way do you mean?"

The colonel put his forearm on the table and leaned toward her. "Tricia, I don't think I've ever seen you blush before. What happened?"

"Nothing happened, Uncle John. He is very different from any other man I've met before, that's all."

Her uncle straightened in his chair. "He is indeed, and I don't intend to ask you to entertain him any more than is absolutely required. I'll protect you from that."

"Thank you, Uncle John, but he did nothing to—"

The colonel leaned across the table and patted her hand. "I'll protect you from him, don't worry." He sat up and put both hands on the edge of the table, as though bracing himself for something difficult. "He'll cause enough trouble with the Indians as it is. That's clear to see. I'll never know why Commissioner Tarking selected a man like that to replace Silvers." He squared his shoulders and pulled in his chin, ready to face the trouble. "But I've learned the hard way. You can expect anything out of Washington. They have no idea what it's like out here, and they won't listen to experienced people like me."

He laughed suddenly and then leaned back and relaxed as he reached for his cup. "After you cut him off, Lieutenant Barkley was not his usual cheerful self last night, was he?"

"What do you mean? I didn't notice anything different."

The colonel chuckled. "Tricia, come now! You hardly paid him any attention. And he positively glared at Sykes whenever you were talking to him."

"Heavens, I hope that doesn't mean Lieutenant Barkley thinks he has a special claim on my attention. I've certainly never given him any cause to think so."

"Perhaps not, but when a man knows he's the youngest, best-looking unmarried officer on a post like this, what do you suppose he thinks?"

Tricia sighed. "I shall have to be more careful when I'm around him then."

"Why?"

"Because I have no special feeling for him, and even if I did, I'm only here another month so there would be no point in letting anything develop."

"On the other hand, you don't need to spoil what pleasure he can get out of your presence, and he is a good escort for you here. The two of you make a very striking couple walking around the parade ground together. Makes an uncle feel proud to see you two together." He touched her hand again. "But tell me, now that you've mentioned leaving, have you enjoyed your stay at this last outpost of civilization?"

"I wouldn't have missed it for anything! It's been so completely different from anything else in my life."

"That's true, and I will say this—you're a great trooper when it comes to doing without all the comforts you're used to."

"I don't really miss them. Oh, a few things maybe. At first I thought I would feel terribly confined, having to stay inside so small a place for so many months."

"But you don't now?"

"How could I when so much happens here all the time? No two days have been the same. Things are so much the same at home."

"Come now, anyone that gets a pretty new dress as often as you do—"

"Uncle John! That seems such a trivial way to spend my time now that I've been here, and it was bad enough before." Her thoughts drifted to her rigidly ordered life at home in Boston. The rounds of teas and parties, the bland, polite young men, an occasional foray into the stinking slums to press bits of charity on the poor and sick. She had wanted to help in a hospital during the war, but her horrified mother had forbidden it. Tricia had become moody and restless, and her constant importuning had driven her mother to consent to a visit with Uncle John in the West.

She went to the kitchen and fetched the coffeepot. After filling their cups, she paused at the dining room window. She could see along the east end of the parade ground where the laundry tents and the guardhouse stood. While she watched, Cole Sykes rode around the corner of the parade ground and headed in the direction of the laundry tents.

Tricia was puzzled as she went on into the kitchen, wondering why her cheeks felt warm again. Surely this wasn't going to happen every time she saw him. She put the coffeepot on the stove and stood with her hands on her hips, staring at the pot for a minute.

As she walked back into the dining room, she tried to think of something else to talk about. She didn't want to discuss Cole Sykes or Lieutenant Barkley with her uncle anymore. She deliberately avoided looking out of the window as she passed it again.

Sykes did not look at the colonel's house as he rode by it, at the same time wondering what difference it made whether he looked or not. The colonel's niece lived in a world completely apart from his. That was easy to tell. He didn't know much about women's clothes, but anyone could see that hers were expensive and elegant. As he turned the corner of the parade ground and trotted toward the laundry tents, he reached up and ran his finger along the knife cut, still healing, in front of his left ear. That was what he knew about, fighting and staying alive when the odds were against it.

There was no hitching rail near the first laundry tent he came to, and after he swung down, he ground-reined his horse and walked to the open tent-flap. The canvas shelter was divided in two, and there was another flap open at the back. From the opening, it seemed more like two tents joined together. At one side he could see the living quarters for the laundress; the other side was where she did her work. Tubs of water squatted on the ground, one of them filled with soaking clothes. A fire burned in a stove covered with kettles of hot water. Even in the early morning, it was steaming inside the tent.

A young woman was leaning over one of the tubs, rubbing a white shirt across a scrub board. She glanced at him over her shoulder and then went back to her work without a greeting. He watched as her hands worked vigorously up and down the scrub board. She was accustomed to hard work, and her hands were red and rough from the hot water.

"What's your name?" he asked, changing his attention to the waggling of her hips and letting her catch his eyes on them when she glanced at him again.

"I'm Libby Jones," she replied curtly, straightening and turning to face him while she reached to her apron to dry her hands. "And who do you think you are?" Her voice made it clear he was wasting his time.

"Someone that needs his clothes washed. Isn't that what you're here for?"

"Ha! You think I'm going to do your clothes? Look, Mister, I do the officers' laundry. That's all. You can take your dirty clothes on down the line. Maybe Mrs. Pearce will do them for you, if she's got time."

Libby folded her round arms over her ample chest, and tilted her head to one side, looking disdainfully up at him. The two top buttons at the front of her dress were undone, and Sykes looked down the opening as he reached to his tobacco pocket. She was a pretty woman in a different way from Patricia Ashley. Without the ceaseless burden of hard work her features would have been fine and her hands small and delicate enough to pass as those of a lady, like Tricia. But her eyes held a bold, knowing look that wasn't ladylike.

"Stand there if you like," she snapped, turning back to the laundry tub as he started to roll a cigarette, "but it won't get your clothes washed for you—or anything else."

He watched the motion of her back while he lit

the cigarette, and then he shook out the match and dropped it to the dirt beside him.

"Do the officers bring their own laundry over here?" he asked.

Libby grinned at him over her shoulder. "What do you think?"

"I think they do. Are you sure that's the only kind of laundry you'll do?"

She looked past him to the colonel's house. "Well—almost all. I have to do hers, too. She's the only woman on the place too fancy to do her own washing."

"Who?"

"Miss Patricia, of course. Who do you think I mean? Can you imagine?" Libby turned back to the tub. "Too damned fancy to do her own laundry!"

When Sykes remained silent, she scrubbed furiously until she finished a shirt, wrung it out, and tossed it into the rinse water. "I'm not washing clothes for the likes of you, Mister. You get one of those fancy uniforms, you know—lots of shiny gold buttons, and I might be interested—if you're not married."

Chapter 6

Colonel Forbes left the house as soon as he finished breakfast, and walked the hundred yards to his office. While he walked he studied the fort. The buildings were sturdy and well placed in a large square. The barracks, the guardhouse, and the trader's store were of stone. He had sold the idea of a fort without walls to the officials in Washington, and he had made it work. It was better to be protected by the vigilance of men than by a solid wall of logs that could give a false sense of security. In any event, the fort was seldom attacked. The day-to-day danger was nearly always to the men out grazing horses, hunting or cutting wood, not to the men in the fort.

As Colonel Forbes walked up the steps to the porch outside his headquarters, he took a deep breath and drew up his shoulders. Fort Mason was an accomplishment of which he had a right to be proud.

Tricia cleared the table and washed the dishes as soon as her uncle left. The hired girl that had been working for Colonel Forbes when Tricia arrived had married almost as soon as Tricia could take over, and there had been no one to replace her. For important meals, like the one the previous night, the woman had agreed to return to do the cooking, but otherwise Tricia took care of her uncle. It surprised her that she mostly enjoyed that task.

That morning she straightened the rooms quickly. Then, fastening a blue and white checked sunbonnet under her chin, she picked up a basket and hurried out of the house and across the end of the parade ground in the direction of the trader's store. She usually went to the store with one of the officers' wives, even though she was allowed to walk freely around inside the fort. This morning, however, she did not want any company.

She glanced in the direction of the laundry tents as she walked. Her uncle had made one thing clear from the first. Even though one of the laundresses was a woman her own age, Tricia was not to associate with her. Tricia had asked no questions about that and always sent their laundry with one of the men. The men had never seemed to mind the request, even though it took a considerable amount of time to carry out the errand.

While she thought about that, she stared for a moment at the tents. Then she stopped short at the corner of the parade ground. Cole Sykes was standing on the porch outside the store. Evidently he had returned from the laundry tents.

She started forward again and, as she walked down the side of the field, she felt her cheeks flushing. This heady warmth no longer surprised her, and she approached Sykes with her head high.

She stepped up to the porch at the far end of the building, and he turned to look at her before he held a match to the cigarette in his mouth. He continued to watch as she walked the length of the porch. At the same time he shook out the match in his hand and flipped it into the dirt beside him without taking his eyes off her.

Even when she looked away for a moment, across the parade ground, he was still watching when she faced his way again. When she was close enough, she met his stare fully and stopped at his side.

"Mr. Sykes," Tricia smiled only to be polite. "How are you today? I trust your dinner agreed with you?"

He pulled the cigarette from his lips and let out the smoke as he looked down her body to the skirt flaring over her hips and then returned his gaze back up to her face. "It was fine," he returned.

Tricia glared at him and was about to protest his bold look when Lieutenant Barkley's voice interrupted them from behind. "Is this man bothering you, Miss Ashley?" he inquired.

She turned quickly to face the officer. "No," she insisted even though her cheeks were more deeply flushed than ever.

The lieutenant stood in the doorway of the store, glowering at Sykes' back, but the agent did not turn to face him. Instead he leaned one shoulder against the post beside the steps and stuck his cigarette in his mouth again as though neither of them mattered to him in the least.

"Oh!" cried Tricia. Haughtily lifting the side of her skirt nearest the agent, she turned away from him and stalked toward the doorway.

Barkley stepped to one side to let her pass, but he did not follow her inside as she expected. Seeing that she was safely standing at the counter on the far side of the store, Barkley stepped briskly across the porch and stopped beside Sykes, holding himself rigidly erect.

"Sir," he barked, waiting until Sykes turned his head and looked over his shoulder at him.

Sykes' face was like stone as he squinted through the smoke. After a moment he turned away and slowly pulled the cigarette from his mouth.

"I am speaking to you, sir," the lieutenant persisted.

"You aren't saying a hell of a lot."

"Miss Ashley doesn't need to be insulted by you."

The agent straightened up from the post and slid his hands to the sides of his waist, his eyes still on the far side of the fort. "Look, army boy—"

"Be careful, sir. I am an officer on this post."

"Well, I'm not a soldier on this post," retorted Sykes. He flipped the cigarette out into the dirt as he suddenly turned to face the soldier. "Whatever you're asking for, get your asking over with. I've got better things to do than listen to a boy in a uniform try to sound important."

William Barkley's eyes flashed as he leaned forward and he poked Sykes' chest with the fingers of his right hand. "You'll listen to me as long as I'm talking, you—"

Before Barkley could finish, Sykes raised his open hand in a backward motion and slammed it across the lieutenant's face. The blow rocked the officer back on his heels, but he was able to catch himself before he fell. As he awkwardly regained his footing, a voice behind Barkley called out.

"Lieutenant!" It was Colonel Forbes' orderly. "The Colonel wishes to see both of you at once, sir."

At the sound of the orderly's voice, Tricia ran to the doorway of the store. She could see her uncle on the porch outside the headquarters building.

The lieutenant stiffened into a military posture

and swallowed carefully while he composed his face. He aboutfaced and walked away, following the orderly.

Cole Sykes glanced at Tricia and turned, walked to his horse, swung up and galloped out of the fort. He kept up the pace down to the river and then walked the sweating animal across the bridge. Once across, he headed into Mason City's dusty main street and loped the length of it, peering at each building.

At the far end of the street, he reversed direction and rode back to the weatherbeaten hotel. Swinging down from his horse, he walked to a shack between the hotel and the dry goods store and stopped in front of its one window. The structure was little more than a lean-to built against the side of the store. Its roof slanted down from the store's wall to the side of the hotel, and its door and window were boarded shut. He doubted if a man his size could stand up under the low end of the roof, but it was the only building in the town that appeared unused.

When he had seen all he could from the outside, he walked into the dry goods store and out through the back way where he could study the lean-to from that side. There was another door but no window in the back wall. Altogether it wasn't more than a dozen feet wide and fifteen feet long.

Returning inside the dry goods store, Sykes approached the man behind the counter.

"Who owns the building next door?" he asked.

"That's hard to say. I've got some things stored in there now, but it was built by a gunsmith, a man by the name of Fred McLeary. Soon after he built it, he got the gold fever and left."

"Looks like the only empty place in town."

"You looking for a storeroom? What for? You're the new agent for the Indians, aren't you?"

"I want an office outside the fort."

"Hell, why? Wouldn't they give you Silvers' quarters?"

Sykes ignored the question. "Can you store your stuff someplace else?"

"Oh, I guess so. If you set up there, it'll probably be good for business in the long run, anyway. Not that those Indians have much money." He laughed as he reached behind him and lifted a key off a nail in the wall. "I'll show it to you, but I can tell you right now you'll have a job cleaning it up enough for an office. It's pretty dusty in there."

The storekeeper led the way out the back door to the lean-to. He unfastened the padlock and motioned Sykes inside the single room.

Boxes and barrels were stacked along the low side of the room under a shelf that extended the length of the building. At the front under the window was a workbench the height of a desk. The three chairs appeared to be in good repair. On the high side were several rows of pegs that could have been used to display guns.

"Tell you what I'll do," suggested the storekeeper. "I'll empty this out for you and get the woman who cleans the hotel to fix it up this afternoon. You want a sign out in front or anything?"

"I hadn't thought about it. I guess so."

"I've got a can of paint open in the store."

"All right. What will it cost me to get this ready?"

"A couple of dollars should do it. I'll have to pay the woman to clean and hire a clerk to watch the store this afternoon. Then I'll work on it myself. The more I think about it, like I said, it'll be good for business. As it is, the Indians do most of their trading at the fort."

The man put out his hand. "The name's Pard Warner."

"Cole Sykes," said the agent, shaking Warner's hand. He gave Warner two dollars before he went out the back door and headed for the hotel to make arrangements for a room. This done, he was in a hurry to get back to the fort and clear out his gear. He stopped briefly at the livery stable and rented a box stall. His horse was lathered and breathing hard when he pulled up at his quarters in the fort.

As Sykes was loading up his horse, Colonel Forbes' orderly approached.

"Colonel Forbes would like to see you, sir," the soldier stated crisply.

"I'd like to see him, too," replied Sykes. "Tell him I'll be there in a few minutes."

When everything was fastened in place, Sykes led his horse over to the rail outside Forbes' headquarters. The colonel did not stand up as Sykes walked into his office. Instead he watched with his jaw set and his eyes narrowed until Sykes stopped in front of his desk. "I hope you're ready to apologize," he snapped, holding his pen in both hands in front of him, his shoulders rigid and set like his jaw.

"Apologize for what?" retorted Sykes, stepping to the end of the desk so that he could see the orderly while he talked to the colonel.

"Sykes, I'm not even going to mention your behavior toward my niece," Forbes began in a voice that made it clear how generous he was being about that, "but striking one of my men is a military matter."

"I'll strike anybody that puts his hands on me, and I've never apologized for hitting anybody yet."

"You don't understand, do you? This is a military matter. It's a matter of discipline."

"You've got no authority over me, Forbes. Don't get to thinking you do."

The colonel jumped to his feet, his voice rising. "If you think you can accept the hospitality of this fort and then go about as you wish, striking the officers, insulting my niece—"

"Your niece must be insulted pretty damn easy, Forbes."

"Leave her out of this," he shouted.

"When she walks up to me and starts talking, she's buying herself in. And your smooth-cheeked soldier boy bought himself in the same way."

"Why you . . . ," Forbes fairly shrieked as he started around the end of his desk.

Cole Sykes turned away. "I'm setting up the agency in town, Forbes."

"In town? What kind of nonsense is that? Now, see here, Sykes. Have you got some kind of notion you can deal with those savages? Why, man, there're thousands of them! Do you think you can deal with them all by yourself? You think you don't need the army behind you?"

Sykes stopped in the doorway and turned to face the colonel. "Look, Forbes, right now we both work for the government, but I don't work for you."

The colonel was livid. "If you think you can stir up trouble around here any way you want and then call on me for help—"

"I will call on you when I need your help. That's your job, isn't it?"

There was no sound in the room behind him as Sykes stalked down the hallway and went out.

Chapter 7

"What do you want on that sign, Sykes?" asked Warner.

"Blackfoot Agency is good enough," he replied. "It doesn't have to be fancy. Can any of the Indians read?"

"I've never seen any that could." The storekeeper laughed as he walked out of the makeshift office.

A half-hour later he returned with the sign, a hammer and a couple of nails.

"Over the door?" he suggested, standing in the opening.

Sykes stepped out onto the sidewalk and perused the building. "Good as any place." He shrugged and reached for his tobacco sack. Farther down the street Hugh Gaines emerged from his blacksmith shop. He mopped his dripping forehead with an old rag and stood for a moment to breathe in the cooler outside air. Spotting Warner nailing up the sign, he stared in curiosity.

When Warner stepped back to admire his work, he beckoned across the street to the blacksmith. "Come on over, Gaines," he called.

Hugh Gaines sauntered across the dirt road, his eyes examining the sign. He was a big man, with the powerful arms and shoulders of a person who uses his muscles for a living. From working in the heat of his shop, his shirt sleeves were rolled high and his arms and face glistened with moisture. His big leather apron flapped against his legs as he walked.

"Blackfoot Agency," he read out loud as he stepped up on the sidewalk. "I'll be damned. So that's why you wanted a place for your horse, Sykes. What happened? Poppa Forbes kick you out?"

"I moved out," explained Sykes, his voice noncommittal.

"Didn't mean to pry," said Gaines. "Welcome to Mason City."

"That's what I say," chimed in Warner. "Won't hurt business at all, will it, Gaines?"

"Hell no. You ever see an Indian with shoes on his horse?"

"No, and I'll bet they got a few thousand head up there, too." The storekeeper waved his hand to the north.

Sykes looked puzzled. Madden had briefed him on the treaty with the Blackfoot, and blacksmithing was one of the services the government was to provide for the Indians. He turned to Gaines.

"You've never seen any with horseshoes?" he asked. "Didn't Silvers get a blacksmith for them? I was told he did. It's in the treaty. He was supposed to."

Hugh Gaines guffawed and jammed his hands on his hips while he looked up at the sign. "Well now, that just happens to be why I ended up in a place like Mason City in the great territory of Mon-tan-y." He emphasized each syllable of the last word. He looked squarely at the agent. "The government paid my way here, all right, but Silvers had no money for me. Leastwise, that's what he said. And no place to work. He didn't know much about the horseshoeing business, anyway. He sent for something he called an anvil, but it was so small. I guess he thought I was going to go from tepee to tepee or something."

Sykes and Warner, who had been listening intently to the conversation, both grinned. "Anyway," Gaines went on, "I told him I only worked for money. He didn't seem to care, one way or the other, so I did what you've just done, Sykes. I found an empty building here and set up a stable and then built the shop when I'd earned enough for it."

Sykes pondered the looks of this dreary town, with its unpainted, unkept facade, and studied the blacksmith. "What did you stay for?"

"The same thing that made me sign up as a smitty for a reservation in the first place." Gaines' smile faded as he spoke, and his mouth twisted belligerently.

Before Sykes could venture another question, Pard Warner interrupted. "We better do this right, Gaines. Let's buy Sykes a drink by way of a welcome to this prosperous little town."

"Sure," said Gaines, smiling easily again. "Then we'll drink to all those thousands of horses without shoes."

It rained for most of the next week, and during that time Cole Sykes worked on the agency building. Warner and Gaines had offered to help, but this was something Sykes wanted to do alone. It was his idea to move into town and it was his responsibility to set up an agency office. For most of his life he had acted on his own and he wanted to keep it that way.

He shored up the sagging wall boards, repaired

the doors and leveled the rough plank floors. As he worked, he mulled over the Indian situation. As far as he could tell, Silvers hadn't implemented much of the treaty. A blacksmith who wasn't shoeing Indian horses, no ration house to store supplies for the Indians—what else hadn't Silvers done? Or, more to the point, what *had* Silvers done as agent? Sykes was sure he had been lining his own pockets, but just how much had he gotten away with? Sykes found himself surprised that the Indians hadn't done more than murder Silvers. Or had they? Now he was beginning to wonder if Sam Ross had been right.

By the end of the week, Sykes was nearly finished. He was just hanging a new kerosene lantern over the workbench he intended to use as his desk when he heard a horse canter up. Stepping outside, he saw Sam Ross pull up short in front of the office.

The scout leaned one arm on his saddle horn and intently studied the sign over the door.

"I'll be damned," exclaimed Ross.

"That seems to be the usual comment," the agent remarked.

"What did Forbes run you out for, hitting Barkley?"

"He did not run me out."

The scout scrutinized Sykes for a moment. "That's not his side of it."

"His side of it isn't something he's likely to talk about."

Ross straightened in the saddle and picked up his reins. "That's always possible. I've got to say though, Sykes, you've got your own way about you."

"What do you mean?"

"Nothing important. Thought I'd ride up to the

camp and see how the gathering is coming. You want to ride along?"

"No, not today, unless you think they'll all be there."

"It's too soon."

"Then I'll go ahead with what I was doing. I want to be able to tell them I've got a ration house started when they're all together."

"A ration house?"

"Yes. There's supposed to be a ration house to store the supplies for the Indians. It's a place where they can come and get the stuff. This building's too small for storing much of anything."

"I never heard Silvers mention anything like that."

"What did he do with the supplies?"

"He always had them brought in on mules, and he'd head out with the mule train into the reservation as soon as it got here."

"Didn't he take you along?"

"Nope."

"Christ, how much of it got to the Indians?"

Although the scout smiled as he looked at Sykes, his eyes were stony. "Damned little," he admitted. Turning his horse into the street, he called back to Sykes, "I'll give your regards to Many Arrows and his warriors. You want me to tell him you made a mistake pulling your gun that day?"

"Yes."

The scout reined up so abruptly that his horse jerked its front feet off the ground and danced sideways. "You do?" he exclaimed.

"I said yes, didn't I?"

"I'll be damned," Ross shook his head in wonderment. He kicked his horse into a lope and did not look back, but rode the rest of the way through town as though he thought Sykes might change his mind.

The agent stood in the doorway, staring after Ross until he faded from sight. Stepping back inside, he settled himself at his desk and for the next hour read the Office of Indian Affairs manual. Finally putting the book aside, he undid his belt and opened the folded leather inside, taking out a hundred dollar bill. They hadn't given him much money to get started on, not nearly enough to do what he was supposed to do, but if he was going to report the progress he had made by the end of the year, he'd better make some.

He stuffed the bill in his pocket and went out, crossing the street to the blacksmith shop. Gaines was working at the hearth, leaning over a red-hot wheel spoke in the fire when Sykes stopped in the doorway. The burly man straightened as soon as he saw the gunman. "Howdy," he greeted Sykes, ambling over to the anvil in the middle of the room. "What can I do for you?"

"Are you busy?" Sykes asked.

"In this town? I've never been what you could call busy since I've been here."

Sykes looked slowly around the shop. "You said you built this yourself?"

"Yep, that I did."

"Where'd you get the wood?"

"Cut it myself. Trimmed it. Took awhile, but like I said, I'm not that busy."

"Who owns that flat land south of here?"

"Whoever squats on it, I guess."

"It's not on the reservation?"

"Well, when you come right down to it, I've heard it said the reservation ends at the river."

"Then this whole town is on the reservation."

"Sounds like it, doesn't it?"

"Good," said Sykes.

Gaines folded his brawny arms over his chest. "You planning on kicking us all off?" he asked suspiciously.

"No, but I might collect a little rent." Sykes grinned as he reached to his pocket and pulled out his tobacco. Eyeing the blacksmith's frown, he explained. "Don't get excited, Gaines. I don't mean dollars. I'm supposed to see that the Indians have a blacksmith. That's what you came out here for, wasn't it?"

The blacksmith nodded, still scowling.

Sykes rolled a cigarette and went to the fire and gingerly lifted out a piece of half-burnt wood to light the tobacco. "I might ask you to do some work for me in your spare time, that's all. By the end of the year I need to show I've made progress in civilizing the Indians. I have to write a report."

"So did Silvers, but he didn't have any money."

"You'll be paid," assured Sykes.

"Well, damn it," Gaines bellowed, "why didn't you say that in the first place?"

Sykes filled his lungs with smoke and exhaled slowly as he walked to the door. "Didn't know I'd have to. But that's not why I came over here. If you're not all that busy right now I could use some help building a ration house. I'm planning to put it on the flat land I was asking you about."

Hugh Gaines followed Sykes out of the shop and stood beside him as he pointed out the spot. "How big a building?" Gaines asked.

"How big can I get for a hundred dollars?"

"Are you talking about both wages and materials?"

"Yes, but I'm planning to work on it myself as much as I can."

The blacksmith broke into a large grin as he studied the ground. "You give me the hundred dollars and all the time I need and I'll have you whatever you want by spring."

Sykes reached into his pocket and pulled out the bill. "It'll be mostly a storehouse," he detailed. "Big and not too fancy."

They had the four corners of the ration house staked out by the time Sam Ross returned. As he rode up, Hugh Gaines called out from the far side of the measured-off area. "Looks like we got a real agent here for a change."

"One that's lucky to be alive, anyway," replied Ross, swinging down from his horse.

"That means something. What is it?" wondered the startled agent.

"Seems like Many Arrows felt insulted enough to get out the war paint, but Flying Hawk insisted on going to see the old medicine man first. The medicine man said no."

"And that stopped him?"

"Of course."

"What do you mean, of course? You can't tell me a young hot-blood like Many Arrows listens to some old codger's advice?"

"You a religious man, Sykes?"

"No."

"Then you aren't going to understand."

"What's religion got to do with it?"

"I said you wouldn't understand."

"I can't understand anything you don't tell me."

Gaines interrupted the two by reaching into his pocket and asking, "You ever see one of these before, Ross?" He held up the hundred dollar bill.

"Where'd you get that?"

The blacksmith grinned at the bill and then inclined his head in Sykes' direction. "U.S. government, where else?"

"If you got a lot of those around, Sykes, you better be careful who you let know about it."

"I haven't got a lot of them. I've got damned few to do what I'm supposed to get done here." Frowning at the blacksmith for a moment, he turned to Ross again. "When do you figure Flying Hawk will be ready with his council?"

"Another week at least."

Ross was still talking when Sykes spotted a group of horsemen at the far side of the river heading toward the bridge. A stocky man with a thick black beard rode in the lead. A little behind him, and leaning slightly in his saddle, was a man with his arm in a sling. Sykes recognized the injured rider. Littan was what the bearded man had called him that day in the street when Sykes' bullet had slammed into his shoulder.

Sykes pushed past Ross and stepped out into the street. The approaching riders clattered across the bridge and into the town. As they rode by on their way to the Trapper's Last Chance Saloon, they gave no sign that they even saw the agent.

"I was going to suggest a drink," said Ross in a low voice as they watched the men dismount and go into the saloon, "but I don't think I will."

By the end of the following week, the log walls of the ration house were three feet high. Sykes drove himself hard, concentrating on the work and trying to hide his concern from Gaines. He would often pause and scan the horizon, half expecting to see a band of warriors swooping down on them. Ross had returned to the Indians, and each day that passed without word from the scout turned Sykes' uneasiness to outright apprehension. He wasn't confident that Many Arrows would not put on war paint.

Sykes was weary, but satisfied with their progress on the storehouse when Sam Ross rode down from the Indian encampment and said the council would take place the next day. That evening Sykes took the agency manual to his hotel room. He studied it most of the night until he was certain he understood everything it said about his contacts with the Indians. Then he pored over the latest treaty that had been signed with the Blackfoot until he could recite it word for word.

Early the following morning, Sam Ross met him in town and rode out with him to the camp. They traveled in silence until they reached the last rise before the grassy plain that Flying Hawk had selected for the council.

As they started up the incline, Sykes turned to Ross with a startled look. "I can hear them already," he tilted his head to one side. The hubbub of shouts, neighing horses and barking dogs blended into what seemed to Sykes a discordant uproar.

"The chiefs don't travel alone," explained Ross. "They bring along plenty of protection as well as all of their own families."

Despite the rising tumult he heard as they topped the hill, Sykes was not prepared for the panorama spread out below him. He pulled up abruptly, staring in amazement at the scene.

"Gives you an idea of what you're here for, doesn't it?" asked Ross, as he drew up beside the agent.

Cole Sykes sat as if stunned. He finally took a deep breath and let it out all at once.

"You should have seen 'em before the smallpox got to 'em," recalled the scout, a note of sadness in his voice. "This isn't anything."

Wherever Sykes looked he saw a sea of motion and color. Hundreds of conical tepees splashed with brilliant designs and animal figures dotted the plain. Warriors pranced their ponies among the lodges, dodging in and out, displaying their horsemanship. Others tended to their bows and lances, while still others sat in groups exchanging greetings and talking. Children called and laughed as they ran to and fro. Dogs yelped and leaped after them.

Some women were bending over the myriad cooking fires scattered over the encampment. Others were erecting lodges. Ross had told Sykes that putting up the tepee was woman's work, but the agent had been skeptical. Now he gazed in fascination as a group of women drove stakes into the ground in a circle and then hoisted up the poles they had tied at their tops. According to Ross, a wealthy brave could have as many as thirty lodge poles and a good number of wives to put them up. The women tugged and hauled the thick buffalo-hide covering over the frame and then set in place the outside pole that held open the flap at the top.

Even at this distance, Sykes could make out the handsome regalia of some of the chiefs. Eagle-feather bonnets draped nearly to the ground, and long-fringed buckskin shirts and leggings were trimmed with porcupine quills and beads and bits of fur. Some had slung robes of beaver and raccoon over their shoulders.

Off to his left, Sykes noticed a group of braves file into camp leading horses laden with the carcasses of antelope and elk. In the distance, to his right, a huge herd of picketed horses grazed peacefully. Over it all hung the soft gray, slowly moving drift of the camp smoke.

The longer Sykes observed the scene, the more he sensed its order. The hundreds of lodges formed an immense circle. Each lodge was surrounded by another circle of tepees. The circle was finally closed when the last group of tepees lifted their poles upward.

"Looks like Many Medicines' band made it," observed Ross.

"How can you tell that from here?"

"That's their place," he replied, pointing to the tepees that had just been erected.

"Ross," Sykes began hesitantly.

"What?"

"Nothing."

The scout chuckled to himself as they urged their horses ahead, easing down the far side of the hill. "I'll tell you if I see any war paint," he laughed. "Otherwise leave your gun—"

"You do that," Sykes interrupted. He swept his eyes over the scores of Blackfoot ahead of him. "I don't think six bullets would be enough this time."

As they approached the encampment a voice called out the scout's name. Ross turned and raised his hand in response. As they trotted through the camp, he spoke a few words that Sykes could not understand to each person that greeted him.

"If I didn't need this job, Ross," Sykes remarked, "I'd say you're the man that ought to have it."

The scout looked thoughtful. "I wouldn't want it." He gazed ahead of him.

"Why not?"

"If you have to ask, you wouldn't understand."

"By God, Ross, is that the only answer you know?"

"For that question, yes."

"I could use more help than that."

Sam Ross smiled. "I don't know as much about you as I thought I did."

"You always act like you do."

"Everyone's heard of Cole Sykes."

"So what?"

"So . . . I'm . . . more pleased to meet you than I expected."

"That isn't what you started to say."

"Maybe not, but it's what I ended up meaning. There's Flying Hawk's lodge."

"I can tell that much," insisted Sykes. "I see the bird painted on the side. "And there's my friend Many Arrows."

Ross jerked his head toward the young chief, who was watching them closely.

"Don't count on him being a friend."

"You think I am?"

They dismounted together, dropping their reins to the ground. Sykes wondered how any horse would remain ground-reined in the din of the encampment, but he followed Ross' example and left his horse where the animal stood.

Many Arrows had already ducked into his father's tepee when Ross took Sykes' arm, holding him back. "Stay outside," he cautioned as he bent to enter the lodge. Sykes started to protest, but thought better of it and remained silent. Once inside, Ross exchanged a few words with Flying Hawk. The chief was flanked by his son and Walks-on-Crooked-Leg. They said nothing.

Outside the lodge, Sykes was growing restless. A group of children had gathered around, staring solemnly at him. Suddenly Ross emerged and, pointing to an open space in the middle of the lodges, he explained that the council would be held there.

"In the meantime," he suggested, "walk around with me and greet the chiefs."

Sykes nodded and the scout led the way. For the next hour they moved among the Indians, stopping at each chief's tepee. They had walked through the entire camp by the time Flying Hawk entered the council circle followed by the medicine man and Many Arrows. The chief moved slowly with the dignity of his office. His son followed behind, bearing himself like his father.

Buffalo skins and blankets had been stretched on poles over an area large enough to shield the chiefs from the sun.

As Flying Hawk took his place, the other chiefs gathered around, placing themselves in their positions of rank. Sykes and Ross joined them, and the parley began.

Sykes couldn't help staring at Flying Hawk. His long shirt of wolf skin was spread over his knees, the tail and paws of the animal draped on the ground. At his side lay his ceremonial lance, wrapped entirely in ermine skin.

The agent could not understand the talk, although he listened carefully, trying to learn a few phrases. A pipe was passed many times, and Sykes accepted it. The chiefs, dignified and aloof, never addressed him directly, although their glances told Sykes his presence was not being ignored.

The council lasted about three hours. Flying

Hawk stood up, and he and the other chiefs made their way to their lodges. Sykes turned to Ross who motioned him to their horses, still waiting patiently where they had been left.

"What did you get done?" asked Sykes, pulling himself stiffly into the saddle.

Without answering, Ross hauled himself up on his horse and galloped out of the camp. Sykes caught up with the scout just before they reached the rise and pulled up close to him.

"What the hell went on back there?" Sykes demanded.

"The chiefs are holding back Many Arrows and the other young braves from putting on war paint . . . for now," answered Ross. "I told them about the ration house, and they said good, it's about time."

"Well, what do they expect then?"

"They expect to get the supplies before it snows."

"And that's all you said in three hours?" Sykes questioned.

"It's about all that concerned you."

Sykes abruptly turned in his saddle. He could hear the sound of beating drums and loud chanting. "What are they going to do now?"

"They'll be dancing and singing and eating and talking the rest of the day and night."

The agent looked at the scout. "We're not invited to that, I suppose."

"Hell, you want to stay for it? Silvers never did, so I just figured you wouldn't."

In response, Sykes pulled his horse around. "I'd like to go back, Ross. I want to see what it's like. Besides, I'm hungry."

The scout grinned. "The Blackfoot don't eat dogs,

Sykes, so you won't have to worry about what's in the stew."

Sykes was already urging his horse toward the camp as he called to Ross, "You ever eat prison food? Dog would taste good compared to that."

Chapter 8

The council fires lit up the plain as Sykes and Ross feasted all night and watched the dancing and chanting and drumming. From time to time, a chief would rise to his feet, and with great formality begin what seemed to Sykes a monotonous and endless speech. After one particularly lengthy oration, Sykes turned to Ross enquiringly.

"Better get used to it," Ross responded. "Just about every ceremony has to have some speeches. They set great store by a good speechmaker. And nobody interrupts either."

It was dawn, and the drums were still beating when Sykes and the scout eased their horses up the rise above the camp.

"How long can they keep that up?" asked Sykes.

Sam Ross looked over his shoulder at the tepee-covered plain. "Longer than I can," he chuckled. "That hard bunk I've got in the barracks is going to feel good. Hope Forbes hasn't got any plans for me today."

"Does he ever?"

The scout studied Sykes' profile as he spoke. "It's a living. I know I should have moved on before this, but I've tried to a couple of times and something keeps pulling me back."

"What's the difference," asked Sykes, "one place or the other?"

"Way I look at it, too."

After that they both rode heavily in their saddles, feeling the lack of sleep and their full stomachs.

Once in town, Sykes continued down the street at Ross' side, not stopping at the livery stable.

"Where you going?" asked Ross as the agent rode along with him.

"It's as good a time as any to see about that supply train coming in."

"See what about it?"

"That they make sure it gets here."

"You think you can get Forbes to help you now?"

"It's his job, isn't it?"

"Sure, but he's got a lot of different ways of going about it."

"Only one that I can see."

"You'll learn."

"What do you mean? Jesus, Ross, why don't you just spit it out when you've got something to say?"

The scout laughed. "Not used to it," he explained. "I'm used to being around those fancy army officers. It's best to tell them what they want to hear."

"I suppose that's something you think I should do."

"I don't know. It's been sort of interesting seeing what happens when you don't."

"Yeah," muttered Sykes.

As they rode into the fort, they viewed the parade ground filled with troopers, the voices of the sergeants raised in sharp commands as the mounted soldiers wheeled through their drills.

Sam Ross turned aside and rode to the front of the barracks, while Sykes loped in the other direction, toward the headquarters building, passing in front of the store and the unmarried officers' quarters. Reaching the colonel's headquarters, he dismounted and walked into the hallway. Forbes' orderly encountered Sykes at the colonel's door and stood there, barring the way.

"Colonel Forbes is occupied, sir," he informed Sykes. "He suggests you see Major Campbell if you have business that concerns the army."

"Is that right?" said Sykes. "And where is Major Campbell?"

"If you'll go down the porch outside, you'll see his office at the other end of this building."

Without another word, Sykes returned the way he had come in. He smiled as he walked along the porch. He'd have done the same thing if he'd been in the colonel's place.

Sykes stopped at the open doorway of the major's office and Campbell looked up at once and motioned to a chair. "What can I do for you, Sykes," he waved impatiently, making no move to rise. A sheaf of papers lay open on his desk and he held a pen in one hand.

"I wanted to see about that freight coming in for the Indians."

"What about it?"

"When do you expect it?"

"Could be here almost any time. The last boat that can get up the Missouri River to Fort Benton this year must have already come and gone. The wagons have to be loaded and the mules gotten at Benton before the train can start. King is the man in charge at Benton. He knows how to run a supply train."

"I'm interested in the kind of protection you're providing."

"What makes you think the supply train needs any special protection?" he asked sharply. The major stuck his pen back in the inkwell. "Half that freight will be for the Indians, and between here and Benton, it's nothing but Blackfoot country. Do you know something we don't?"

"No. I don't want anything to delay it, that's all. There's not much time before the first snow, and the Indians need those supplies."

"Look," said Campbell, his tone exasperated, "the wagons don't even have to be reloaded before you can take the supplies to them."

"All right," nodded Sykes, "I understand that. But you're not sending any men out to see it gets here?"

"No, not unless we have some reason to. King has his own guards."

Sykes abruptly turned his back on Campbell and stepped out into the warm sun on the porch. He watched the cavalry on the parade ground, wheeling and turning in their drill, the red-faced sergeants shouting the orders. Plenty of time to drill their heads off, he thought, but no time to escort a supply train. He was beginning to wonder for what reason these troopers were here.

His eyes strayed to the colonel's house at the far end of the parade ground. He was about to step off the porch when Patricia Ashley appeared in the door of her uncle's house. Turning her face away, she shook out a rag with one hand, the dust from the cloth flying around her. Momentarily, Sykes' thoughts drifted to Tricia and her smooth, pale skin and slim figure.

He shook his head and rubbed his hands over the

day-old stubble on his chin, blinking his eyes wearily. He needed to clean up and get some rest. Besides, a woman like Tricia was Barkley's type. And he had more important things to think about.

He unhitched his horse, swung up and, circling around the drilling troopers on the parade ground, loped out of the fort.

Once in town, Sykes fed and watered his horse, and headed for his room at the hotel. Maybe later he could add a room to his office, but for now there was no space in the building for living quarters. He skipped breakfast, still full from the Blackfoot feast, and went straight to his room. After shaving, he pulled off his shirt and boots and sank heavily onto the bed. But he couldn't sleep. He lay there staring at the ceiling, finally getting up and walking to the window. "Where the hell is that supply train?" he muttered. "And why is Forbes so reluctant to send out an escort?"

Chapter 9

The council fires had turned to ashes, the women had dismantled the lodges, packing them on their horses, and the chiefs, with their families and warriors, had dispersed to their winter camps. The council was over.

In the still dawn, Many Arrows made his way through the tepees to his horse, staked out beside the river. The pony whinnied and danced his feet as Many Arrows slipped the length of raw-hide rope from the animal's neck. The young chief fastened a half hitch in the middle of the rope and looped it firmly over the pony's lower jaw, drawing it taut. He threw the two ends of the rope over the horse's neck and leaped to its back. Turning toward the pasture above the camp, he kneed the pony into a lope.

Breathing in the cool morning air, Many Arrows thought of the decision of the chiefs not to go to war. Perhaps it was wise. Still, he felt shame and sadness that his people, once powerful and prosperous, were now confined to what land the white man was willing to give them.

He recalled the stories the old men told of how their domain had reached far into the land to the north and into the great western mountains. As a boy he had listened in awe to the tales of brave, fierce warriors whose lances were once festooned with the scalps of trappers and traders who dared trespass on Blackfoot land, taking their beavers and game. Proud, defiant, his people had kept the white intruders at bay for many seasons.

But it was not the white man's weapons, nor even his numbers, that had conquered the Blackfoot. It was the white man's disease, the sickness they called smallpox. Three times in his own father's life, this plague had swept like a prairie fire through their camps. Weakened, their warriors and hunters decimated, his people could no longer withstand the always increasing number of settlers invading their land.

But these were bitter thoughts, and he put them out of his mind. "We can still hunt the buffalo and the elk," he mused, "and still keep our horses." Many Arrows smiled to himself as he trotted toward the grazing pasture and his herd of sleek ponies. He had nearly a hundred war and hunting ponies. With such wealth, he could walk with assurance and dignity among his people.

He thought with pride of his favorite hunting pony, the glossy bay with one white foot. He had caught the horse himself, singling him out from a band of mustangs. He had roped him and thrown him to the ground, blowing his own breath into the animal's nostrils so the horse would know who was master. He had broken him to ride, taking him to the deepest part of the river where it would be more difficult for the wild stallion to buck and plunge. Many Arrows laughed softly when he thought of how many times he had been flung into the water. He had never beaten the mustang into submission, as he had heard white men did, but had trained him gently and patiently until he was the quickest and most fearless of all in the hunt.

The young chief cantered along easily, staying close to the north fork of the river until he reached the grove of trees at the bend. Easing his horse up the slope above the trees, he topped the rise and stared below him in stunned amazement. Where scores of horses had grazed before, now only a dozen or so remained, scattered over the flat plain. His throat tightened and his handsome face twisted with anger.

Cursing, he dug his heels into his horse and plunged down the slope. He galloped in a circle around the edge of the grazing land, anxiously searching the remaining animals for his bay stallion. But all he saw were appaloosas, the gray horses with spotted rumps that white men called "Indian ponies."

His mind churned at the thought of his horses, his wealth, stolen from him. Finally, he slowed his quivering pony and trotted for the cover of bushes at the side of the south fork of the river. Dismounting, he began searching the ground for signs of the direction in which the horses had been driven. When he found the tracks, they pointed across the south fork. The herd had been run off the reservation.

Many Arrows walked slowly back to his horse, his eyes still studying the ground. Suddenly he stopped and dropped to one knee. He picked up a small, rounded piece of white paper and sniffed at the shreds of tobacco still clinging to it. Straightening up, he put the cigarette stub in the pouch at his side.

The camp was beginning to stir as Many Arrows pounded into the circle of lodges and reined up before his father's tepee. Kills Bear and several other warriors gathered around the lathered pony.

"What is it?" Kills Bear questioned as Many Arrows jumped from his horse.

"The horses are gone from the grazing land!"

"What? All of them?"

"Almost all of them. See for yourself. Get Runs-at-Night and Long Tomahawk and as many of the others as want to go. I will tell my father, and then I will join you at the South River. We will follow them."

"Is it not too late?"

"They are off the reservation lands now, but they are still our horses. We will take them back." Many Arrows turned and strode toward his father's tepee. Kills Bear ran through the camp, calling out to the young men that he knew would want to go. Hearing the commotion, Flying Hawk stepped through the lodge opening and encountered his son.

Many Arrows told his father what had happened and showed him the piece of cigarette he had found. Flying Hawk turned the paper over in his hand and then sniffed at it. "It is white man's tobacco," he stated, handing it back to his son.

"Yes, and among the tracks of our horses were tracks of horses wearing iron shoes. That means white men's horses. We will go after them. I will fill my pouch with bullets, and then I will lead the others."

"Where did they go?"

"Across the South River."

"Then you will not go after them. We have signed the treaty. We must not follow them off our own lands."

"They can't have our horses!" Many Arrows cried angrily. "What else will we have of our own if they take our horses as well as our hunting ground?"

"The bluejackets will go after them. It is their work now. They have also signed the treaty." Even while he spoke, Flying Hawk frowned in the direction of the fort and his voice was hesitant. The new agent must be told about this.

"But we cannot wait for them!" demanded Many Arrows. "By the time they decide to do anything they'll blow their bugles for an hour first, and then the horses will be gone too far."

Flying Hawk looked intently at his son, holding him with his eyes. A half dozen of the younger men had gathered behind Many Arrows, standing belligerently and nodding their heads in agreement with the young war chief's words.

"Many Arrows," lectured Flying Hawk sternly, "first you will go with me to see the white man, Sykes." Then he glanced past his son at the warriors. "All of you, we will go together."

Cole Sykes straightened up from his work and glanced in the direction of the fort. His eyes widened in surprise as he watched Flying Hawk, Many Arrows, and a dozen other Blackfoot warriors ride up the hill toward the gate of the fort. At once the agent turned to Gaines, who was sawing a board in half.

"You got a horse ready?" he asked.

"Sure, take the buckskin in the first stall." The blacksmith's eyes narrowed as he glanced toward the file of braves across the river.

Sykes walked rapidly to the stable, led the buckskin out and swung into the saddle. He touched his spurs to its flanks and loped to the bridge.

Entering the fort's gate, Sykes could see the mounted Indians grouped in front of the building he had been offered for the agency. He loped toward them. At the same time, Sam Ross strolled from the headquarters building and walked to the Indians.

The two white men reached the warriors together. Sykes swung his horse around to face the chief, and Ross stopped beside the agent.

"Tell them where the new agency is," requested Sykes. "I want them to go down there to talk business."

For several minutes, Ross spoke to the Indians. Sykes scowled at the scout, wondering exactly what he was telling them. It seemed like a lot more than he had asked Ross to relay.

Flying Hawk spoke a few words in return, his face impassive.

"He says okay," translated Ross. "Wait a minute and I'll get my horse."

While the scout hurried back into the headquarters building, Sykes reached to his pocket and pulled out his tobacco sack. He had a cigarette going by the time Ross returned and headed for the cavalry stables. His smoke was nearly finished when Ross rode up from the stables.

"I noticed you took the time to tell Forbes you were going," mentioned Sykes, as he turned his horse and rode beside Ross.

"I work for him, don't I?" retorted Ross, staring ahead of him. "You might want to remember that."

"Is he threatening to keep you away from me?"

"No, he's a fairer man than that, Sykes, no matter what you think of him. If you're going to be so damned independent, it wouldn't hurt you to learn to talk to these people yourself."

"I've been thinking that."

They rode through the gate in silence, Ross at the chief's side, Sykes beside the scout. Many Arrows stayed a stride behind his father on Flying Hawk's other side. Reaching the bridge, Sykes turned to the interpreter. "Who goes across first?" he asked.

"It's not like in the lodge. Just show a little respect, that's all."

"Thanks for the lesson," said Sykes.

Ross frowned as he glanced questioningly at Sykes, and the agent turned and met his stare. Ross nodded and held his horse back so that Sykes and the chief rode across the bridge together. Ross followed at Many Arrows' side, and the group continued down the main street in the same order until Sykes motioned to the agency building.

As Ross pulled up beside the chief, he pointed to the sign and translated it into the Blackfoot language. Then he turned to the agent. "You're the host here," he said.

Without responding Sykes swung down, tied his horse to the hitching rail in front of the hotel, and motioned for the others to follow his example. When they had all dismounted, he led the way into his office.

There were still only three chairs in the room and Sykes arranged them in a half-circle. He then sat down in the one on the right and indicated that the chief should sit in the one in the middle. He directed Many Arrows to the third chair. "Tell the rest of them I'm sorry there aren't more chairs," said Sykes. "I will try to have more by the next time."

Ross squatted on the floor next to Sykes as he spoke to the Indians. The warriors sat to the left of Many Arrows, nearly completing a circle around the room.

"Do they expect some kind of ceremony here, like at the tepee?" asked Sykes.

"No, you're in charge here. You can do it your own way."

"All right, explain to them that this is the place for them to come when they want to see me. Tell them I'm staying here in town at the hotel. They're welcome to come here or the hotel anytime. This way they don't have to go past the guns at the fort every time they wish to talk to me. I want them to understand I am not part of the army, and Colonel Forbes doesn't give orders to me. When you think they have that clear, ask them what they want."

Sykes sat without moving and watched Flying Hawk as the chief and Ross spoke back and forth for several minutes. He glanced only once to Many Arrows, who was staring at the open doorway, appearing not to listen.

"Sykes," explained Ross when the chief finished speaking, "someone got off with a whole passel of their horses."

"What! How many horses are you talking about?"

"Almost a hundred."

"Christ! Who? Some other Indians?"

"Many Arrows tracked them. He says not. He says he saw signs of white men. There were tracks of shod horses."

For the first time Many Arrows turned and looked squarely at Sykes.

"You think he knows what he's talking about?" asked Sykes, without taking his eyes off Many Arrows.

"I never saw anyone better at reading signs."

Cole Sykes looked away from the Indian and turned to the scout with a frown. "Let's ride out and take a look. Will he go with us?"

"Don't accuse him of lying, Sykes," the scout cautioned.

"Jesus," he cursed, "I'm not accusing anybody of anything. I want to see for myself where it happened and how it happened."

"You want me to get some troops to go with us?"

"Why? So they can trample up all the evidence?"

A trace of a smile flickered in Ross' eyes as he

looked from Sykes to Many Arrows. "Silvers always did, that's all."

When Ross spoke to the chief again, Flying Hawk nodded his head and then pointed to Many Arrows, Sykes and Ross.

"The three of us?" asked Sykes.

"Yes."

"Good, let's get going while the tracks are still fresh."

Their horses kicked up a cloud of dust as they rode out of town, Sykes, Ross, and the two chiefs leading the other warriors. Pard Warner stood silently at the entrance to his store, watching apprehensively. Gaines peered out from his blacksmith shop. A group of men pushed their way through the swinging doors of the saloon and gathered sullenly on the board sidewalk. Some pointed and muttered, others fingered their guns. As the braves passed the hostile stares of the townspeople, the angry murmur of voices died, only to rise again as Sykes and the Indians reached the outskirts of town.

Sykes turned to Ross, his face grim. "I guess the Indians don't come into town much."

"No, they don't," Ross replied, spurring his horse toward the camp. "They're not welcome there."

Reaching the edge of the camp, Flying Hawk turned to his braves and spoke sharply, pointing to the lodges. The braves milled around the old chief, their voices angry. Sykes wondered if they would obey Flying Hawk's obvious order to stay in the camp.

As the agent and Ross exchanged glances, Many Arrows trotted to his father's side and spoke briefly. But the old chief shook his head and turned his horse toward the lodges. For a moment the braves hesitated and then galloped off after Flying Hawk. Many Arrows motioned to Ross and Sykes, and the three rode off toward the river.

Leading the way, Many Arrows followed the route he had taken earlier, pointing to what he had seen and to his own tracks as he had followed the signs.

Sykes dismounted several times to study the signs for himself, asking for an interpretation of Many Arrows' explanation until the agent understood all that the Indian implied.

While they loped across the flat to the other branch of the river, Sykes rode at Ross' side. "How important are these horses to them?" he asked.

The scout looked straight at Sykes. "They count their wealth in horses," he replied.

"Are these all they have?"

"No, but it's a lot of them, and most of them were Many Arrows'."

Moments later, Many Arrows halted them at the river where the agent could see the tracks beside the water without dismounting. He stared at the clear print of a horseshoe outlined in the mud.

Damn, he thought to himself. It must have been white men who ran off the horses. But who, and where had they taken them? Sykes thought of the smoldering faces of the young warriors as they had clustered around Flying Hawk. The old chief still seemed to be in command, but how much longer could he control his resentful braves? He had to get those horses back before the Indians decided to do it themselves. He might need Forbes' help at some point, but for now he wanted to follow these tracks alone.

The voice of Many Arrows interrupted his

thoughts. The Indian reached to the leather pouch at his belt and loosened the cord at the top as he spoke.

Sykes' eyes questioned Ross. "He says he has something he found on the ground here," the scout interpreted.

Many Arrows stretched out his hand, palm up. There, in the center of his hand, lay the stub of a cigarette. The war chief's eyes focused on Sykes, and he held his hand directly toward him.

As soon as Sykes saw the cigarette stub, he lifted his eyes to stare directly at Many Arrows. Abruptly, the agent picked up his reins, and turned his horse toward the horseshoe tracks in the mud. He walked his horse slowly beside the tracks into the water, leaving another set of hoof-prints. Turning his horse back, he pointed first to the other tracks and then to his own.

Many Arrows returned the cigarette stub to his pouch, ignoring the tracks Sykes had made. As Sykes splashed out of the water, he smiled at Ross. "Checked them out a long time ago, I suppose," he concluded.

Chapter 10

"Tell Many Arrows to go back to camp and stay on the reservation," Sykes ordered Ross. "I'll follow these tracks and see where they lead. You tell Forbes I may need some of his men as soon as I find out."

"You planning to go by yourself now? You better wait for me, at least."

"No. They're too far ahead now. Do what I told you." Without waiting for further argument, Sykes plunged into the water and struck out across the river. He pulled out his rifle and held it high as his horse swam through the deeper water in the middle and finally struggled out on the opposite bank.

Once at the top of the bank, Sykes reined in and studied the land ahead of him in the direction the tracks led. It was a grassy plain, like the one nestled between the rivers, and it extended for more than a mile ahead of him. The course of a stream through the middle of it was marked by clumps of brush along its banks. At the far edge of the plain, foothills sloped up, and along the upper part of the foothills a ridge of rimrock jutted above the dark green of the pine trees. The rocks were so sharply eroded that they looked impassable, although above them, from what Sykes could see, the land was flat and bare of trees. The tracks headed directly toward the hills, but there were no horses in sight on the plain.

Riding across the flat, he stayed close to the brush and trees along the stream, his eyes watchful. The grass was tall and thick, and it was easy to see where the horses had been driven through it.

At the bottom of the foothills, Sykes headed into the brush beside the stream, out of sight of the ridge above him. Moments later he rode into the pines. As he had expected, the tracks led to the place at which the stream coursed through the rimrock. Approaching the bottom of the cliffs, he could see the narrow cut made by the flowing water. It was gradual enough for horses to climb the hill beside it.

As soon as Sykes was sure of the route the thieves had taken into the hills, he circled back to where there was cover from above, searching for a different path to the top. After riding for more than a mile without seeing another place that he could get a horse up, he doubled back to check the other side of the stream.

Sykes searched unsuccessfully for a different path up the rocks. He finally took cover behind a pile of rocks and dismounted. Taking his rope and his rifle, he clambered to the bottom of the ridge of rocks rising sheer above him. For the next hour, moving slowly and staying out of sight, he searched for a way up the rim-rock on foot. The only way he could find to negotiate the vertical face of the rock was to climb up by rope.

He searched the cliffs until he saw a pinnacle above him that he could get a loop over. He uncoiled his rope and shook out the noose. On the third try he dropped the rope over the pinnacle, pulled it tight and leaned his weight against the end of the rope. Tying his rifle to the end of the rope lying on the ground, he pulled himself hand over hand. Once over the top, he hauled up his rifle, coiled the rope and hid it close to the top of the rocks.

When Sykes looked around him, he was disappointed. It had looked flat up here from the plain below, but he was still a long way from the crest of the hill. He climbed the rest of the way. Reaching the top, he saw the land was not plateau as he had expected. He cursed to himself when he saw how deeply the plateau was cut with canyons and ravines. It was no place to cross on foot, especially in highheeled boots, but he had no choice.

He looked for a higher ridge and headed for it. It took another hour to reach the top of the second ridge, but from there he could see where the stream that flowed across the higher level dropped down over the side.

Sykes was damp with sweat and breathing hard. As he pulled off his hat and drew his sleeve across his forehead, he saw a thin line of smoke, as if from a campfire, rising from a valley ahead of him. The haze from the fire hung in the air halfway across the plateau.

The sun was low in the sky, and the smoke was at least an hour ahead of him. It would be nearly dark before he could get back to his horse. Having come this far, he wasn't going to stop now. He jammed his hat back on his head, checked out his rifle and started toward the haze.

As he crossed the plateau, he watched for landmarks to help him get back in case it was dark. As he climbed the last ridge above the valley, he slowed his pace. Whoever had stolen the horses would know enough to have guards out in Indian country. He crouched over as he crossed the last few yards to a spot from which he could see down into the valley.

At the same time he heard the sound of a hammer striking metal. A moment later, he could see what appeared to be a permanent camp. Several tents had been pitched, and in the center of them a blacksmith was at work. There were two corrals below the tents and another one above, all three filled with horses, Indian horses, he'd be willing to bet. The smoke he had seen was coming from the blacksmith's fire. In the center of the corral above the tents, a wrangler had tied a horse to a snubbing post, and he was struggling to get a saddle on its back.

It was easy to see that the Indian horses were rapidly becoming white men's horses, and from the appearance of the men in the valley they were well experienced at their work.

Sykes hurried from his hiding place as soon as he saw all he could and started the long walk back. It was dark by the time he reached the spot where he had left his rope. As he bent over to pick it up, he stiffened suddenly and stared at the edge of the cliff. He moved cautiously toward the edge, keeping low so that he would not be silhouetted against the stars as he peered from behind a rock.

While he strained his ears for any sound, he heard a metal horseshoe strike a rock below him. A moment later he made out the light and dark pattern of a spotted Indian pony, and then a second one.

The dark forms astride the ponies were hard to make out, but he could see the outlines of bare shoulders, and across one man's back what looked like a quiver of arrows. He could swear he saw the barrel of a rifle sticking up behind the other man, probably strapped to his shoulder somehow. Barely breathing, Sykes peered intently into the night until he was certain they were leading his horse away.

He rose to one knee. "Damn them," he cursed softly, his anger rising, "why the hell are they after my horse?"

Sykes jerked his rifle to his shoulder and aimed at the nearest white spot. He tightened his finger on the trigger, the white spot still in his sights. Then muttering to himself, he lowered his rifle and watched as the forms disappeared into the shadows.

The Indians had left him no choice about where to get another horse. He was still sweating from having walked and scrambled over the rocks. His feet were too sore to move very fast, and he took his time heading back to the outlaws' canyon, feeling the temperature drop as he walked. He carried his rope with him this time, slung over his left shoulder so that he could use his rifle if necessary.

By the time he reached the valley a second time, there was no sign of activity around the corrals and tents. For two hours he circled the camp until he located all of the guards, and then he moved down through the trees above the uppermost corral. A dozen Indian ponies milled around in the corral, probably the ones the thieves intended to work the next day. This looked like the best place to try for a horse. He would rather have one of the outlaws' horses, but they were picketed too close to their tents.

Sykes moved slowly toward the corral, letting the horses get accustomed to his presence slowly. Whenever the horses showed signs of restlessness, he stopped and waited until they ignored him again. Reaching the back of the corral, he circled around to the gate, studying the horses inside, choosing the one he wanted. He opted for a big bay, larger and more powerful than the others. Because of his own size, he would need a large horse to get away from the outlaws.

As nearly as he could tell, none of the horses in the corral had been shod. As he studied their feet, he recognized the white stocking on the left hind foot of the big bay. It was Many Arrows' horse.

Still moving slowly and deliberately, he slid both of the gate poles back from the opening and lowered their ends to the ground far enough away from the gate post to make room for the horses to get out. Then he stepped to one side, shook out the noose in his rope, and waited.

The bay was the first horse to sense the opening. The huge animal lowered its head as it stepped through and then tossed it high as though tasting its freedom. At the same time, Sykes dropped the loop of his rope over the horse's head and jerked the rope tight as he ran forward. He pulled the animal away from the press of horses following its lead through the gate.

Reaching the horse's head, he looped his line over the animal's lower jaw, the way he had seen the Indians control their ponies. Before he could haul himself up on its back, one horse whinnied and the others began snorting. They stampeded toward the tents.

The bay plunged backwards, shying away from Sykes. At the same time the agent heard a shout behind him. He threw down his rifle and fought the rope with both hands until the animal stood quietly enough for Sykes to jump on his back. He struggled to turn the horse in the direction of the trees above the corral. Guns flamed in the darkness as the animal plunged ahead, and Sykes let the horse have its head. Bullets clipped through the trees around him as he rode into their shelter.

For the next several minutes he gave all of his attention to staying on the horse's back and keeping the long end of the rope from falling and tangling around the horse's feet. There was no time to duck the branches that whipped across him. He took their sting in his face until finally the bay slowed to the climb out of the canyon. He was then able to bring the horse under control and turn it higher up the hill. He had to ride straight up the side the rest of the way to avoid the guard at that far end of the canyon. He hoped an animal without shoes could hold its footing on the steep rocks. A moment later the bay struggled over the top in a slide of rocks and dirt, and Sykes reined him to a walk into the darkest grove of trees ahead of him.

For several minutes the guns continued to fire below him, and Sykes wondered what their target was. He hoped they were shooting at each other and that their aim was good. The guns finally stopped and aside from the horse's heavy breathing, the only sound was that of its nearly silent hooves treading on the pine needles.

He galloped through the darkness until he came upon a stream which he followed down to the lowland. He emerged on the plain about five miles from the fort. By the time Sykes rode in through the gate, the sun was up, and soldiers on the parade ground were standing inspection. Although he was chilled through, he sat erect on the horse's bare back as he trotted past them.

At the headquarters building, he waited on the porch for Colonel Forbes to appear at his office. He rolled a cigarette and stood smoking and watching the troopers.

Sam Ross emerged from the cavalry barracks and, spotting Sykes, hurried toward him. The scout looked over the bay. "You know whose horse you've got there, don't you?" he asked as he stopped at Syke's side. His voice showed his concern.

"Yes."

"Where'd you find it?"

"I didn't find it. I stole it."

Ross turned quickly away from the horse and glared at the agent.

"I stole it from the outlaws," explained Sykes.

"Where were they?"

"Above that rimrock."

"It's pretty rough up there."

"They've got quite a set-up. They're holding the horses in corrals while they shoe them and break them to the saddle."

"I'll be damned. Sounds like they've been there for a while then. How'd you get close enough to steal one of the horses?"

"I had to. It was that or walk back."

"What happened to your horse?"

Before Sykes could answer, Colonel Forbes approached. Stepping up on the porch, he brushed by the two men and into the hallway. Sykes and Ross followed the colonel.

"Good morning, Ross," the colonel greeted the scout and ignored Sykes. "You may come in, Ross, if you wish to see me."

"It's Sykes that has something to say," indicated the scout.

"He may come in, if you say so, Ross."

Sykes ignored the officer's affront and told his story as briefly as he could. The colonel stood behind his desk until Sykes finished. Then he sat down, put both hands on the edge of the table, and braced himself against the back of his chair. His voice was controlled and formal. "And now, Sykes, if you had listened to reason, if you had listened to people who know more about this country than you do, you'd have had enough troops with you to have captured them right then and there."

"If I'd taken troops with me, those outlaws would still be shooting down on us from the rimrock. They had half a dozen guards above the rock and they could have kept your whole company busy long enough to get those horses out some other way. I am willing to bet on that."

The colonel sat forward and leaned an elbow on his desk. "They could keep a whole company out but you went right in there? Do you expect me to believe that?"

"I went in a mile away from there, up a rope."

"Ha!" Forbes sat back again. "And now you say you just happen to have one of Many Arrows' horses?"

Sykes face grew dark and he stepped toward the desk.

"Easy," Ross grabbed Sykes' arm.

Sykes stared at the colonel for a moment and then reached for his tobacco sack as he stepped back. "I came to ask what you know about outlaws in this area," he said dryly.

"I don't know of any at all, unless you want to call some of that riffraff living in town outlaws. However, as far as I know they confine their dealings to the town. They're only interested in what they can steal from the soldiers. Most of their business is the kind we don't allow here in the fort, Mr. Sykes. Of course, you must know that already, since you have chosen to live among them."

The colonel stood up, as though accepting the honor of having won a major battle. "And now," he motioned to his orderly beside the doorway, "I suppose you want me to send some of my men up there after the horses for you?"

"They're gone by now, but you do what you want, Forbes," replied Sykes. He turned, and the orderly stepped out of his way. He glanced over his shoulder before he went out. "You're right about one thing. I do know a lot about horse thieves."

Chapter 11

"Well, Patricia, what can you expect of a man like that?" asked Lieutenant Barkley, taking the cup of coffee she held out to him. He smiled knowingly at her.

Tricia did not return his smile. She did not notice how even and white his teeth showed beneath his perfectly trimmed mustache, or how he had combed his wavy brown hair so carefully around his ears. "How would I know what kind of man he is?"

"Cole Sykes is a criminal, an outlaw, that's what he is. I just heard that they took him out of prison to give him this job—"

"But that's ridiculous."

"Well, if he's only supposed to see to the hostiles—who knows, perhaps they couldn't get anyone else to do it?"

Tricia poured herself a cup of coffee and walked to the chair on the other side of the fireplace. Settling down, she daintily placed her feet on the small needlepoint-covered stool in front of her. The needlepoint was one of the things she had done since she had been there.

"I thought it was a more important position than that," she said, frowning slightly as she lifted the cup to her lips.

"They gave it a fancy title, Assistant Superintendent or something, but it isn't anything. It's only until the new governor is appointed, you can be certain of that. And what's there for him to do of any importance, anyway?"

"I'm sure I don't know what he's supposed to do."

"Keep the Indians from stealing each other's horses, I guess, or let them, better yet. They need to be kept busy."

"Well, that may be, but let's talk of something else, William. Somehow I don't enjoy thinking or talking about Mr. Sykes. Everything seemed so peaceful before he got here." She stared straight ahead.

"That kind always makes trouble wherever they go, but I'll say no more if you don't want to."

Tricia sighed and turned to Barkley. "I have only a few more weeks here. What have I missed seeing?"

"You didn't need to remind me that you are leaving." Barkley leaned toward her and searched her eyes. "Why do you have to leave? Can't we do something to keep you here? Can't I do something?" His voice was cajoling.

Tricia laughed lightly as she sat back in her chair, away from the eagerness of his expression. "Now, William, can you imagine my staying here all winter? Uncle John says it's simply dreadful. He says I'm lucky to be leaving before the first snow, even leaving as soon as I am."

"Patricia, I—I won't be in this godforsaken place forever. I wish—" He fumbled with his cup.

"Oh," said Tricia, interrupting him as she stood up, "let me fill your cup again. Where will you be going after this, do you think?"

"I don't know. It all depends on what I can do

here. What I show I can do. I'm hoping for a promotion, of course, but they're not easy to get anymore, not since the war ended."

"Heavens, what's there to do here except ride your horse around the parade ground?"

"That's not funny, Patricia," he said stiffly. "As a matter of fact, it is a very great problem to me. I need to show that I can handle men in battle. I was still in West Point at the end of the war, and as far as the army is concerned, I'm untried in warfare."

"Well then, surely you're happy that Mr. Sykes will be able to stir things up for you."

"I thought you didn't want to talk about him."

"I don't. Let's talk about the party Uncle John said he would have for me before I leave."

"But I don't want to think about your leaving."

"Oh dear, and now we're back to that again. This conversation doesn't seem to be getting us any place. Why don't you finish your coffee and then let's go for a walk. I'm told there won't be many more nice days like this, and the nights are certainly getting cool enough, aren't they?"

He stood up as soon as she suggested the walk and carried his cup to the tray. "I can't think of anything I like better than walking with your hand on my arm." He added boldly, "I'm at least touching you."

Tricia fidgeted with her cup and then set it down. "Lieutenant Barkley, you're not supposed to think of it like that."

"Don't tell me that you think of it some other way?" His tone was demanding now. "I don't want to hear it, if you do."

He stood over her, his smiling eyes boring into her. Tricia reddened and turned away quickly. Why had she immediately compared his height to Cole Sykes', and then felt relief that he was a little shorter?

"I'm sorry if I'm being too bold," Barkley apologized, aware of Tricia's consternation. He moved a step away. "But you are a beautiful woman, and this place is a long way from *our* world, your world and mine . . . I thought . . ."

She forced herself to smile and then laughed as she walked past him toward the front door.

"Come along, William," she beckoned. "Let's go for that walk. I'll just stop by the store as long as I'm out." She took a moment to study herself in the hall mirror, and then patting her hair into place, she picked up her basket and stepped out the front door. She waited on the porch as Barkley closed the door behind them. The morning shadows were still long in front of the buildings, but the air was fresh, and as she took a deep breath, her eyes paused on the horse in front of the headquarters building.

"That's strange," she exclaimed.

"What?" asked Barkley, holding out his arm for her.

"Why doesn't that horse have a saddle? I've never seen one there before unsaddled." She rested her hand on his arm as they descended the steps together.

"And it's tied with a rope instead of a halter," Barkley noted. "It looks like an Indian horse to me. That is strange." Barkley was puzzled, but his thoughts were on Tricia. He smiled and looked past her at the men on the parade ground, as though he wanted to make certain they saw him walking with her. "I've never seen any of them come here alone before. One of them, at least, must have enough sense to come to your uncle for help instead of—that man you don't want me to mention."

The two moved toward the parade ground. The lieutenant laughed as he looked down and caressed the back of her hand. "Do you want to go around the other side of the parade ground so you won't chance meeting the savage? It'll be farther to walk, but that suits me better anyway."

Tricia glanced behind her at the laundry tents and then looked ahead at the horse. "No, Uncle John has suggested I stay away from the tents over there."

While Lieutenant Barkley grinned in the direction of the tents, Cole Sykes emerged from the headquarters building and walked to the Indian horse. As soon as she saw him, Tricia gasped slightly. Barkley faced squarely ahead and then scowled at the agent.

Colonel Forbes' orderly and Sam Ross followed a few steps behind Sykes, but as soon as the orderly saw Barkley, he hurried past the other two men and headed directly toward the lieutenant and Tricia.

There was a look of anticipation on Barkley's face by the time the orderly stopped in front of him, standing stiffly at attention.

"Colonel Forbes wishes to see you, sir," saluted the orderly.

"Thank you. Tell Colonel Forbes I'm on my way." He smiled down at Tricia. "I'm sorry to cut this short, Patricia, but at least I'll get you home safely. You can see there's trouble, and I'm quite certain our friend brought something for me to do."

He turned toward her uncle's house, but Tricia held back. Lifting her hand from his arm, she insisted, "No, I'm going on to the store, but don't you keep Uncle John waiting. You know he doesn't like that." Her eyes followed Sykes as he led the pony away. "Mr. Sykes is leaving, William, now you go on."

"No, I'll see to your safety first."

"I'm quite all right, William. I'll walk slowly until he's gone. You go ahead." She touched his arm and gave it a push, and finally he strode ahead to the headquarters building. On the steps, he turned and raised one hand to her. But Tricia's eyes were still riveted on Cole Sykes, and she did not see Barkley wave until it was too late to respond.

When Sykes and Ross stopped at the store, Tricia made sure Barkley was out of sight, and then started walking rapidly toward the store. Reaching the porch, she hesitated for a moment, looking at the open doorway. Then she turned her back to the store and faced the Indian pony tied at the railing.

From inside the store, Sykes saw her in the doorway. Her back was to him, the sunlight from the east outlining her figure and striking through her hair. He studied the slender line of her back as he walked toward the door.

Tricia heard the sound of his boots as he approached the doorway, and she moved quickly down the porch. Lighting a cigarette, Sykes stepped out into the sunlight and approached her. He blew out a cloud of smoke over her head.

"Mr. Sykes," she exclaimed, turning as if startled.

"Don't act so surprised," he grinned sarcastically. "You knew I was coming, and you were waiting for me."

"Was I really? How can you be so sure?"

"What do you want, Miss Ashley?" he asked crisply.

Tricia lifted her chin haughtily. "I want to know what you and Lieutenant Barkley were fighting about the other day."

"He shoved me, and I hit him. It wasn't what I'd

call fighting. Your uncle saw to that when he called it off."

"I mean—why?"

"I'd hit anybody that poked their fingers into me," he replied coldly.

"Anybody? Even me?" Tricia asked, her voice flirting with him.

"Don't be silly."

"I was not silly! Now," she demanded, "I want to know why William shoved you in the first place."

"Are you afraid he'll get hurt? You want to protect him?"

"He does not need my protection," she replied sharply. "Lieutenant Barkley is a very brave and honorable man." She put a hand to her hip. "For heaven's sake! You are a difficult man. I can certainly see how you've managed to get everyone here against you."

She started to flounce away and then paused. "You still haven't answered my question."

"Which question?"

"I've had enough of that kind of answer," she snapped.

"You're raising your voice again. You'll get Barkley here in a minute."

"So—it did have something to do with me."

"He claimed I insulted you. Were you insulted, Miss Ashley?" Sykes put the cigarette to his lips and grinned at her through the smoke, watching her eyes.

"No," she answered. She drew herself to her full height. "A lady *cannot* be insulted by anyone like you!" She turned and stamped down the steps and walked rapidly in the direction of the colonel's house.

Sykes heard a chuckle behind him, and he turned abruptly. Sam Ross was standing with one shoulder against the side of the doorway. Sykes had been caught off guard, and he didn't like it.

"Little spitfire, isn't she?" said Ross.

"Shut up," retorted Sykes.

"Oh," drawled Ross, straightening up in the opening. "Sorry, I didn't think that'd mean anything to you."

Sykes turned away and flipped his cigarette into the dirt beside the horse. "It doesn't," he said, starting down the steps.

Ross raised his eyebrows at Patricia Ashley's back and sauntered across the porch, his face expressionless. "What are you going to do with that horse?" he asked as Sykes unhitched the bay.

"Trade it for my own."

"Look here, Sykes," Ross began. "You're not sure . . ." The scout stopped in mid-sentence.

"Looks like you lost your rifle, too, or did you leave it with your horse?" he asked bluntly.

Sykes jerked the rope free of the hitching rail and stood there coiling up the long end of it until the horse started to back away from him. At once he jerked the horse toward him again and held the rope taut, staring at the animal steadily while he took a deep breath. After a moment he glanced at Ross over his shoulder.

"You ever try to get on one of these unsaddled bastards while it's shying away from you and you've got a rope in one hand and a rifle in the other? They were shooting at me before I could get away as it was. I didn't have time to do anything except leave my rifle on the ground."

Sykes faced the horse again, and without waiting for a response from the scout, moved cautiously to its side. This time he mounted with a single try. He turned the horse away from the rail and looked down at Ross.

"Could you tell Many Arrows I've got his horse down here at the agency and that he can come and get it? Tell him he can ride mine on the way."

"How do you know he's the one took it?"

"I don't for sure, but it's my guess. Tell him and see what he says."

"All right," Ross agreed, "and I'll come in with him, too, so there won't be any misunderstandings."

Sykes nodded his thanks and spurred the horse toward the gate. Almost involuntarily, his eyes slid sideways to the colonel's house just as Tricia paused at the doorway and looked in his direction. He jabbed the horse's flanks and galloped through the gate.

The sun warmed his shoulders by the time he reached the river, and he walked the bay across the bridge and along the street. Dismounting at the hotel, he entered the dining room. Sykes shared his breakfast with three other men at the large table in the middle of the room. They ate in silence, the three men watching the agent furtively. When he had eaten, Sykes went to the dry goods store to look over the case that held guns and knives. The only rifles he could see were on the wall behind the case. As he stood looking them over, Pard Warner walked around behind the case and rested his hands on top of it.

"What can I do for you, Sykes?" he asked. "You need some ammunition?"

"Are those all the guns you've got?" Sykes pointed to the wall toward the short-barreled Sharpes carbines that hung there, light rifles used a lot during the recent war.

"Yep. I haven't got anything here as good as the one I saw on your horse the other day."

"Those carbines are too light. I want a better range."

"Well, that's all I've got. They might have something better at the fort," suggested Warner. Then he laughed. "If they'll sell anything to you. I heard old Forbes has really got his tail in a crack over moving the agency out of there. Tell you what, though. You see something you want up there, I'll go trade 'em for it if you need me to. We trade back and forth all the time. Forbes wouldn't have to know."

Sykes turned away from the case. "I'll see what they have later."

Out on the sidewalk, Sykes stopped and rubbed his eyes. He felt drained and weary. If he waited for Many Arrows in the agency office, there was a good chance he'd fall asleep, and he didn't want to be caught by the Indians that way. After a moment he walked down the street to the Trapper's Last Chance and pushed through the doors.

Although the morning was still early, he was not the only customer in the saloon. As he walked toward the bar, a man shoved away from it and turned toward him. Although the man's right arm was in a sling, it took Sykes a moment to realize that it was Littan, the one he had shot his first day in town. Littan's whiskers had grown into a dark stubble over his chin, and his hat was tilted low over his eyes. From the expression on his face, he had no trouble recognizing Sykes, but he said nothing as he sidled past the agent and out through the doors.

Sykes watched Littan's disappearing back and then moved along the wooden counter to a spot where he could see most of the room in the huge mirror behind the bar. He leaned both forearms on the bar's edge after he motioned for a drink. He stared into the mirror at the still-swinging doors, while the bartender poured a shot of whiskey.

The bartender stood silent and unmoving until Sykes took a coin from his pocket and dropped it on the bar.

"Wasn't that Littan?" Sykes asked at the same time.

The bartender, a shabby little man with a scrawny neck, set the bottle under the bar and picked up his bar rag. He carefully wiped where there was no spill. "You think I ask that kind what his name is?" he replied, his face sullen.

"There were several others with him the last time I saw him," Sykes persisted as he lifted his glass.

"They've been gone awhile," the bartender answered shortly.

"Thanks," Sykes uttered sarcastically, picking up his glass and walking to the table by the front window.

He was already fighting sleep, and he did not sit down. Standing with one foot on the seat of the chair and one arm across his upraised knee, he watched the street.

The minute he saw Ross canter into view, he knew the scout had been unsuccessful. Somehow, he had half expected that Many Arrows would not make a deal concerning his horse so quickly. Besides, he grudgingly conceded to himself, he hadn't gotten their herd of ponies back, and now he was beginning to wonder just when and how he would.

Ross reined in as Sykes pushed open the saloon doors and stepped out to greet him.

"I guess I should've told you it wouldn't be easy," Ross said half apologetically.

"What does he want now?" Sykes asked in exasperation. "His horse is as good as mine, maybe better. You told me the bay was his best hunting pony. He's not losing anything, and he damn well doesn't need the saddle."

"He wants to see his horse first. I can understand that."

"You understand too damn much about them. All right, I'll go with you. I want my saddle back, and I don't have the time now to train the bay the way I want him."

Abruptly, Sykes turned from Ross and headed for Pard Warner's store, barking over his shoulder to the scout, "I'm not going out there without a rifle, though."

The agent stamped into the dry goods store and emerged within minutes with a Sharpes carbine, stuffing ammunition into the breech. He leaned the rifle up against the hitching rail and vaulted onto the skittish stallion. He leaned awkwardly over the animal's neck and grabbed the rifle by the barrel.

Ross chuckled at the maneuver. "Now you know why the Indians put straps on their guns."

"It'd be just as smart to have a saddle with a rifle boot," he snapped to Ross' back as the scout loped away.

Sykes touched the bay with his spurs and the animal lunged forward. As they approached Ross, the bay flattened his ears and, straining against the rope bridle, pulled ahead of the scout's horse.

Ross laughed. "Sure can tell that's Many Arrows' horse," he called to Sykes. "He's used to being out in front."

As the riders came into view of the camp, Ross pointed to the grassy meadow above the lodges. "He said he'd meet us there." Before Sykes could respond, the scout turned to him. "Look, Sykes, there's going to be a lot of ceremony to this. Just like in the council. You have to . . ."

"Jesus, what for?" the agent exploded. "It's my own damn horse and he stole it."

"Like I was saying, Sykes," Ross explained stonily, "you have to remember a horse is one of the honors of war to the Blackfoot. Their horses were taken, so they feel they have a right to take others. Right now, Many Arrows has another feather in his bonnet for taking your horse, and he'd hate to give that feather up."

"But there isn't any war," Sykes persisted, "and he stole . . ."

"Sykes," Ross warned, "I've been trying to explain that it isn't stealing to them. This could mean a lot of trouble if you don't handle it right. Besides," he added slyly, "you didn't get their horses back for them."

"All right, all right," the agent conceded, "I'll try to do it their way."

They urged their horses up the incline and reined in at the top. In the middle of the field, ten mounted braves had arranged themselves in a semicircle. In their midst was Many Arrows, astride a spotted pony. His face and chest were splashed with brilliant streaks of color, and his head bore a short, eagle-feathered bonnet, trimmed with wolf fur, to which he had proudly added another feather just that morning.

In his hand, the young war chief clenched a short bow made of buffalo bone. One of his most valuable possessions, the bone had been traded for two ponies with a Crow warrior. The war arrows in the otter-skin quiver slung over his back were designed for a human enemy. Many Arrows himself had fashioned the long, cruel barbs on the arrowheads so that the head would remain in a wound after the shaft had been withdrawn.

Sykes started at the sight of the young chief and the other braves. They were also daubed with paint, and feathers and quills poked at various angles from their shining black hair. Some held lances at their sides, and others had strapped their short bows over their shoulders. Two of them grasped their coup sticks, the short clubs with which they clouted a foe at close range.

Sykes scanned the row of Indians for a yellow-grey horse, his buckskin. "I don't see my horse," he growled at Ross as he shifted his rifle higher across the bay's shoulders.

"Hold on, Sykes," the scout cautioned, "you're not going to see your horse here. This is ceremony, like I told you."

Ross moved slowly across the meadow, beckoning Sykes to follow. Struggling to keep the bay stallion from dashing toward the other ponies, the agent pranced toward the warriors. The two stopped a dozen feet from Many Arrows, and Ross turned to the agent. "They haven't got any guns, Sykes. Hold your rifle by the barrel and set the stock on your leg. And don't look so ready to shoot."

Sykes glared at the scout, but did as the man advised. At the same time, the braves slowly extended the half circle and gathered around the two men, nearly enclosing them.

Sykes clenched the barrel of his rifle and stared straight at Many Arrows. "Tell him why we're here, Ross," he ordered, his voice toneless.

Ross and Many Arrows spoke for several minutes, and then the scout turned to Sykes. "He says the buckskin is his now, but he'll trade with you for the saddle."

Sykes fought to keep his face from betraying his surprise. "I'll be goddamned," he breathed hoarsely. "That's about the. . . ."

Ross shifted uneasily in his saddle, and Sykes paused. Still staring directly at Many Arrows, the agent let several seconds pass. Then he turned to Ross. "Ask him what he wants for the saddle."

The glint that flashed in Ross' eyes betrayed his surprise. "You mean you're going to let him have it?" he asked.

"You ever spend any time in a territorial prison, Ross?"

"What's that got to do with it?"

"I'll tell you some time," Sykes said impatiently. "Right now I want that saddle even if I do have to train this damned horse of his. What does he want for the saddle?"

Ross pointed to the agent's hand around the barrel of the Sharpes. "He wants that rifle."

"Jesus—" Sykes drew in his breath. "Is that a fair trade?" he questioned Ross.

"It'd be a damned smart one."

"Tell him I want to see the saddle first."

"Now you're talking," Ross sighed with relief. The scout exchanged some words with Many Arrows. The chief motioned to one of the braves behind him and then swung his arm in the direction of the camp. At once the warrior turned his pony and raced away.

Chapter 12

Corporal Rich Eddy stood patiently beside his horse on the parade ground, waiting with the rest of the men for the order to mount. His clear brown eyes scanned the horizon as he reached up to pull his trooper's cap farther down over his thick red hair. His young face was unlined and smooth. He had decided to forego the drooping mustache grown by many of his comrades.

The afternoon sun had lost some of the heat of summer, but it was still hot on his back and shoulders, and the sky was clear, unbroken by a single cloud as far as he could see. There was anticipation among the men that he felt strongly in himself. Chasing horse thieves, whether they were Indian or white as the new Indian agent claimed, meant action to the men. None of them had been out of the fort on anything but a woodcutting or horse-grazing detail since they'd tried to find Silvers' murderer.

With the others, he turned his head as Lieutenant Barkley trotted from the officers' stables. Sergeant Pearce barked out the order to mount, and Eddy settled into the saddle with a sigh of pleasure. From the way his mount shifted its weight under him, he was sure the animal knew they were going to do more than wheel and swerve on the parade ground.

Corporal Eddy, slim and assured, sat his horse with the ease of someone who had grown up riding. He realized how much some of the men needed the daily drills. Men like Lew Miles, for instance, who was letting his horse toss its head high enough to get behind the bit, had never owned a saddle horse. He would have to speak to Miles about not letting his mount get the best of him, but not this afternoon.

The corporal stared straight ahead as the lieutenant trotted briskly down and back before the line of men and horses. When Sergeant Pearce shouted the order, Eddy moved out into position.

The detachment left the fort riding four abreast, Corporal Eddy in the front line of men and Sergeant Pearce to one side, where he could see the entire column of men and horses. Lieutenant Barkley rode alone at the head of the detail. As soon as the troopers passed through the gate, they wheeled to the right and followed the course of the river.

They stayed off reservation land, turning east as the river turned, even though it was a long way to go, and then northeast again until they began to climb to the shadowy, pine-covered foothills. As they rode up the slope Eddy could see the spires of rimrock rising above the pines. They reminded him of pictures he'd seen in his school books of fancy churches in Europe. He grinned and flexed his shoulders when he thought about how far away he was from that school and how much he would rather be where he was now, with a good horse under him riding in all that open space.

He could see a half dozen antelope off to his right, close enough to be an easy target with the rifle he had under his leg. He followed the antelope with his eyes as they leaped away from the dust and clatter of the cavalry horses. Eddy was concerned about the swirling dust cloud. He swept his gaze over the foothills. If the horse thieves were still up there, they ought to know the cavalry was coming by now. The dust they stirred up would be visible for miles.

Barkley turned the soldiers aside before they reached the trees and followed a narrow branch of the river up to higher ground. Climbing into the pine grove, the men broke formation to dodge between the trees. Where the trees were the thickest, they spread out in single file.

Barkley signaled a stop a hundred yards below the rimrock, and spoke for several minutes to Sergeant Pearce before the sergeant called to Eddy. As Corporal Eddy rode forward, he saw that the stream had cut through the rimrock wide enough for riders to ascend. Sergeant Pearce explained that he wanted the corporal and his men to scout ahead.

"Yes, sir," Eddy responded, "but are you certain that's the only way up? We'll have to go one at a time most of the way. If there's anyone up there—"

"You heard your orders," Barkley snapped. "Get that horse moving."

Eddy turned his horse at once and rode briskly past the officer as he motioned to his men to follow. When he was above the main body of troopers and his horse had settled into the climb, he called over his shoulder to the four behind him.

"Drop back," he ordered. "Give me twenty, thirty feet of lead, and then keep me covered." He paused for a moment before he went on. "Johnson, if anything happens to me, you're in charge."

Eddy pulled his rifle from the saddle boot and held it in front of him. He searched the rocks and trees above him as he let his horse pick its way up the rough incline. Glancing at the ground beside him, he could easily see that a large number of horses had gone up that way recently, most of them unshod.

Eddy felt his senses sharpen the higher he climbed, and he was relieved that he could still command the steadiness that he always had when he chased four-footed game. He'd hunted ever since he'd been old enough to handle a gun, and this didn't seem as different as he'd thought it might. Moments later, riding over the top of the rimrock without seeing anyone, he felt a sense of disappointment.

He stopped and studied the tracks ahead of him while he waited for Johnson and the men. He turned as he heard them clatter over the top.

"Did any of you see anything?" he asked.

Johnson shook his head along with the others. "I didn't, and you can bet I was looking hard enough."

"All right, then, wait here. I'll go down and tell Barkley it's clear. Keep a sharp watch while I'm gone. It looks like they went over that ridge, but stay here until I get back. Then we'll check the ridge out next."

Still holding his rifle, Corporal Eddy made his way slowly down, his mount bracing itself at the steep places. He watched around him as carefully as he had before. There was always the chance the horse thieves had led them into a trap that was now closed behind them. Again he saw nothing, and when he reached the trees, he loped the rest of the way toward the waiting troops.

"What did you find?" asked Barkley as Eddy pulled up.

"Nothing, sir, except the tracks of the horses. Most of the horses were unshod, but there were some tracks of horseshoes mixed in."

"You think you can read tracks like a scout, do you?"

"I've done a lot of hunting, sir."

"For horses?"

"No, sir. I guess not."

"No matter anyway," shrugged the lieutenant, turning toward the hill. "If there's no one up there, Sergeant, give the order to proceed."

"Lieutenant, sir," interrupted Eddy. "If you don't mind, I'd like to go on ahead. It's not as level up there as it looks, and the tracks go over a ridge close to the top where there could easily be an ambush."

Barkley scowled at the young cavalryman and then waved his hand in the direction of the rimrock as though it were not important one way or the other.

At once Eddy touched his spurs to his horse's side and headed for the hill. This time he pushed his mount to the climb as fast as the horse could take it, loose rocks rolling down the cut behind him. Reaching the top he beckoned to the other men.

"Cover me the way you did before," he commanded. His expression was serious as he cantered by the soldiers. Then he grinned, sweeping his eyes over the ridge ahead of him.

Barkley let him ride as scout all the way to the valley where the Indian horses had been held. Riding into the thieves' camp, Eddy saw the trampled ground where tents had been pitched. The stone circles that had enclosed their fires were still filled with charred wood. While he waited for the main body of the detachment to arrive, he dismounted and walked slowly around the corrals and the tent area. Passing the largest fire pit, he stopped, reached down, picking up a horseshoe nail lying beside one of the stones. He looked from the nail in his hand into the ashes and partly burned pieces of wood. After a moment he dug out a piece of wood and smelled it to see how recently it had been burned. As nearly as he could tell, it had been burned within the last day or so.

Several empty cartridge cases were lying not far from the fire pit, and he was inspecting one of them when Lieutenant Barkley and the soldiers galloped directly into the camp. The horses trampled the ground, churning up dirt and dust. Eddy had kept his own men clear, and he was certain there would have been more to see and collect in the way of evidence. But he said nothing about it as he walked toward Barkley.

"I found these here, sir," he said, extending his hand.

The lieutenant peered down at Eddy's hand for several seconds and then looked casually away. "Sergeant Pearce, it's getting late. This looks like as good a place to camp as any. Give the orders."

The detail broke camp at dawn the next morning and followed the tracks up the valley. This time Lieutenant Barkley rode in the lead. After a mile, the ground turned rocky on both sides of the stream and the trees were so dense that the column could never thread its way through them. Another half mile of clattering over the rocks or riding in the stream bed brought no sign of the horses. Barkley signaled a halt.

"We might as well turn back," he decided, looking at the trees ahead of him. "They could have left the water a half dozen places in the last mile, if they came this way at all."

"Yes, sir," agreed Pearce. "I think you're right, and from what I can see of the sky we've got a humdinger of a storm brewing over us, too."

The lieutenant squinted up. Only a narrow strip of blue sky shone through the trees lining the banks, but what he could see was already filled with dark clouds. Suddenly a rush of wind whistled down the canyon. Barkley turned his head quickly away from the gust and settled his hat lower on his head. "Let's go," he ordered, pulling his horse around.

Chapter 13

Cole Sykes ate breakfast early, and then gathered up his saddle, blanket and bridle from the livery stable and carried them out the back to the corral. He fetched the bay and led it slowly out to the corral. For several minutes he led the horse around the enclosure. When the stallion continued to walk by itself, Sykes gradually let out the lead rope and backed toward the snubbing post in the middle of the corral, carefully watching the way the horse moved in its iron shoes.

Hugh Gaines appeared and climbed the fence behind the agent, leaning his elbows on the top rail.

"Looks okay to me," commented the blacksmith after a few minutes. "I don't see any problem."

"Neither do I," said Sykes, but he continued to scrutinize the bay's gait for several minutes after the blacksmith left. Finally, he pulled the horse to the snubbing post and tied him there.

For half an hour Sykes moved his hands over the animal, talking softly to it, letting it get accustomed to him. He picked up each leg and cleaned out the hoof, even though Gaines had done it the night before. Then, still murmuring soothingly to the bay, he set the saddle blanket on its back. He had seen Indian horses with blankets on them, and the animal accepted the covering without resistance. The stallion stood quietly as Sykes threw on the saddle, hooked the stirrup over the saddle horn and reached for the cinch. Its ears pricked up as the agent lifted the cinch into place. Then suddenly they flattened and the huge beast snorted and with a heave, hunched its back as Sykes pulled tight on the cinch. The bay fought the snubbing rope, jerking away from the agent as far as it could. Despite the horse's struggles Sykes stayed beside it until he had the cinch as tight as he wanted it. Then he walked over to his bridle hanging over the fence and stood beside it, his back against the corral, observing the horse while he smoked a cigarette.

By early afternoon Sykes had the stallion trained to the saddle and bridle, and when it would obey the pressure of the reins, the agent trotted out of the corral and headed for the fort. The parade ground was empty when he arrived. He rode straight to the middle of the field, galloped the horse down the center, reined up sharply at the far end, turned and then spurred the bay into a dead run toward the gate. When there was still no problem that he could see with the iron shoes, he loped to the store, swung down and tied the horse. "That's just the beginning," he told the horse, stroking its soft nose. "You've got a lot more tricks to learn, but that's enough for today."

He strode across the porch and then stopped in the doorway just as Patricia Ashley turned from the counter and glanced in his direction. Seeing him silhouetted in the entrance, she turned quickly back to the counter. Ignoring her back, Sykes entered and walked to the gun case. He stood looking over the weapons, but his mind was on Tricia and the sound of her voice. It had been sweet and friendly before he approached. Now she was speaking sharply to the clerk.

The clerk's attention was on Tricia, and Sykes grew impatient. He stepped to her side and motioned to the clerk.

"Excuse me a moment, Miss Ashley," the storekeeper said. "What can I do for you, Sykes?"

"Are those your only rifles?"

"Yes."

"One of them looks like an Indian had it."

"The one with the nailheads all over the stock?"

"Yes."

"You're right. They always trade in their own guns when I have anything better. I get some good ones, and they seem to know it the same day. You might find something better at Warner's."

"He's got nothing but carbines. I want something heavier."

"Well, I can't help you now. Sorry," he answered.

Sykes walked to the doorway and stopped in the entrance, looking at the heavy clouds forming over the hills beyond the fort. He folded his arms across his chest and leaned one shoulder against the side of the doorway.

It was several minutes before he heard Tricia bid the clerk good-bye and heard her footsteps coming toward him. She stopped behind him abruptly, but he did not move out of her way.

Sykes made her wait a full minute before he turned slowly to face her.

Her mouth was set in a straight thin line, and her eyes were fixed on the open space beyond him. He still did not move out of her way. If she wanted to go through the door, she would have to turn sideways to get past him.

"Excuse me, Mr. Sykes," she said icily. "If you don't mind—"

"You can get through there," he drawled. "You don't think I'd know enough to get out of the way of a—lady—do you?"

She continued to gaze past him. "I am quite aware that when I said that to you I was not being polite either. You do not need to remind me of it every time you see me."

Sykes pulled off his hat and bowed slightly as he stepped aside.

Tricia glided haughtily through the doorway, and then turned her head away from Sykes, but not before he could see her lower lip tremble and her eyes close tightly as she walked to the edge of the porch. She stood there uncertainly, with one hand over her face.

He stared at her trembling back as he settled his hat on his head. Ambling across the porch to his horse, Sykes pulled his reins free and swung into the saddle. Tricia's face was still buried in her hand when he crowded his horse against the edge of the porch. She did not see him reach for her. She felt a strong arm grasp her, and before she could protest, he lifted her into the saddle in front of him and spurred his horse toward the parade ground.

"What are you doing?" she gasped, clutching his arm with both hands.

"You looked as though you didn't want anyone to see you crying."

"Mr. Sykes, this is absurd!" Tricia's voice quavered. Tears streaked her face, and the agent gently brushed one hand over her cheek.

"Don't you touch me!" she protested, pushing herself back against his arm.

"Touch you? How can I help it now? You're practically on my lap, and I've got my arm around you."

"And right where everyone can see!"

"Is that what's bothering you? What if no one could see? Would it be all right then?"

"Mr. Sykes!" Her voice now took on the sharp edge that had come into it as soon as she saw him.

"I don't like the way you talk to me," he said.

"And just what is wrong with the way I talk?"

He smiled. "Why don't you use your sweet voice and say things like, 'Look, Cole, see how the grass is growing down there, and look at those clouds in the sky. See the way they're moving like that'?" He spoke in a calm, conversational tone, and while she looked down at the grass and then up at the sky, he twisted in the saddle and studied the clouds around them.

"I think we're going to have a storm, Tricia," he whispered, his voice soft and friendly. "Do you see those dark clouds over there?"

"Mr. Sykes—"

"Nope, that's not the way I said to talk."

"Will you please take me back to the store," she insisted, her voice harsh with the effort to control it.

"Have you ever been caught out in a prairie storm?" he asked, still studying the dark, almost black clouds drifting toward them.

"No, and I do not intend to be. I've heard about them."

While she spoke lightning streaked across the sky and crashed in the hills beyond the fort. A drop of rain splashed heavily on the back of her hand.

"Oh!" she exclaimed, wiping at the wet spot with the other hand. "You can take me directly home now."

"I think we should finish our little ride first."

"We have finished our ride, Mr. Sykes. Take—me—home!" her voice rose to a near scream.

Another drop of rain pelted her skirt as Sykes turned the bay in the direction of the gate.

"No—oh!" She softened her voice. "Cole," she pleaded, "please take me home. I'm not dressed to be out in this."

He spurred his horse across the parade ground and put his hand on her waist. "It's all right," he assured her. "I've been caught out in rain a lot worse than this is likely to be."

Tricia started to protest again, but Sykes urged the stallion ahead faster. Her hand tightened on his arm as she set her mouth firmly and remained silent.

They dashed through the gate and down to the river. Sykes turned aside before he reached the bridge and rode along the bank until they were below the town and out of sight from the fort. By the time he pulled up, the rain was streaming down in a regular pattern and the temperature was starting to drop.

"This'll be a good place to watch the storm," he said as he rode part way up the bank and stopped. "We're not high enough to be struck by lightning—those trees up there will get it before we do—and we're far enough above the river so we won't get caught in a flash flood if there is one."

"Mr. Sykes, I am not dressed for this, and I'm cold already."

"What did you call me?" He tightened his arm around her shoulders and pulled her close to him.

"Cole," she whispered, her voice softening a bit.

The lightning brightened the sky again for an instant, and the thunder that followed broke and crashed around them. At the sound, Tricia flung both arms around him and hid her face against his shoulder. At that instant, the rain became a downpour. In moments their clothes were soaked through.

Sykes laughed as the next bolt of lightning struck, closer still, and he fought the nervous stallion as the thunder cracked again. He held Tricia tight against him, balancing them both to the motion of the prancing horse. The bay calmed down, but shifted uneasily under them. Sykes laughed again, looking up at the sky.

"Oh, Cole," Tricia shuddered and pressed her face against his shoulder.

"Don't you like it?" he grinned.

"No!" she answered emphatically, lifting her head a few inches and looking up at him. Her eyes were wide with fear and her soaked hair was plastered around her face. "Please."

He lowered his head over her so that his hat kept the rain from her face. "It's all right. You don't think I'd take you where it was really dangerous, do you?" he asked, looking into her eyes.

The lightning streaked again and she closed her eyes for a moment. He could feel her shiver as the thunder crashed over them. Then she opened her eyes and looked up at him, questioning what she could see in his face.

Sykes gazed tenderly at Tricia and brushed the wet hair from her cheek. His hand lingering on her face, he lowered his head until his lips touched hers. Her mouth, wet with the rain, was warm and soft, and she made no effort to move away. Lifting his head slowly, he saw that her lips were parted and her eyes still questioning. She seemed to have forgotten the storm.

Suddenly he wanted to get her away from there, out of the rain. He wanted to take her where it was dry and warm.

"I'm sorry," he said quickly, spurring the bay

around. "I didn't really mean for you to be cold and miserable."

"Cole," she said, smiling at his frown and speaking in the voice he had asked her to use. "I'm terribly, terribly cold, but I'm not sorry. But now, please, if I don't shiver myself right off the back of this horse first, I do want to go back."

The stallion was still climbing the bank from the river when Lieutenant Barkley, at the head of the returning detachment, appeared behind them. The men and horses did not seem weary. They looked as if they'd had a good rest the night before, even though now their uniforms were soaked and heavy with the rain.

As soon as he saw Patricia, Barkley ordered the detail into the fort and spurred his mount toward her and Sykes.

"Miss Ashley," he called out, his voice reaching her through the storm. "Are you all right?"

"Blast," Tricia blurted out the unaccustomed word. "What will I say?"

Her eyes flashed with a trace of humor as she glanced up at Sykes. "He'll never understand this. He's much too proper."

The agent smiled down at her. "You want me to do the explaining?"

"No," she exclaimed. "How do I know what you'd say?"

Tricia smiled at the lieutenant as he stopped in front of her. "I'm quite all right, William," she said in her most proper voice, a voice that belied her present appearance. "It's good of you to see to us, but we were just on our way back."

Cole Sykes could feel how hard she was trying not to shiver.

"We seem to have gotten caught in a storm. You'd think Mr. Sykes would have seen it coming, wouldn't you?" She looked up at the agent, a trace of mischief in her eyes. "But you're not from this part of the country, are you, Agent Sykes?"

"No," he answered, staring solemnly at Barkley and touching a spur to his stallion's side. The bay jumped suddenly in response to the jab and Sykes wrapped both arms around Tricia. He continued talking as though nothing had happened. "Where I come from it's so dry the wind mostly just picks things up and carries them away. We're always glad when it rains, and we go outside to enjoy it."

Barkley looked grimly down at Sykes' arms around Tricia's waist. "That horse of yours isn't very well trained, is it?" he asked contemptuously.

Sykes shifted one arm slightly, as though to take it away, and then rested his hand lower on the far side of Tricia's waist.

"He's doing okay," said Sykes. "He only learned about saddles this morning."

Barkley stretched sideways in his saddle, leaning to investigate the single white foot. "I know that horse! That's an Indian pony." He spit the words out.

"Yep, just a pony," retorted Sykes, openly studying the lieutenant's smaller horse, a horse that had always looked sharp on the parade ground, but didn't seem to have much left to it now.

"Gentlemen," Tricia broke in, her voice tinged with anger, "I'm cold and soaked through, and I'd like to get back to the fort." She didn't seem to notice that as she spoke she had folded her arms over her waist and her arms were resting on Sykes' hands. "I'll make some coffee for you and Mr. Sykes, William, but we must get back."

"I'll have to report to Forbes first," said Barkley as he lifted his reins. He was annoyed, and his voice was sullen. "Patricia, what were you doing out here, anyway?"

"I'll tell you later," she waved to him as he straightened in his saddle and turned his horse toward the fort.

Waiting until Barkley was out of sight, Sykes spurred the bay ahead, and Patricia settled herself against his chest. The thunder rolled around them again, and she started. "I don't think I'll ever get used to it, Cole."

"That rumbling reminds me I'd better get you home before Barkley tells Forbes where he saw you. I don't want to hear that bugle calling everyone to arms."

"You'd certainly deserve it. I have no idea how I'll get my hair dry in time for dinner tonight."

"It looks all right wet."

He felt her take a deep breath, but she did not respond to his comment.

When he lifted her down in front of her house, she ran up the steps and hurried inside without looking back at him or the passing troopers, who were staring at her.

Chapter 14

Lieutenant Barkley rode directly to the headquarters building and dismounted. He was standing on the porch, stamping his feet to get the water off his boots before he went inside, when Cole Sykes rode into the fort holding Patricia in front of him. The lieutenant turned away at the sight and strode through the door.

The heels of his boots struck loudly against the boards in the hallway as he walked to the colonel's office. Reaching the doorway, he stopped. His eyes narrowed and his mouth was set in a harsh line. He waited in the doorway until Forbes looked up.

"Barkley," inquired the colonel, rising from his desk as soon as he saw the lieutenant's face. "What happened?"

"If you look down the hall, sir, you'll probably still have time to see for yourself." The lieutenant stepped backward out of the doorway and pointed to the outside door.

At once Colonel Forbes stalked past Barkley and into the hall. Even before he reached the front door, he could see Cole Sykes lower Tricia to the ground. While he watched, his niece flew into the house and the agent turned his horse away.

The colonel stood stiffly inside the open door, his

arms folded over his chest, until Sykes had traversed the length of the parade ground.

"There are strange things going on around here," muttered Barkley, standing at attention behind the colonel.

"There certainly are," replied Forbes, turning toward his office.

"For one thing, I'd like to know why he hasn't given that horse back to Many Arrows," Barkley spat out angrily. "I suppose he's fleecing them all on the side."

"I don't know," Forbes remarked, "but I'd expect it of a common criminal, wouldn't you?"

"Yes," said Barkley.

Colonel Forbes picked up his pipe as he sat down and held it, unlighted, while he stared out toward the parade ground for several minutes. Sheets of rain were still driving against the window. Barkley waited in silence, his hands behind his back, his face a mask of self-assurance.

The colonel sighed and looked away from the window. Then he straightened in his chair and set the pipe down without lighting it. "What is your report of the expedition?" he asked, his tone formal.

"We saw very little, sir. There were a few horse tracks here and there, and we did find a canyon that had some cut poles in it. I presume that's what Sykes was calling a permanent camp with corrals and all. The poles looked to me as though they could have been left there by a settler at some earlier time. I found no evidence that horses were being shod by the dozens, and certainly no blacksmith shop in the middle of nowhere. It was a fanciful story on Mr. Sykes' part, I'm afraid. Why he would make it up I can't imagine. That's one of the strange things I mentioned."

"Covering up for something else, I suppose. Is that all of your report?"

"Yes, sir, and I expect by now this rain has washed away what little we did see."

"All right. Thank you, Barkley. You're dismissed."

Barkley saluted smartly and strode out.

Waiting until he was certain the lieutenant had taken care of his horse and then gone to his quarters, Forbes sprinted through the rain to his house. As soon as he was inside he called out.

"Tricia, where are you?"

He heard the door to her room open above him, and he bounded up the steps. "What did that scoundrel do to you? Are you all right?"

Tricia was waiting for him in the upper hallway. She had changed her dress, but her hair was still hanging wet around her shoulders, and she was holding a towel in her hands.

"Yes, I'm fine," she assured him. "This is quite a storm, isn't it?" she continued brightly. She sensed that he had seen her with Sykes, and she wanted desperately to avoid the subject. She rubbed her hair vigorously with the towel and turned away from his apprehensive face.

"What were you doing with Sykes?" he demanded.

Tricia stopped drying her hair and stammered, "I . . . well . . . I . . ."

"Young woman, you had me worried a little before, traipsing off to town, acting strangely around that agent, and now this." Forbes' face reddened. "You're making me think . . . I don't know what you're making me think."

Tricia bristled at the implication. She drew herself

up and her chin jutted forward. "Uncle John, I'm sorry if I've upset you. But I've never been out in a storm like that. It was beautiful and frightening and . . ." she hesitated, searching for the word, "and exciting. You know," she went on, her words tumbling out, "I've tried to do the things you wanted me to. But I feel useless here. Today out on the prairie, in that storm, I felt strong and alive. It made me feel as though I want to stay here forever."

Taken back by her intensity, Forbes started to admonish her about Sykes, and then thought better of it.

Tricia broke the awkward silence. "You're home early, Uncle John. Do you want to eat now?"

"No," he said, turning away. "I have a few more things to do at my office. I only came home now because I was worried."

"There's nothing to worry about," she said emphatically.

"You haven't convinced me of that, Patricia," he said as he started down the steps.

When her uncle closed the front door behind him, she walked back into her room and stood thoughtfully in front of her mirror, holding the towel to her hair.

"Tricia Ashley," she spoke out loud, studying her reflection, her flushed cheeks, her bright eyes. "You talked back to your uncle, and you covered up for Cole Sykes." She thought about the touch of his lips and wondered about her feelings for him.

During the night the storm abated, and by morning it had passed. After breakfast Cole Sykes once again took the bay stallion to the corral behind the livery stable. Barkley had been right, the horse wasn't trained well yet. As he swung into the saddle he wondered if he'd ever tell Many Arrows all of the things that buckskin horse could do. He shook his head as he thought how Many Arrows had beat him out of his horse, and nearly out of his saddle. He was irritated about the second carbine he'd had to buy.

He had to train the bay to stand ground-reined. Hauling a huge wagon wheel from Gaines' shop, he tied the ends of the reins to the spokes as the wheel lay on the ground. The stallion jerked and plunged, but couldn't pull loose from the wheel. When Sykes untied the reins, leaving them dangling, the animal shied away and danced backwards. Sykes tied him to the wheel several more times that morning. But it wouldn't do to push the horse too far, or he would never learn.

He was just untying the bay for the last time when he heard a bugle sound at the fort. The blast was louder and more urgent than usual, and it was a call he hadn't heard before. Almost at once he saw a man dash across the bridge, and head up the hill for the fort. He ran to the street, where several other people were heading in the same direction. Hugh Gaines came out of the stable.

"What's happening?" asked Sykes.

"You heard that bugle, didn't you? That's their call to bring in the woodcutters and all the stock that's out grazing. Most of us figure it's a good time for us to be inside the fort, too."

Gaines threw off his leather apron and hurried for the bridge along with the others. Sykes swung into his saddle, and then reached down and patted the stallion's neck.

"Okay, White Foot, looks like we've got some excitement here." Leaning from his saddle, he pulled open the corral poles and loped into the street.

Ahead of him three women ran toward the bridge,

clutching their long, hooded capes around their churning legs. One cape flew open, and Sykes saw a thin nightdress. He couldn't see their faces, but he knew who they were. Usually, these women lounged around the saloon or in the hotel, their round arms and bosoms exposed in their tight satin dresses.

Reaching the fort, Sykes reined in and waited for the women, then followed them in. He heard a man's voice call out to them, and one woman waved gaily.

When Sykes galloped up to the hitching rail at the headquarters building, Sam Ross stepped down to greet him.

"Looks like you took good care of the ladies, there," he grinned slyly in their direction.

"What's going on?" asked the agent, ignoring the scout's comment.

"Forbes just found out they lost some horses last night during the storm. He always calls everybody in when something like that happens. This time, he figures the Indians were replacing their stock."

"Were they?"

"I'd have to see it for myself."

"Then let's get out there before the army tramples everything up."

All of the townspeople had made it into the fort by the time the two rode out through the gate. Looking south, Sykes saw a herd of cavalry mounts being driven toward the fort by men in army uniforms.

"They've got a few left," observed Sykes dryly.

"That looks like the main bunch of them, all right. They only lost a couple dozen up north, next to the reservation."

They turned in the direction Ross indicated and rode watching the ground ahead of them until they saw signs of recent grazing. Slowing their horses, Ross and

Sykes studied the tracks around them. For over an hour they rode back and forth across the army horses' grazing land, each time getting closer to the river that separated the fort area from the reservation.

Finally Sam Ross pulled up, staring at the ground in front and crossing his arms over his saddle horn. "I'll be Goddamned." He breathed each word slowly and distinctly.

Sykes stared down at the ground near Ross. "What is it?" he asked. Then he froze in amazement at the tracks in the dirt between the clumps of grass, the tracks of unshod ponies.

Chapter 15

The paunchy man's moustache and beard were as black as his broad-brimmed beaver hat. He was not tall, but his shoulders were wide inside his heavy coat. He sat his horse between the empty rope corral and the Indians riding toward him without taking his eyes off them. He knew they could see the half dozen guns behind him, covering him, and he didn't bother to take his own rifle out of its boot.

When the Indians were close enough, he counted the horses they had brought with them, eighteen in all, and all good cavalry stock. He took the time to study each of the horses while the warriors halted the mounts a hundred yards away. Then Many Arrows rode forward and the man kneed his own horse into motion. They met in the middle of the open space, facing each other.

The outlaw moved his hands in the sign for a trade, and when Many Arrows nodded, he went on in the sign language. It was a half-hour before they agreed on the bargain. Many Arrows turned and signaled behind him, and the braves drove the army horses toward the rope corral. The young chief then took the bottles of whiskey the outlaw gave him and stuffed them in a large wolfskin pouch slung over his shoulder. The rest of the warriors joined Many Arrows, and the braves loped toward the nearest trees. Moments later the Indians separated and rode into the woods.

Colonel Forbes was standing at the window when Cole Sykes and Sam Ross walked into his office. Forbes moved over to his desk and sat down before he spoke to them.

"So you think you saw something out there my men did not?" he asked, lifting his eyebrows.

"Yes," answered Sykes, ignoring the disbelief in the officer's voice. "There's a chance the horses were taken by the Indians, all right."

"A chance? I guess so! Sykes, there's no one else around here that steals horses, no matter what you claim you found up in the hills. Lieutenant Barkley saw nothing resembling your report. What you haven't learned yet is that the savages do nothing but steal horses back and forth. And it does not concern the army until something like this happens."

"What are you planning to do?"

"We've learned before we won't get them back. They're very clever about that, but we'll have to teach them a lesson, of course."

"Like what?"

"They came off the reservation to get them, didn't they?"

"It looks like it," Sykes conceded.

"Well, I'm surprised you're admitting it."

"Look, Forbes, I need some time to talk to them."

The colonel pushed back from the desk with both hands and laughed, his eyes mocking the agent. "I've heard how successful you were at getting your own horse back. I understand you now have nothing but an Indian pony to call your own. Tell me, is it big enough for you? Does it have pretty spots all over it?"

Sykes took a step forward. "You saw—"

Ross cleared his throat loudly, and the agent hesitated. He forced the anger out of his voice before he went on. "It has one white spot," he said evenly.

The colonel leaned forward again, his smile now a threat. "You can talk to them all you want, but we'll see they stay on the reservation after this—any way we have to."

Sykes turned and walked out, and a few moments later Ross followed him.

"You going up there now?" asked the scout as soon as he caught up to the gunfighter.

"Yes."

"I'd better come along then."

"I want to take a look around the camp before I start talking this time," Sykes explained. "Riding across the river doesn't prove they stole anything, and the only place we saw their tracks was next to the water."

Ross said nothing in response, but he was frowning as he swung into the saddle.

They rode directly for Flying Hawk's camp. About a mile from the lodges, the riders turned aside and circled the camp, staying out of sight from the tepees and the young boys with the grazing horses.

Completing the circle, Ross and Sykes rode into the camp from the fort side, as though they had come directly from there.

Ross looked around in surprise as he swung down. There were only women and children in sight. As they went past Many Arrows' tepee, Ross poked his head into the opening. "Nobody there," he muttered, as he straightened again. His frown deepened as he moved his eyes over the camp. When he called out to a woman carrying a child up from the river, she answered him and then slipped into a lodge above the trail.

Ross looked around him one more time. "This isn't a good time," he decided. "We'd better come back tomorrow."

"Why?"

"They've got likker from some place," Ross said grimly.

"How?" Sykes exploded. "That's against the law."

"How the hell do I know? They traded somebody for it, what else?"

"What have they got to trade?"

"Let's get out of here. We can talk about it later."

Impressed by the urgency in Ross' voice, Sykes swung into the saddle without asking any more questions. As he picked up his reins, he reached to his hip and checked his Colt.

They rode side by side away from the camp without appearing to hurry. Both searched the brush and trees beside the river, and this time Ross said nothing about looking behind them.

They were a half mile from the camp when they saw the first of the Indians. The braves were not sitting silently in a half circle. They were whooping and waving their lances as they broke out of the woods. Nearly a dozen men rode full tilt, some still held whiskey bottles in their hands. Many Arrows rode at the head. The war chief lunged ahead on Sykes' stolen buckskin horse, a horse the agent knew had never been outrun. The Indians were between the town and the two riders.

Sykes motioned quickly to Ross and reined his horse away from the warriors. The scout followed his lead at once. At the same time the Indians veered at an angle, attempting to intercept the white men while they were still on the reservation.

"Looks like they've got paint on this time," yelled Sykes.

"We got to get to those trees first," gasped Ross, "or they'll cut us off."

Ross' face was strained and grim. Sykes leaned over his horse's neck and dug in his spurs. Almost at once he started to pull ahead of the scout. The agent felt a surge of satisfaction with the power he could feel under him. He let the bay out more, and the animal responded again, pulling farther ahead. The stallion ran as though it had raced before, and it ran as though it knew nothing about losing.

He reached the trees beside the river far ahead of Ross. Pulling his rifle, he dashed into the woods and then reined up and turned back, waiting for Ross. Reaching Sykes, the scout peered back over his shoulder through the trees. One of the Indian horses was riderless, but still running with the others.

"Too damn drunk to ride," said Ross, his voice disgusted.

"How dangerous?" barked Sykes.

"How dangerous were you at that age full of cheap whiskey?"

Sykes looked down at the carbine in his hands. His expression was bleak. The braves were pounding toward them at full speed, Many Arrows in the lead. Sykes raised the carbine and aimed carefully. He squeezed off his first shot and a black and white pinto close behind the chief screamed and fell. Its rider sprawled to the ground over its head.

While Sykes aimed again, Ross' gun blasted beside him, and a second horse went down heavily. At Sykes' next shot, a third horse reared and pawed at the air, squealing, its drunken rider struggling to cling to its back.

Many Arrows signaled, and the braves halted their headlong rush long enough for two of them to ride to the fallen men. While they hauled the reeling braves up behind them, the others raised a loud cry and poked their guns in the direction of the trees. They began firing wildly.

"Come on," Ross rasped. "We've got a chance to get away while they're stopped." He dashed to the river bank and then rode along it in the direction of the town.

With Sykes following his lead, Ross splashed through the stream for a hundred yards and then reined in. He raised his hand while he listened to the drunken shouts of the Indians. After a moment, he started ahead again at a faster pace, reloading his rifle as he rode. "We may be okay," he guessed. "They're arguing about what to do."

Sykes rode up to Ross' side.

"That was real progress," he spat out the words and shoved the carbine down into his saddle boot in disgust.

Ross pondered for a moment. "Might not be as bad as you think. When they're sober, they'll probably realize we only shot at the horses. In the condition they were in, we could have killed some of them easily."

"I'm not counting on them waking up tomorrow and feeling grateful."

"Well, they won't be, but you got to remember you started the shooting."

"I didn't see you standing around waiting to shake their hands," he said sharply.

"I wasn't. I don't tangle with them when they've been drinking. Most of those young ones didn't know me when I lived with them. I don't know what they'd do."

Once in town Sykes stopped in front of the livery stable. "I found out one thing today anyway."

"What's that?"

"This stallion of mine's a damned good horse." He reached down and stroked the animal's lathered neck. The stallion snorted softly and trotted into the stable.

Chapter 16

When Andrew Madden left the commissioner's office, deep lines plowed a furrow between his eyes and his jaw was set. In his hand, he held the letter from Colonel John Wesley Forbes, a letter that certainly made it clear what kind of choice Cole Sykes had been for an agent in the field.

And it didn't make Madden feel any better now that he could say "I told you so." He should have known better than to mention Sykes' name aloud when Tarking had asked him who the toughest so-and-so out there was. Didn't Madden know Tarking well enough to realize the commissioner would do something just like this?

As soon as Madden reached his desk, he sat down and read the letter through again. It was addressed to the commissioner and written in a deliberate and precise hand that indicated the importance of the writer.

It read like the logbook of someone who ought to be in prison. First the arrival at the town, not the fort, and the delay in announcing who he was and why he was there. Madden had seen the town, not that you could call it a real town, and he knew what went on there. And then a shooting, completely unexplained, before Sykes finally presented himself at the fort. His complete refusal to accept the prudent help offered by Colonel Forbes, although he had managed to accept an invitation to dinner. Then the final insult—striking an officer.

"Inexcusable!" cried Madden angrily. The chief clerk stood up and paced around his office before he picked up the letter and finished reading it. Nowhere was there mention of a single activity expected of a field representative of the Office of Indian Affairs.

So, he'd moved the agency office into a shed and taken a room in the hotel where the town's loose women were allowed. Then he had slept while the Indians stole cavalry horses. And if all of that wasn't bad enough, Commissioner Tarking had thought it was funny!

Madden turned and stared in the direction of the commissioner's office. No matter how much Tarking wanted Grant's success in the upcoming election, the commissioner didn't wish it one particle more than Chief Clerk Andrew Madden. At the same time, Madden tried not to think of Tarking as a member of the President's Cabinet.

The clerk threw the letter down on his desk. A half-hour later, still on his feet and no closer to a solution, he picked up the desk calendar that listed his engagements for the rest of the year. He replaced it and resumed his pacing. There was no way that he could clear his calendar for a trip out there now, and the winter snows would be coming soon, if they hadn't already. All he could do now was hope that the train with the Indians' supplies, their blankets and food, axes, kettles, cloth, hay and oats, was getting through on schedule and not late as it had the previous year. Maybe the arrival of the supplies and the cold weather would be enough to keep things settled down until after the election, when he hoped to hell he could get Sykes replaced.

Dear Assistant Superintendent Sykes:

I am in receipt of a letter from Colonel John Wesley Forbes which enumerates the events at and around Fort Mason since your arrival there. From the contents of the letter I have concluded that I must not have fully outlined to you the duties and responsibilities of your position. This letter is an attempt to remedy that situation.

Enclosed is another copy of the *Procedures Manual.* I suggest that you read it carefully from cover to cover. There is, in particular, an entire chapter on the protocol of relationships with the army, its officers and men. In the letter it sounds as though Colonel Forbes has been very patient and understanding of your breaches of this protocol, but I am confident that when you know the "rules," you will be most willing and anxious to follow them exactly.

Let me also call to your attention the chapter in the manual about the mandatory *Annual Report.* This report should be every bit as carefully prepared as the manual indicates because it becomes a matter of permanent record here in Washington. If you need to have someone else write the final copy for you so that it will be completely legible, as befits a permanent document, I am confident that Colonel Forbes can supply you with the necessary help.

The most important requirement, however, is that the document be a report of *progress* in the work of the Agency. As you can imagine, ample funding for the Agency depends upon the achievement of the goals set by Congress and the President for our programs. Those goals, *I cannot emphasize too strongly,* are to make the Indians Christians, educate them, teach them the skills of agriculture, and provide the advanced technology of our age by supplying them with blacksmiths, good hunting rifles, wagons, etc. An important part of their education must involve their learning the economics of our advanced civilization, and particularly they must learn the concept of private property. In other words, Mr. Sykes, *they must not steal any more horses*. You need to convince them of that immediately.

As a last item of business, I would like to remind you we had assumed that by now whoever murdered Silvers would have been brought to justice. You'll want to be sure the matter is fully investigated and its resolution included in the *Annual Report*. You must realize that the only "law" out there at this time is provided by the army, so I am certain you can understand the importance of repairing your relationship with Colonel Forbes. He will instruct you in the best procedures to follow in apprehending the murderer. Listening to people who have more experience in a particular area is not a sign of weakness, Mr. Sykes. It is a sign of wisdom.

Unfortunately, in reading over this letter before closing, I find it sounds more like a lecture than I had intended—

Cole Sykes flung the letter across the room. It struck the window and then fell, its pages out of order, on the desk. He tilted his chair back against the wall and reached for his tobacco. After he had rolled a cigarette he stared at the wall across from him for several minutes without lighting it. Then he rose and stood in the doorway while he lit the cigarette and smoked it halfway. With the cigarette in the corner of his mouth, he returned to the desk, picked up the letter, folded it and stuck it in his shirt pocket. He took his sheepskin coat off its peg and carried it with him across the street to the livery stable.

The agent rode out of the stable and on up to the fort. Inside the gate, he immediately turned toward the barracks. He did not look in the direction of the headquarters building as he hitched his horse, walked up the steps, and went in.

Sam Ross was sitting on the edge of his bed talking to Corporal Eddy beside him in the next bunk. When the scout saw Sykes in the doorway, he finished what he was saying and then stood up and went to the door.

"Let's have a drink," said Sykes.

"Where?"

"The commissary here will do."

The scout followed Sykes out, and then they walked together to the bar at the end of the commissary building. As soon as the bartender poured their drinks, Sykes motioned to a table at the far end of the room where they would be away from the nearest soldier.

"What's on your mind?" asked Ross curiously as they sat down.

Sykes took the letter out of his pocket and tossed it on the table in front of Ross. Then he sat back in his chair and sipped at his drink while the other man read.

Sam read the entire letter without touching his glass. Then he placed it on the table, carefully arranging the pages together, picked up his glass, and held it in front of him. "Let's drink to Colonel John Wesley Forbes," he toasted, "and all his mighty experience in the area."

"I'll drink," muttered Sykes darkly, "but not to that."

Sam Ross slapped one hand over his heart and closed his eyes as he put the glass to his lips. "I've never seen him ride out through that gate since he first rode in," confessed Ross after he swallowed the whiskey. "But I can understand why. He's pretty comfortable where he is. Got all the comforts of home, nearly—'cept one, and as soon as Tricia leaves, he'll get himself another hired girl to help out with—things around the house. You can bet on that."

"I'd like to know what progress Silvers reported last year," growled Sykes, glowering at the letter.

"Well, he kept Forbes happy. He worked at that. Could be that's all you need to do. Then write anything you want in your report."

"I'm thinking of riding out to see Flying Hawk again and asking him what he wants the most. I can't do everything it says in that letter at once, but I'll have to do something."

Ross picked up his glass and looked over its rim at Sykes as he took another sip. "You know, I can't figure you out. Everybody's heard of Cole Sykes. When I saw you down in Kansas five years ago, you—"

"I know what I was."

"Well, *was* is a good word, but what I can't figure is what you're doing in a job like this."

"You would understand if you'd spent any time in a territorial prison."

"They straightened you out, is that it?"

Cole Sykes laughed humorlessly as he put down his glass. He sat back and folded his arms over his chest. "I'm on a furlough, Ross—for as long as I last in this job. Then I go back."

"What kind of a deal is that?"

"I can tell you it wasn't Madden's idea. He told me Tarking thought of it, but Madden disagreed."

"That's too bad. There's been a Madden in that bureau as long as I can remember. You'll want to satisfy him if you can. He's likely to be there after Tarking's gone."

Sykes rose slowly and picked up his letter. "You think I haven't figured that out? I've got five more years on that sentence, and I'm going to show some goddamned progress every year." He turned toward the door. "Give me half an hour, and we'll take a ride."

"You going to see Forbes?"

"No, his niece." Sykes looked back at the scout. "I don't mind showing some progress in a job I've said I'd do, but I won't be licking the colonel's boots at the same time."

Sykes heard Ross chuckle as the agent stepped out the door. He walked to his horse. A gusty cold wind was blowing from the north and thick clouds had covered the sun while he was in the bar. He put on his coat before he climbed into the saddle and then he pushed the right side of it back so that it was behind his gun. Riding to the other end of the fort and around the corner of the parade ground, he let his hand hang over his gun. His jaw was set and his face expressionless. He had never gone out of his way to see Patricia Ashley before, but he figured he owed something to the colonel for that letter.

She answered the door as soon as he knocked, as though she had seen him coming and was waiting. She was smiling. "Cole," she greeted, her eyes friendly. "I'm glad to see you, but Uncle John isn't here."

"I didn't come to see your uncle."

"Oh? Well—" She looked around her, and then smiled warmly as she opened the door farther. "Please come in if you came to see me."

He did not smile in return, and when he spoke his voice had an edge to it. "Tell me when it's time to leave. I guess I'm not too proper at these things."

Her smile faded and her hand still held the doorknob after she closed the door. "What's the matter?" she asked, her voice puzzled.

He stared at her for a minute, his eyes hard, his hands knotted in fists on his hips. In response she tilted her head to one side and her eyes filled with concern. Before she could say anything, he turned away. "Nothing that has anything to do with you," he mumbled as he walked into the front room.

"Why don't you take off your coat and sit down while I make some coffee?"

He heard her step behind him on the wooden floor between the rugs, and when he faced her again, she had one hand out to him as though ready to take his things. "I didn't come here to see you," he admitted. "I came here to make Forbes mad."

"Well, I'm sure you will, if he knows about your being here, so you might as well have the coffee."

"No, I've got work to do. I don't have the time."

She glanced to the window and then walked

toward it. "Cole, come here," she said as she stopped in front of the glass and leaned forward to look outside.

He followed her to the window and looked out over her head, trying to see what had taken her interest.

"Cole, do you see how green that grass is? And look there, see those clouds? I think we might have another storm." Her voice was gentle. She continued staring out the window, standing with her back to him. He knew she was waiting for something.

He gazed at the grass and the clouds, and then he looked down at her and sighed deeply. "I'm sorry I sounded like that."

"Now we're even, aren't we?" she replied. She turned to face him, her expression one of anticipation. He put his hand out toward her arm, and she blushed. Suddenly she looked confused and, stepping quickly by him, she walked to the rocking chair beside the fireplace and sat down. She motioned to the chair across from her and folded her hands in her lap. "I shall be going home soon," she informed him. "Uncle John says the supply train is due any day and the air certainly feels like snow already."

"The snow's not far away," said Sykes, still standing by the window. "There could be some in those clouds."

"Uncle John will have a good-bye party for me the night before I go. Will you come if you're invited?"

"He won't invite me here again."

"The party will be for me, not him."

"Why would you ask me?"

"Because I'd like you to come." Her tone was open and frank. "I enjoyed our ride that day, Cole, truly I did. I'll think about it often when I'm back home."

"Are you coming back here?"

She stared into the fireplace, and while he waited for her answer he studied her profile. It took her several minutes to decide on her reply, and then she did not look at him as she spoke. "I don't know," she whispered, as though she wondered at her own response.

He waited until she turned and met his eyes, and then he walked out into the hall. "I expect this has been as long as I should stay," he said, opening the door.

Chapter 17

On the way around the parade ground, Sykes could see Forbes' orderly standing in the doorway of the hall to the colonel's office. He raised one hand to his hat when he was certain the orderly was watching him. Ross was still in the bar, and while he waited for him, he untied his horse, dropped the reins to the ground, and walked a dozen yards away.

The horse shifted at the rail, but stayed until Sykes whistled softly. The stallion pricked up his ears and lifted his head far enough for the reins to clear the ground. Then he trotted to Sykes.

"Nice trick," Ross observed approvingly as he walked past the agent toward the cavalry stable.

Sykes led his horse alongside the scout as far as the gate, and waited there while Ross got his horse. Thoughts of Tricia came into his mind, and he tried to sort them out. He had seen the consternation in her face as he reached out to touch her. She seemed to want him near her, but then she had withdrawn from him. He shook his head, puzzled and confused himself, and turned his thoughts back to the job at hand. "Besides," he said to himself, "she'll be gone before the first snow."

Riding through the town with Ross, he asked

about Forbes and how he had handled Silvers' murder. "If the Army's the only law around here, what did the colonel do after Silvers was killed?"

"Forbes, himself? He never left his office. Never even saw the body that I know."

"Who did?"

"The detail that went out to bring his body in. I went with them, so did Captain Olin."

"Where did you find him?"

The scout twisted in the saddle to point behind him. "Down there."

"Off the reservation?"

"Yes, in those hills, the farthest ones you can see."

"What was he doing down there?"

"He didn't tell me," Ross grinned.

"I thought he never went outside the fort without part of the army behind him."

"That's when he was expecting to meet with some Blackfoot. And that's as far as Forbes knows. But Silvers drank a lot, and he liked the entertainment here in town. Spent quite a few nights here that Forbes probably never knew about. The colonel would have him over to dinner, and they'd drink a little sherry, maybe, and have dinner, sit around afterwards talking and smoking their pipes. Then after Silvers went back to his quarters, maybe an hour later, he'd ride into town."

"He must have gone farther than the town a few times."

"At least once," Ross replied dryly.

Sykes studied the scout's profile. "You know something you're holding back," he accused.

"I don't have anything more than suspicions, and the man's dead, so I figure to let him rest. I'll tell you this though, you're already a better agent than he ever was. I guess that's about all that matters to me. We've done enough to the Blackfoot without his kind making things worse."

"I've got orders, Ross. I'm supposed to find his killer. I've got to show it on my report, and the report's due at the end of the year. And chasing a killer is the only part of this job I've had some experience in."

The scout returned Sykes' steady look for several seconds and lifted up his reins. "Then you're going in the wrong direction."

"You think there's still something down there to see?" Sykes pulled up and faced the hills Ross had pointed out.

"I don't know. But you better see where it happened."

"We can't get there and back before dark, can we?"

"No."

"Then I'll make up a bedroll and meet you across the bridge in a few minutes," suggested Sykes. Ross nodded and turned away, and Sykes trotted to the hitching rail in front of the hotel. As he went past the saloon the swinging doors moved, but no one had gone in and no one came out while Sykes had tied his horse. He stood so that he could see any movement in that direction, and when he was certain he was being watched, he did not go into the hotel. Instead, he crossed the street to the blacksmith shop and stood inside the doorway talking to Gaines for several minutes.

During that time, he saw no further movement of the saloon doors. Before he left he stepped into the shop.

"Do me a favor after I leave, Gaines."

"Sure, what can I do?"

"See if anyone in the saloon pays attention to

what I'm doing when I leave here. If you're standing in the doorway when I ride out in a few minutes, I'll know they did."

"You think your friend with the bad shoulder might be looking for you?"

"I don't know. He ought to be getting the use of his arm back by now if he's going to."

"Can't see how he'd be asking for a second lesson from you. Especially now that he knows who he was up against."

Sykes checked his Colt before he walked out of the shop and crossed the street to the hotel. Without looking directly at the saloon he couldn't be sure, but he thought he spotted a face in the shadows behind the doors, even though the doors remained motionless.

Up in his hotel room, Sykes made up a bedroll, and once down in the street, he tied it securely behind his saddle. At Warner's store he bought enough food for several days. By the time he had his supplies tied in place, he saw Ross on the way down from the fort. He swung into the saddle and headed out to meet him.

Sykes waved his hand to the blacksmith, who was standing in the entrance of his shop as the agent went by, but he did not look behind him. Gaines was facing the saloon, and his shotgun was leaning against the doorway.

At the other side of the bridge, Sykes and the scout turned and rode south. Sykes was silent for the first mile. Then he twisted in the saddle and studied their back trail. "Now let's get out of sight," he said.

"What for?"

"I want to check behind us without being seen."

The scout leaned over the far side of his horse and touched his stirrup. When he straightened again, he pointed to the left, where a stream had cut a ravine, and then veered in that direction. "Could be someone back there, all right."

Ross led the way to the edge of the ravine and down over the side, angling across the steep drop to the bottom. Before he started down, Sykes glanced along the stream's course. It was more than a ravine. The creek wound back and forth across a wide flat area, and all the space between the bends was filled with brush, high enough in most places to hide a horse and rider.

Ross continued in the lead, following what looked like a game trail to the nearest bend in the creek. "What kind of a hiding place you looking for?" he asked as he moved into the brush.

"One with a back way out. If it's the same outfit that was in town the day I got here, we might need to make a run for it."

"It's not too likely they'll follow us into this puzzle," laughed the scout. "But we might as well lose our tracks for a ways. Then we'll stop where we can see the place we came down."

"Go ahead."

As they pushed farther into the brush, Sykes wished he had a pair of chaps to cover his legs. The stallion didn't seem to care how close it came to the stiff short branches. No wonder the Indians wore full-length, buckskin leggings even when their upper bodies were bare.

A dozen yards later the only way through the brush was in the stream itself, and they splashed along for several minutes before Ross pointed to a rocky spot on the opposite shore. They rode out of the water across the rocks and into the brush again.

Moving into the brush, Sykes looked back at their

tracks. They'd left no sign except for some moisture on the rocks, and that would dry fast enough.

The scout finally pulled up in a small clearing where there was enough space for the horses to stand without disturbing the bushes around them. They dismounted, ground-reining their horses away from the bushes.

Sykes continued to follow Ross as they took their rifles and went farther into the brush. A moment later Ross stopped behind a pile of rocks at the base of the ravine's far side, facing the place where they had entered.

They spread apart so that each could see a different part of the opposite bank and then settled down to wait. It was half an hour before Sykes thought he heard the sound of horses and turned his head to listen. Hearing the sound again, he glanced at Ross, and the scout nodded.

At first he could not tell how many there were, but as the horses neared the ravine it sounded like only two or three at most. Sykes slowly lifted his rifle and aimed at the place he expected to see them.

The men had been tracking, all right. One was still watching the ground at his horse's feet when the two of them rode into sight. The other man held a rifle in his hands and was studying the brush ahead of him. They stood at the edge for just a moment before both of them turned and rode rapidly out of sight, back the way they had come.

"They've got it figured," said Ross. "They know we're here."

"Looks like it, but we'd better wait a while. There might be a way they can get behind us."

"There is."

"If I wait here, can you cover it?" Sykes asked.

The scout nodded. "When you're ready to leave, climb that bank behind us and then ride a half mile due west. I'll catch up to you as you go."

"All right," agreed Sykes. He watched Ross move silently away from the rocks and into the brush. He waited for another half-hour without seeing or hearing the two men again.

It was late in the afternoon when he rode out of the ravine, and as soon as Ross joined him, they headed to the southwest.

"You see anything more?" asked Ross.

"No."

"Neither did I. They knew we were down there all right."

"I don't figure them for being dumb."

"Good idea not to. I haven't seen any signs that they are."

"We won't make it to the hills before dark now," noted Sykes.

"No, and you won't be able to see what you're down here for after dark. We better hole up for the night and check it out first thing in the morning. You ready for snow?"

"Yes." As the gunman glanced up at the clouds, the first flakes swirled in the wind.

Colonel John Wesley Forbes was smiling as he left the headquarters building and walked along the end of the parade ground toward his house. The men had finished the flag-lowering ceremony on the parade ground, and the fort appeared empty. In this weather most of the soldiers stayed inside during their half-hour of leisure before the evening mess call.

Enough snow had fallen already to show his foot-prints, and more of it was in the air. Despite the cold the colonel continued to smile until he reached his porch. Then he straightened his expression and opened the door.

As always, Patricia had the table set and the candles burning, and he could hear her moving around in the kitchen. The smell of the food being prepared filled the house, and a fire crackled in the fireplace.

Forbes went upstairs to his bedroom and changed his uniform coat for a smoking jacket. Downstairs he plopped down in his favorite chair beside the fire. The fire seemed more than necessary that evening. It was a pleasant companion, hissing and burning brightly, in contrast to the blackness and cold outside. It also reminded him that he must tell Major Campbell to check the supply of wood for the fort and increase the wood-cutting details, if necessary. There would be long periods in the months ahead when they would be snowed in.

He picked up his pipe and the small knife he used to clean it and started to scoop out the inside of the bowl. His expression was one of contentment.

"You look pleased about something, Uncle John," remarked Tricia as she walked from the kitchen to the dining-room table. She was carrying a covered dish, and having set it on the table, she turned to face him, her hands at her waist, smiling.

"Oh, just a small matter, my dear, a small matter."

"What is it?"

"Nothing of interest to you."

"Well, it must be some kind of military secret if you won't share it with me." She turned and walked back to the kitchen, and Forbes watched her back, grinning now.

A few minutes later, as they sat down together at the table, the colonel was still smiling.

"All right, Uncle John, this isn't fair. I haven't known a single thing to smile about all day, and you seem to have lots of things."

The colonel laughed loudly. "You are persistent, aren't you? Well, if you must know, I've had a response from the Office of Indian Affairs to the letter I sent Commissioner Tarking. He said that he had turned the matters I told him about over to Chief Clerk Madden to straighten out, and it's my guess we'll have a new agent here soon."

Patricia's face grew dark. "Why should we? What did you do?" she demanded, her tone impertinent.

"Come, come, Tricia," he coaxed. "Why are you frowning? Surely you'll agree it is my duty to inform them in Washington when they do anything so clearly a mistake."

"What did you tell them?" She tried to control her voice.

"Why, the truth, of course, that Cole Sykes is worse than no agent at all. It wasn't difficult to substantiate. I merely listed everything that has gone wrong since he arrived here. We had none of that kind of thing while Silvers was here, nor while we were waiting for Sykes to arrive, I might add. However, as you know, Mr. Sykes shot one of the citizens in the town the very day he arrived, even before he reported to me."

"He didn't have to—report to you, did he?"

"Tricia, what's gotten into you? You seem upset about something. It was my business to inform them about this man's troublemaking. After all, there is no one of higher authority in this part of the territory, is there?"

Patricia stared steadily at the bowl of potatoes as she handed it to him. "What was in the response you received?" she asked.

"It explained a great many things, I can tell you that, and Tarking wrote the letter himself. He said he had thought what we needed out here was someone tough enough to handle ambushing hostiles and also someone whom—" The colonel cleared his throat before he went on. "Someone whom nobody would miss if he weren't successful." He smiled at Patricia as he returned the bowl of potatoes. "What explains everything, of course, is that they got Mr. Cole Sykes out of prison for the job. It seems we now have what used to be a high-priced, gun-for-hire here among us."

"Lieutenant Barkley has already mentioned that he was in prison. But a gun-for-hire? I don't understand." Tricia set the bowl down.

"I understand that he hired out to the cattlemen in Texas, guarding the cattle drives, things like that, but knowing him as I do, I'm sure he would shoot at anything or anybody he was paid to kill. A hired killer is probably a better name for him."

"Why was he in prison?"

"The commissioner said it was for killing three men. He understands that Sykes killed three armed men over a card game. If they'd been unarmed, I presume Sykes would have been hanged instead."

"That's terrible!" she exclaimed. Her face betrayed her consternation.

"Yes, Patricia, and who was it told you what he was like in the first place?" The colonel stopped with his fork halfway to his mouth. "Think of the danger you were in the day he carried you out of here. I should have put him in the guardhouse for that and left him there."

"I wasn't in any danger that day, not from him."

Forbes put his fork down and rested his hand on the edge of the table. He straightened to his full height. "I can see you're no judge of character."

Tricia stood up and walked hurriedly toward the kitchen. "I think I left something burning on the stove," she mumbled. Returning a few minutes later, her face was composed, and she immediately changed the subject. "When do you think the supply train will be here?" she asked.

"Any day now. I'd say it's overdue already. You're thinking about that party I promised you, I hope. Too bad you won't have a new dress to wear, but as far as I know there isn't a seamstress within hundreds of miles."

"I have a dress I haven't worn yet," she said. "And I've been making out the invitations. As soon as the supply train gets here, if you would please send your orderly over, I'll have him deliver them."

"Of course, my dear. That's a fine idea. You certainly know the protocol by now. In fact, you'd make an excellent officer's wife." He looked at her knowingly, immediately pleased with himself. "I can't believe how well you've adapted to all this." He waved his hand in the general direction of the outdoors. "Although not all forts are like this one. This is much larger and better than most—if I do say it myself. I've seen to that."

Patricia went to bed early even though she did not feel sleepy. She needed time to think about what her uncle had told her at dinner, and she couldn't do it around him. Instead of falling asleep at once, she lay awake, staring into the darkness over her bed. The moon broke through the clouds, flooding the room with its pale light. She got up and stood at the window, gazing out at the fort.

Only a few more days and she would be gone, probably never to return. She felt a sadness every time she thought about it. It was beautiful in the moonlight, and so peaceful. There were no carriages rattling by on the cobblestones, like at home, nothing to break the beauty and peace of the night, now even more startling with the snow.

She stood there until she shivered from the cold, and then climbed back under the feather quilt, still not feeling sleepy. She lay there, her body growing warm again. Finally she felt drowsy, and then her thoughts turned, as they always did lately, to the man she tried not to think about when she was wide awake. Her mind was in a turmoil as she thought about what her uncle had just told her. Cole had killed three men over a card game? It was a good thing she was leaving, she thought, as she turned on her side and pulled the covers high around her shoulders.

In the next instant she heard the pounding of hoofs and a man's voice shouting. By the time she was up and putting on her wrapper, there were several men's voices, all shouting at once down at the far end of the fort, and she could hear her uncle moving around in his room. Moments later she heard him run down the hall. As he dashed down the stairs, a knock sounded at the front door. Tricia opened her door a crack to listen.

"Colonel Forbes, sir, a rider has just come from the supply train!" The young man's voice was excited, and he was breathing hard after running all the way from the gate. "He's badly wounded, sir. The train is under attack. He said he barely managed to get away."

"Where's the train now?" demanded Forbes as he stepped outside and closed the door behind him.

When Tricia could hear no more, she went back to her bed and sat dejectedly on the edge of it. She sat with her hands folded in her lap, not feeling the cold, not moving even when she heard the bugle call and the tumult of men preparing to ride out. She was supposed to have gone home with the returning supply train, but surely it was not safe enough now. She sat there, lost in her thoughts. Probably she would not leave until spring.

Chapter 18

Despite the snow Ross suggested they make camp without a fire. They wolfed down cold beans and then slept in turns in a brush-filled depression. By dawn they were in their saddles again. Leaving the camp, Sykes looked at the tracks they were leaving in the snow. The sky had cleared overnight and the temperature was still below freezing. Their tracks would remain unless the sun melted the snow during the day.

"We'll be in the trees later," Ross commented as he glanced in the same direction. "There's probably not much snow up there."

"I hope not. That's a damned clear trail."

When they reached the trees, he could see that Ross had been right, and the pine needles cushioned the sound of the horses at the same time. They climbed through the trees for a half-hour before Ross called a halt.

"We'll go on foot from here," he pointed to the outcropping of rock ahead of them.

"We're going up there?" asked Sykes, incredulously. From where the agent sat, he could not see a path to the top.

"Too bad you haven't got some moccasins," said the scout. "Makes climbing a lot easier." He swung down and pulled a pair of fringed moccasins from his saddlebag and exchanged them for his riding boots.

Sykes followed Ross to the base of the rocks and then climbed after the scout as best he could. Halfway up, Ross stopped and waited for Sykes. The moccasins clung to the rocks in places where Sykes' leather boot soles would not hold, and the agent had to take a longer way around. He was beginning to wonder if this effort was worth it just to see the spot where Silvers had been killed. Sykes was sweating freely under his coat by the time he reached the ledge at the top where Ross had finally stopped and lay on his stomach, peering over the side.

Sykes dropped to all fours when he saw how carefully Ross was squinting past the top. Then Sykes flopped to his belly before he reached Ross' side. The outcropping overlooked a deep canyon filled with trees and brush. At the end of the valley, and above them in the mountains, a waterfall dropped for a dozen yards, the sound of it roaring in the space below them.

"What's that over there?" Sykes pointed to the far side of the canyon. "Looks like the tailings from a mine or something."

"It is. There's a mine up above that you can't see from here. At one time it had a rich vein of gold in it, but the streak was too short to pay well for long, and nobody else ever found any gold around here. Not that they didn't try. That was back in '53 when this was still Blackfoot land. When the one vein gave out it wasn't worth the risk to try and stay here. It had already cost the miners a few scalps to get out what they did."

"And this is where they found Silvers?"

"Just about. His body was down at the bottom end of this canyon."

"Why the hell did they figure the Indians did it when it's so far from the reservation?"

"Well now, I can't say as the Indians have always stayed put like they're supposed to. Especially the young ones. This was always their land before, and that waterfall was a favorite place. They figured the Under Water Persons made it especially for their own benefit, and they came here to pray. It was a kind of a sacred place. The Blackfoot didn't take to white men digging into the side of the canyon like that. Flying Hawk was young then, and he was just like Many Arrows is now. I rode with him and his warriors then. It was some time, I can tell you." The scout chuckled softly, a touch of nostalgia in the sound, and then he was silent as they studied the canyon below them.

When they had seen all they could from the rocks, they went down to their horses and rode to the lower end of the canyon. After Ross pointed out where Silvers' body had been found, they headed back to the fort.

It took two days for the remains of the supply train to reach the fort, and the first report Sykes got was that the mules carrying the supplies for the Indians had been the hardest hit. The winter supplies for the fort had been in heavy wagons, and most of those were still intact. While Cole Sykes stood on the porch outside the headquarters waiting for the last wagon to come in through the gate, it turned dark, but he could see the wagonmaster riding toward him as the last wagon rattled into the fort. Captain Olin rode toward the headquarters building at the wagonmaster's side.

When the captain pointed Sykes out to him the agent saw the wagonmaster shake his head in Sykes' direction. Sykes stepped to the edge of the porch as the men swung down, and began speaking. "I'm Cole Sykes. You're supposed to deliver the Indian supplies and the money box to me."

Sykes saw at once the man was not using his right arm. "I'm sorry. I know I am, but I can't," the wagonmaster replied. "The money box was the first thing they went after."

As the man walked up the steps Sykes saw the hole in his coat and a dark stain where the blood had soaked through.

"I want to hear all about the attack," said Sykes.

"Come on in with us then. You can hear about it while I report to Forbes, but I'll sit down if you don't mind while I talk." The wagonmaster was a short man, but stocky and powerfully built, and only his pale, drawn face showed what it cost him to keep moving.

Sykes stepped aside as the two crossed the porch and then followed them into Forbes' office without waiting for an invitation. Forbes stood up and motioned Olin and the wagonmaster to the chairs in front of his table. Sykes stepped to the window and leaned one shoulder against the wall.

"What is your report, Captain Olin?" Forbes sat down and looked at the officer.

"We found the wagon train where we had been told, sir. The wagons were nearly in a circle, but not completely. The attackers left as soon as they heard us coming. Six men with the wagon train were killed, and as far as I know all the others were wounded. It was dark, of course, and we did not see the attackers clearly. The wagon train had lost so many of their animals that it has taken us the last two days to cover the twenty miles to the fort. We had no trouble ourselves, however. That's all I know from what I saw myself, sir."

Forbes turned to the wagonmaster. "You're Ray King, aren't you?"

"Yes."

"All right, Mr. King. Let's hear the rest of it. My orderly will write down what you tell us."

"We had scouts out ahead like we always do in hostile country. We knew how close we were to the Blackfoot."

"Their reservation is the other side of here. Why were you expecting trouble from them?" Forbes questioned closely.

"I've been taking wagons near Indian reservations too long, Forbes. We always keep a watch out. And we had enough warning this time, but we were a little careless. We were all carrying new Winchesters, so we thought we'd surprise them with that, like the fight down at the Wagon Box that time, but they must have had them, too."

"The Indians? Where could they have gotten them?"

"Well now, some of the men told me they saw more than just Indians. And I could have sworn I saw a man with a bushy dark beard, but I don't know. The moon came out before it was over, so we saw a few of them when they were riding off."

"You did see Indians, too?"

"Oh sure, and we got the arrows to prove it. A couple of the wagons looked like porcupines after they left. Some of them must have run out of ammunition or they didn't have guns."

Sykes straightened away from the wall. "Did you see the Indians?"

"Yep, we saw them. They always take their wounded with them, you know that, and we were able to see one of them while he was picking up another."

"How was it they took their own supplies?" asked Sykes. "They'd have gotten them anyway."

"Olin told you we didn't have time to finish getting the wagons into a circle. That was because we were trying to get the mules inside before we closed it up. But when they hit us with the same fire power we had, it was all we could do to protect ourselves, and I ordered my men to save the wagons. You don't think I'd put Indians ahead of the people here at the fort, do you?"

Sykes leaned against the wall again without answering. A few minutes later, when the wagonmaster finished his report, Sykes walked out of the office.

Sam Ross was standing on the porch when the gunfighter came out of the building. "How bad is it?" he asked.

"You saw the half dozen mules that came in?"

"That's it? For all of them? For all winter? Why that won't feed them for a week."

"They may have their share already."

"So somebody's trying to blame the Indians for it, are they?"

"King claims he saw them picking up their wounded, and there were arrows in some of the wagons."

"If you were white men dressed up like Indians, you'd pick up your wounded, too, wouldn't you?"

"I guess so, but it sounds to me like they were in it together. He said he saw a man with a dark beard, too. Those Indians got that whiskey from somewhere, and I wouldn't be surprised if there isn't some connection."

"Yeah, I know."

"King says the wagon train had Winchester rifles

and figured they could pull off another Wagon Box. But whoever attacked had guns also."

"One of 'em might be that rifle of yours."

"It probably was. Ross, I don't know a lot about Indians, but I sure as hell know when it's time to get rid of some outlaws." He looked in the direction of the town as he spoke. "So far they've stolen horses, sold whiskey to the Indians, and helped them rob a supply train. I think that's enough to shoot on sight."

"Wait a minute, Sykes," the scout cautioned sternly.

The agent turned and met the scout's disapproval. "I wasn't going to," he explained. "I'll give them a fair break before I shoot."

Sam Ross folded his arms over his chest and leaned against the post next to him. "They can't get another supply train through before spring now. The boats can't get up to Fort Benton, even if the wagons could get through to here after that. The only thing that's going to save the Blackfoot from starving now is a good hunting season, and some of those rifles would make a lot of difference."

"I haven't been able to find any to buy around here, and I haven't seen any of the Indians with one."

"I saw a bunch of them down there." He nodded in the direction of the supply wagons below the parade ground. Then he glanced at the sky. "Tomorrow you'll have to tell the Indians they either go hunting or starve, but it would help if you could take a fancy new rifle or two with you."

Sykes laughed but there was no humor in his voice. "You think Forbes will let me have some?"

"No, not likely."

"Then maybe the outlaws will."

* * *

Cole Sykes left his horse at the livery stable and walked to the Trapper's Last Chance. There was no one he recognized in the place, but while he stood at the bar, sipping a drink, Littan came in through the back door and headed for the bar. Recognizing Sykes, he stopped and leaned his left arm on the bar.

As soon as the bartender filled his glass, Littan lifted it, downed the whiskey and then, glaring at Sykes, walked out.

Sykes finished his drink in the next swallow, and left quickly. He ran along the sidewalk and around the corner to the back of the building where he caught sight of a horse and rider. The outlaw was already moving away, heading north in the direction of the Indian camp. Sykes dashed to the front of the saloon, watching the far end of the street. Crossing the street toward the livery stable, the agent kept his eyes on Littan's back, making sure the man did not turn around.

Sykes saddled up quickly and galloped after Littan, keeping behind the buildings. He stayed a dozen yards to the side of the trail until he caught up to the outlaw. Then he stopped and listened.

At first the silence was broken only by the breathing of his own horse. Suddenly he heard the sound of creaking leather ahead of him. He was closer than he thought, and he reached down and pulled his Colt. After a moment he kneed his horse cautiously toward the sound, leaning forward at the same time, peering into the darkness.

In the next instant, an orange flame spurted in front of him, and he heard a bullet explode. As the stallion lunged to one side under his spurs, he fired several times at the place where he had seen the flame. Then he dropped behind his horse's neck and rode closer to the place where the man had been waiting.

It was deadly silent. Sykes pulled his carbine and swung out of the saddle. He inched forward in the darkness, his rifle in his left arm, his Colt ready in his right. It was fifteen minutes before he found the body, sprawled out a dozen feet from the outlaw's horse. The agent approached carefully until he was sure Littan was dead, and then he went to the outlaw's horse, pulled the rifle out of the saddle boot and inspected it. It was what he had been looking for.

"I'll leave your horse," he muttered at the body, "so they'll know I'm not an Indian. But this rifle is just what I was after."

He rode back to town off the main trail, the way he had come out.

Chapter 19

Many Arrows started up at the sound of the distant shots. They were below the encampment, but closer than the town. When Red Beads stirred beside him and opened her eyes, he put a hand on her shoulder and motioned her to be silent. She sighed as she moved close to the warmth of his leg and pulled the buffalo robe higher around her shoulders.

While he continued to listen, he pushed the robe away from his legs and moved as though to get up. In response, she put her hand on his thigh, and then when he hesitated she put her arm around his leg and held it to her. "Don't go, Many Arrows. You've been gone too much."

"I must see what guns those are," he paused, settling back a little closer to her.

"It's cold out there and warm in here."

"Red Beads," he whispered as he ran his hand down her side and over her hip. "You keep the robe warm, but I must see why there was shooting. If someone is coming, I must see who it is before they see me." He moved his hand over her hip again and for a moment pulled the robe over both of them. Then he stood up. It was cold in the lodge, and he drew on his leggings and shirt as fast as he could. Wrapping a blanket around his shoulders, he picked up his rifle. The shots seemed to have been close, and he decided against going for his horse, which was picketed close to his tepee.

An hour later he returned to the camp leading a horse. He untied his buckskin horse, and still leading the other animal, rode to the main band of horses on the meadow above the encampment. At the meadow, he took the bridle and saddle off the horse and turned it loose to join the others. He hauled the saddle into the trees beside the river and hid it. He carried the bridle back to camp where he could use the leather for other things.

Red Beads was half asleep when he slid down inside the robe, and she murmured to him, asking if everything was all right. He felt the warmth and smoothness of her body against the thick hair of the inside of the buffalo robe. He told her that everything was well.

At dawn, Many Arrows appeared at the lodge of Runs-at-Night, who lay with a bullet hole through his thigh. He saw that the medicine-pipe man and the warrior's wife were still there, and waited until they came out.

"Walks-on-Crooked Leg, is his Spirit still strong within him?" asked Many Arrows anxiously when the old man stopped beside him.

The medicine-pipe man nodded. "Yes, his Spirit is willing that he should live, and it is with him."

"Good. Is he awake? Does he ask to see me?"

"It will help him to see you."

Many Arrows waited with respect while the medicine-pipe man walked away, one leg crooked and unbending, both hands clutching the bundle of his sacred medicines. Then Many Arrows pushed aside the lodge flap and stepped in. As soon as Runs-at-Night greeted him he walked to his side, sat down and asked, "Can I do anything for you?"

"No, Walks-on-Crooked-Leg has taken care of me. There is medicine on the wound and it is much better."

Many Arrows stayed for several minutes more. When he saw that the brave wanted to rest, he returned to his own tepee for his morning meal.

He ate with his eyes on Red Beads as she moved around the fire to serve him and then feed First Moon. She was tall and still slender except for the child he could see would come soon. Her arms were long and slim, and she moved with an ease that was a pleasure to watch. She had made her hair smooth again after the night, and she was wearing her favorite necklace, the one fashioned of red and orange beads. He never tired of looking at her beautiful, smooth face.

As he gazed at her, she glanced in his direction. Her face brightened, as though she knew what he was thinking.

Before he finished eating, the dogs in the camp started to bark, and at once he stood up and went to the lodge opening, motioning at the same time for Red Beads to stay behind him.

Outside, he saw his father emerge from his lodge and he started toward him. As he did so, the medicine-pipe man came out of the chief's tepee behind Flying Hawk, and together they stared at Many Arrows until he reached them.

Cole Sykes and Sam Ross dismounted at the edge of the Blackfoot camp. They had taken the shortcut from the fort, riding directly across the grassland instead of following the winding of the river.

As Sykes walked forward into the circle of lodges he put his hand to his mouth and then moved it rapidly away, fingers extended, the sign for talk. At once the three braves turned and went into Flying Hawk's tepee.

Sykes followed them inside and paused at the opening, waiting deliberately until Flying Hawk was seated and had motioned for the agent to sit. Continuing to move deliberately, Sykes walked behind Many Arrows and the medicine-pipe man as they leaned forward to make room for him.

While Sam Ross took his place, Grabs Thorns left the fire and moved to the women's side of the tepee.

They waited until the chief signaled he was ready to listen, and then Ross spoke for several minutes in the Blackfoot tongue. Although Sykes searched Flying Hawk's face while the interpreter spoke, he saw no change in the chief's expression.

Flying Hawk said nothing for several minutes after Ross finished speaking. Then he turned, his deep black eyes looking directly at Sykes as he asked Ross a question.

"He wants to know what you are going to do now," explained Ross.

"Tell him that first I need to notify the other bands. Ask him if there is anyone here who can do that for me?"

When Ross spoke again, the chief remained silent, although he nodded his head.

"All right," Sykes continued. "Now tell him I'll write to Washington to see if there is any other way supplies can be sent here to replace the ones that were stolen, but that will take time. Ask him how much food he has put away for the winter. How long can they make it on what they have?"

Sykes listened, trying to make out as many of the words as he could while the two men spoke back and forth for several minutes.

"He says they were counting on the supplies they had been promised. He said to remind you that the treaty forced them to give up much of their hunting ground in exchange for the supplies, and already there is talk of giving up more land, but now you do not deliver the supplies."

"Ask him about the Indians that were with the attackers." This time while Ross spoke to Flying Hawk, Sykes turned away from the chief and watched his son. Many Arrows met the agent's stare and held it until Sykes looked back at the chief.

"He says he did not send anyone to do that. He says the reason they have kept the camp here so long is to wait for the supplies. Why would they try to steal them?"

Sykes did not respond to the question. Instead he looked around the lodge for a moment. "No matter what he says, they'll have to hunt now," he said, frowning at Ross. "Ask how many rifles they have. They're going to need them."

"None," said Ross a moment later.

"You have one, and there's the one I got last night. That's not enough. We'll have to get more from the fort somehow. Where's the best hunting this time of the year?"

"Are you going hunting, too?" asked Ross with surprise in his voice.

"Yes, and so are you. Where's the best hunting?"

"Flying Hawk says there aren't many buffalo left around here. Not enough to count on finding them in time. He thinks maybe the bands farther north and east can, because they're farther from the fort and the mining camps. These people would be better off trying for elk and deer in the mountains because the time's so short. The elk should be starting down after that snow. There'll be some risk getting caught up there themselves, that's all."

"We're good enough riders. We ought to be able to see a storm coming and get out ahead of it."

"They have to take the whole camp, Sykes. The women'll have to be there to take care of the meat, dry it and make pemmican if it's going to last. They'll have to be where they can get berries, things like that. The men don't do that kind of work, and they wouldn't have time to even if they did."

"All right, if that's the only way—tell them to get ready. How long's it going to take?"

Ross talked with the chief for a few minutes.

"They can't leave until day after tomorrow."

"I thought they had these lodges so they can move fast."

"They can move their stuff fast enough, but they have to go through their hunting ritual or they won't have any luck."

Sykes leaned in the direction of the interpreter as he spoke. "You mean they have to have a ceremony first?" he asked.

"Hold it," warned Ross. He frowned at the agent until Sykes straightened up again.

Sykes took a deep breath before he went on. "Tell them I'll see if I can get some more guns in the meantime. We'll need them that much more, the longer they delay."

* * *

Many Arrows stood beside Flying Hawk as the two white men left the camp. As he turned to his own tepee, his father stopped him, and he followed the two older men into the chief's lodge again.

When they were seated, Flying Hawk stared steadily ahead of him toward Grabs Thorns, who was kneeling beside the fire, stirring the meat in the pot.

"You led the young men against the supply train?" he asked after a moment.

"Yes," said Many Arrows.

"The Man-with-Blackbeard was with you?"

"Yes."

"Was Runs-at-Night the only one wounded?"

"Yes."

"Why did you go against our own supplies?"

"I didn't know they were ours. It looked like an army train. Man-with-Blackbeard said there would be many horses and we could get some back for the ones we had lost, but there were only a few horses. The rest were mules and oxen."

"Before they have brought our supplies on mules. You could not tell from that?"

"Many of their trains come with mules. I could not be sure from that. We only wanted the horses. The agent stole our horses as soon as he got here." His eyes clouded. "We wanted to take his."

"Where are the mules and their burdens now?"

"Man-with-Blackbeard took them. He gave us three horses and an iron kettle that one of the mules carried."

"And he gave you more of the strong water from the place where they make it?" When Many Arrows nodded, Flying Hawk fixed his eyes on the fire for several moments before he stood up. He waited until the others followed his example, and then he turned to the medicine-pipe man. "We will prepare for the hunt."

Many Arrows stepped closer to his father. "The supplies that we need for the winter are at the fort. They are still in wagons. Why do we hunt when they owe us the food? The treaty you signed gave us the food. It is ours to take!" The young chief raised his voice.

"We cannot fight during the winter snows," his father replied calmly. "If this man, Cole Sykes, can get us the supplies we have been promised, then we will not be at war. But if we must go to war for what is ours, it cannot be before next spring."

"There are no walls around the fort. We can get the supplies tonight. I will paint myself for war, not the hunt!"

"No, Many Arrows. You will pray and paint yourself for the hunt. If your luck is good, you will know that this is how we are to feed our people now. They will not build walls around the fort before spring."

Once they were out of sight of the encampment, Sykes pulled up. "I'm going to find out who was in on that attack."

"How are you going to do that?"

"If there were a lot of shooting, some of the Indian horses would have been hit, wouldn't they? This is a good time to take a look at the savages while they're thinking about something else."

"I don't think there's *any* good time to go prowling around Blackfoot ponies."

"You don't have to go with me. Go on back to the fort. After I'm through here I'm going down to where Silvers was shot to see if I can find some stray mules."

"Do that instead then. Let me check the horses. The Indians will ask me questions if they see me before shooting. Then I'll ride down to the mine in case you need me. If we can get that money back—"

"If the Indians don't already have it."

"You'll know that easy enough. They'll have to spend it either in town or at the fort."

"Or make necklaces out of it."

Ross looked steadily at the agent for a moment. "You think they're that dumb?"

"No," admitted Sykes. Then he laughed as he reached for his tobacco, at the same time studying the sky. "Even if they do have to sing and dance while it snows them out of the mountains."

"It's not just singing and dancing for the fun of it like you're making it sound." Ross picked up his reins and turned his horse's head in the direction of the grazing pasture. "It's a lot more like singing hymns and praying, though I guess you don't know about that either."

Cole Sykes tapped tobacco into a paper without responding.

"Where'll I meet you?" asked Ross as his horse moved away.

"You won't," said Sykes. "I'll see you back at the fort some time tomorrow."

Ross pulled up again. "You aren't planning to try something down there by yourself, are you?"

"It depends."

"You'd better wait for me, Sykes. I know my way around this country."

Sykes lit his cigarette and picked up his reins, turning away from Ross. "If you're so set on night riding, check that rimrock again where I found the horse corrals. They might think it's safe to go back up there by now."

Many Arrows strode to the edge of the camp and stood looking in the direction the white men had gone. He would do as his father commanded, but he could not agree with the decision. All around him he sensed trouble, the feeling that events were not in harmony, not the way that was best for him and for his people. When he turned back into the circle of lodges, his heart was heavy and he stopped again, thinking about how he felt.

A moment later he walked to his tepee and entered it only long enough to get his rifle, fill a pouch with dried meat, and snatch a blanket to wrap around him in the cold of the night.

Red Beads watched in silence until he turned toward the opening. "When will you be back?" she asked with anxious eyes.

"I don't know," he said shortly. He left without looking at her, and walked to the spotted pony he had outside the camp, one of the few horses he had left. Once on the pony's back, he kneed the animal in the direction the two white men had gone.

Cole Sykes put his coat on an hour before dark and buttoned it around him. Later, as he neared the valley where Ross had shown him the mine, he unfastened it far enough to clear the top of his Colt. It was dark by the time he reached the entrance to the valley, and a sharp wind blew down the canyon. As he moved into the wind toward the side of the canyon where the mine was, he paused and sniffed the air.

The smell of wood smoke and something else he

couldn't identify drifted toward him. He swung down at once and led his horse higher into the trees. He tied the bay to the trunk of a tree with a short rein so that the animal could not lift its head to whinny. Then he pulled his rifle and began walking up the canyon's slope on foot. Before he reached the mine, the pines gave way to a grove of aspen. As soon as he stepped into the grove, he stopped and swore to himself. The dried leaves on the ground crackled under his feet, and he could advance only a few inches at a time. While he moved slowly ahead, the smell in the air became stronger until the odor was unmistakable. It was the smell of a distillery.

When another leaf cracked under his boot, he scowled and headed down the slope and across the valley floor to the pines on the other side.

A few minutes later he could see a fire at the base of the pile of tailings below the mine shaft, and the sour-mash smell was stronger than before.

In the light of the fire, he counted eight men. There were sure to be others tending the still, and probably a guard or two around the camp. It was more men than he could handle by himself.

For the next hour he moved silently in a half circle around the fire and then back again, noting the guards above and below the camp and the place where their horses were picketed. He did not see any mules with the horses.

As he passed the camp a second time and started down to cross the valley floor below, a rock rolled under his foot. He dropped quickly to his knees behind a bush and lowered his rifle to the ground so that the fire could not glint off the barrel. At the same time he heard a call from the guard below him, followed by the roar of a gunshot echoing through the canyon. He dropped lower into the shadows and peered in the direction of the shot. It couldn't have been intended for him. When he looked back at the fire, the men around it had disappeared into the dark. Any one of them might be coming in his direction.

A moment later, he heard cursing, and one of the outlaws called out, "All right, men. It's only one of the Indians. Let him come into camp."

"You better tell him we made a mistake," answered the guard. "We shot his horse."

Many Arrows held his blanket high around his shoulders with one hand and his rifle in the other as he walked past the guards into the camp. At the same time three of the outlaws returned to the fire and stood behind it watching the Indian. A heavyset, bearded man stepped into the firelight and walked to meet Many Arrows. The Indian signaled for a moment in sign language, and the white man turned, looking around him into the darkness.

"There's someone else here," he shouted, his voice piercing the silence. "Spread out, see what you can find!"

At once the men disappeared into the darkness. Sykes gripped his rifle. They'd be between him and his horse in a minute, and there was a good chance that if they moved faster than he did, they would find the bay before he could reach it.

At least he'd learned for certain that Many Arrows and the outlaws were in it together.

Starting back the way he had come, he saw a man's form suddenly loom in front of him. Sykes had one advantage. Everyone here was his enemy. The man fired one instant before Sykes pulled the trigger. Now the agent no longer attempted to move silently. He sprinted across the floor of the canyon, keeping himself as low as he could yet still moving freely. Bullets were churning the dirt around him as he started up the far side, and he sprawled behind a pile of rocks before trying to go along the side of the canyon. They had him located well enough, and it was a good hundred yards to his horse.

He lay at full length behind the rocks, listening to the sound of men climbing toward him from several different directions. While he waited, he switched his rifle to his left hand and drew his Colt. There was no problem with distance. He lay quietly, trying to discern whether they were approaching him from the front or from the sides. When they were almost upon him, he rose to his feet behind the rocks, his legs spread, his weight forward, ready to move. As the first head and shoulders came into sight, he fired. Then, quickly, he fired again to his other side.

He heard a scream, and then plunged down the side of the canyon, running in a broken line, crouching. He felt a sudden tug at his coat sleeve as a bullet whizzed by, and another slammed into the side of his boot heel so that he tripped and nearly went down. But he managed to keep going, scrambling and dodging until he reached his horse.

Many Arrows stood by the fire, quietly watching the outlaws return to the canyon. He could tell from the expressions on their faces that the agent had gotten away, but he felt nothing for them. Hadn't he followed Sykes to this place to warn them? And what had they done but shoot his own pony from under him?

He waited, his blanket high around his shoulders, until the outlaw, Man-with-Blackbeard, walked to the other side of the fire. He could sense that the man was raging inside.

Many Arrows slipped the blanket from his shoulders and dropped his rifle down on it so that he could talk with his hands. He indicated why he had come, and then asked why his horse had been killed. Blackbeard turned and spoke to one of the other men before he offered Many Arrows a horse to replace the dead pony.

Many Arrows agreed to the exchange and waited for the horse to be brought to him. The men around the fire were silent as he led the horse a few yards away. There was only the rope that had been used to tie it, but he looped it over the horse's jaw and climbed to its back. As he rode away he could tell that the animal had been trained in the Indian way.

He traveled a short distance from the campfire, then turned aside and began climbing the valley floor. After a few minutes he stopped and listened to the night around him. When he heard no sound behind him, he went forward another hundred yards. Then he rode to the floor of the canyon and headed for the flatland beyond. He had lost one of his best ponies, but at least he had another to replace it.

He stopped at the bottom of the canyon where a flowing creek joined the larger stream below. He prayed to the Under Water Persons before plunging in. Suddenly he heard the sound of horses behind him. Looking back, he saw two of the outlaws riding up on either side of his horse. By their manner, he knew they had come for the horse, and their guns were already aimed in his direction.

He pulled his knife from its sheath as he slid forward over the horse's neck. At the same time the guns blasted behind him, and the pony screamed. Many Arrows leaped to the side of the nearest outlaw and, as he jerked him from the saddle, thrust his knife into the man's body and then twisted, holding the body in front of him as a shield before the other outlaw could fire again. As Many Arrows held the limp body, the other horse, shying away from the smell of the blood, bucked and plunged. With the outlaw's back to him, the Indian flung the dead man down and ran to where he had dropped his rifle.

Cole Sykes pulled up short and listened to the sound of guns firing behind him. He couldn't imagine what the outlaws could be shooting at now, except maybe the Indian and Many Arrows wasn't a man he planned to worry about anymore. He started ahead, frowning, and reined in again at the sound of a single shot.

Abruptly he turned his horse in the direction of the canyon and waited. If Many Arrows was in trouble with the outlaws, it was his own problem. Then, despite his decision not to be concerned about the young chief, Sykes changed his course and headed to where he thought Many Arrows was likely to pass on his way back to the Indian camp.

As he waited, he saw the war chief loping along in the distance. He wasn't sure whether or not he was relieved that Many Arrows was safe. But he was numb with weariness. He headed directly for town, put up his horse, and went to his room.

After a few hours sleep, he had breakfast and headed once more for the fort. He was standing on the porch outside the barracks when Sam Ross rode in.

The scout loped to the hitching rail in front of Sykes, a disgusted expression on his face. As he dismounted, he nodded his head. "Yeah," he said. "They were in on it."

"Anything doing at the corrals above the rimrocks?"

"Nothing I could see."

"Well, I found where they brew the whiskey."

The scout finished tying his horse before he turned toward Sykes. "Where?"

The agent pointed to the southwest, in the direction of the mine. "Be a nice chore for the army, don't you think? They can break up the still while we go hunting."

Chapter 20

At dawn the next morning, as Sykes rode across the bridge, the first of the wagons from the supply train left the fort, and he stopped to watch it. He rode slowly up the hill so he could see each wagon as it went by. He wondered which one Patricia Ashley would be in.

He could see a detachment of cavalry forming inside the fort, probably to accompany the wagons. That was one duty Lieutenant Barkley was sure to take for himself, Sykes thought, and the officer was sure to find a reason to ride beside her wagon all the way.

Sykes reached inside his coat for his tobacco, and he had a cigarette going by the time the third wagon passed him. She wasn't in that one, but she would be somewhere near the front. He couldn't imagine her in the back of the train, behind everyone else. For that matter, he couldn't imagine her on a wagon train at all. He had never seen her wear the sort of clothes worn by women traveling in wagons, although once she had worn a sunbonnet. He searched the sky as the next team of oxen started through the gate.

What was she going to think when she saw him sitting there as though he was waiting to say good-bye? He frowned as the wagon moved into sight. What the hell difference did it make what she thought? If he wanted to watch the wagons go, he could.

Tricia wasn't in that one or the next one, and in the break behind them, he rode through the gate into the fort. His cigarette was nearly down to a stub, but he left it in the side of his mouth as he rode past the last of the wagons. Unless she was hiding, she hadn't been in any of them.

He stopped and looked at the departing wagons, staring after them while he took the cigarette butt out of his mouth and flipped it away into the dirt. Then he leaned his arm on the saddle horn and watched Lieutenant Barkley lead his men out of the fort. As Barkley passed Sykes the officer's eyes were fixed on the wagons and he did not appear to notice the agent. But Sergeant Pearce raised his hand in a greeting and several of the other men followed suit. When the column of cavalry was out of the fort, Sykes scanned the length of the parade ground to the colonel's house. Was she still here? He straightened slowly, his eyes on the house. What difference did it make to Cole Sykes if she was?

While he told himself again that it made no difference, his horse suddenly moved forward across the parade ground. When it was clear where the stallion was headed, the front door of the colonel's house opened and Patricia Ashley stepped from the entrance. She was gathering a shawl around her shoulders, and even at that distance he could tell that she was waiting for him.

He held the bay to a walk for a moment while he puzzled over the feeling that had surged through him as soon as he'd seen her. Then he shook his head as though it needed clearing and let the horse break into a lope. He didn't want to keep her waiting in the cold any longer.

When he did not jump down to her, she stepped off the porch and stood beside the horse.

"Why didn't you go with the wagons?" Cole asked.

"Don't you think it's too dangerous right now?"

"They're sending damn near a whole platoon with it, looks like. What are you going to do, take the stage from Helena down to the railroad?"

"No. That doesn't seem any safer to me. It's forever being held up, isn't it?"

"Well, what are you going to do?"

"I'm staying here all winter."

"When you don't have to? No one would do that."

"Cole, are you calling me a—"

"No," he assured her quickly.

"It's possible, of course, that I've gotten a taste for, oh, something different than another winter in Boston."

"Like what? Lieutenant Barkley?"

She laughed for a moment, her eyes looking into his. "Heavens no. He's what I'd call an ordinary man. There are lots of men like William in Boston. Many of them, especially at the parties and dinners."

"What, then?"

"Oh, things that aren't all planned ahead." She hesitated, still watching him. "Like riding in a raging storm—and being kissed when you're soaking wet and shivering."

He ran the back of his hand over the side of his chin, feeling the sharp whiskers. He took off his hat and ran his fingers through his hair, though he knew it was too long to stay in place. It blew across his forehead as he continued to look at her.

There was a thickness in his throat that he had to

swallow before he could say anything. "Did your uncle want you to stay?"

"I'm not certain, but what else could he do except say that he was very happy to have my company for as long as I wish? He did say Lieutenant Barkley would be very pleased."

Sykes settled his hat on his head and jammed it low over his eyes as he turned his horse toward the parade ground. "I'm sure he will," he called over his shoulder.

"Where are you going?" she asked.

"I've got business with your uncle."

A few minutes later Sykes stopped in front of the colonel's desk and waited until Forbes acknowledged his presence. Corporal Eddy was at the orderly table by the door and Sam Ross sat in the chair by the window.

"What do you want, Sykes?" snapped Forbes testily.

"I found the still where they've been making the whiskey they trade to the Indians."

"And now you've decided you need my help?"

"Breaking up a still sounds like something your boys can do," replied Sykes. "I can tell them right where it is."

The colonel stood up. "Mr. Sykes, you have a way of being very unpleasant no matter what you say."

"So do you," retorted Sykes. "Only you're not as honest about it. I don't like being treated as though I'm still wet behind the ears."

Ross cleared his throat without looking at either of the men, but the sound ended the exchange and the colonel sat down again. "It'll have to wait until Barkley gets back. I've only got two squads of cavalry left. That's as low as I intend to let our defenses get here."

"It'll wait. The Indians will be too busy for a while to drink the stuff anyway."

When Sykes made no move to leave, the colonel raised his eyebrows. "Is there something else you want?"

"I need some of those Winchesters that came in on the wagon train."

"Some of them?" he asked. "I can understand one for yourself—"

"I need them for the hunt."

"For the Indians? Never, Sykes! You think I'd give them guns like that? That's the kind of gun that cost you the Indian supplies in the first place. They already have more than they should."

"They don't have any that I've seen. It was the outlaws with them that had those Winchesters."

"Well, what's the difference? Sykes, you must be out of your mind to request that. Do you think I would give the enemy my best weapons?"

"If they don't have a hell of a hunt right now, they're likely to starve to death when the snow hits. There's hardly any game left near them. They've cleaned it out waiting for their supplies."

"No, Sykes. No matter what you say, I'm not parting with those rifles."

"Then how about a loan of a dozen of them, just for the hunt? It's my job to see the Indians don't starve, and I'm going to take care of it somehow."

"Just what do you mean by that?"

Corporal Eddy stood up. "Colonel Forbes, sir," he interrupted. "May I speak to the point, sir?"

"What do you want, Eddy?" The colonel's annoyance showed as he turned to the young soldier.

"If you're only concerned about getting the rifles back, I'll volunteer to go along on the hunt."

"You'll what?"

"The Indians will also need to learn how to use the guns, sir, and that's what I'm good at. I am—if you'll pardon my being the one to say so—an excellent shot. I could be of help to the Indians, and I could keep track of the guns and see that they're returned."

The colonel leaned against the back of his chair and laughed. Then he raised a hand to his eyes as though to wipe away tears. "Tell me, Eddy, how do you plan, all by yourself, to see that a dozen or so thieving, bloodthirsty, Blackfoot warriors return those guns after the hunt?"

In the silence that followed, Sam Ross spoke in a calm voice. "If they promise ahead of time, they'll return them. And we can use the kid if he's that good with the guns. You're here to keep the peace, aren't you, Forbes? What's the risk of a dozen guns, if it works?"

"I wouldn't put *any* guns in the hands of Indians, if I could help it, let alone those." Colonel Forbes looked stonily at each of the men in turn. Then he leaned forward on his forearms and looked thoughtfully at the scout. "Sam Ross, I've learned to respect what you say. I want you to know that if it weren't for you, I wouldn't listen to a word of this." He glanced at the other two men, making sure they had taken in his words. "And if I don't get those guns back, I'll personally throw you in the guardhouse for lying to me."

"I understand," replied Ross, eyeing Sykes as he stood up. "I'm willing to take the chance."

They could hear the beat of the drums and the chanting of voices as they rode over the rise and down into the circle of lodges. The three white men stopped outside the camp and waited for the drumming to stop.

"We'll stay here until they tell us to come in," explained Ross. "We don't want them blaming us for bad luck on this hunt."

Corporal Eddy looked from one to the other of the men. "I've heard about that drumming," he commented, "and it sounds just like what I've heard."

"How's that?" asked Ross.

"It kind of makes the hair on my neck stand up."

The scout laughed. "If that does, you ought to hear 'em when they're painting for war. All their war songs end in a wolf howl, and you can't tell it from the real thing except that it's ten times louder than any wolf pack you ever heard. Especially if you're right there in the lodge with them."

"That'd be something," said Eddy. "I'd like to hear that sometime."

"You can't unless you're one of 'em. Being a warrior is like belonging to a secret society. It's part of their religion. They don't let outsiders watch what goes on."

Cole Sykes turned toward the scout. "I suppose you were one of them."

"When I was younger," he sighed. "I'm too old now."

Corporal Eddy looked eagerly around while they waited. It was the closest he'd been to Indians without a couple dozen other men armed and ready behind him.

The sound of voices was still rising from the camp when two women emerged from the circle of lodges and moved down the trail to the stream. The younger of the pair glanced up and saw Eddy staring at her. She lowered her eyes quickly. The older woman tugged at her arm, and she followed after her, raising her eyes once more to see the corporal still gazing at her.

"That's Night Quail," Ross explained when the two women were out of sight. "Pretty, isn't she?"

The corporal frowned at Ross for a moment before he crossed his hands over his saddle horn. "She's only an Indian," he mumbled.

"Yeah," muttered Ross sourly, turning away.

Taken aback at the edge in the scout's voice, the young corporal studied the set of Ross's jaw, and then said quickly, "But she is pretty."

Climbing into the mountains, the band left the wind of the plains behind them and almost at once the sky began to clear. The older men took the lead with Flying Hawk while half a dozen of the younger braves trotted along each flank, guarding the rest of the camp. The women and children followed the men. What they could not get on their ponies' backs was dragged behind the animals on travois that the women had made from lodge poles. The poles along the sides of the horses were tied together over the horses' shoulders. The other ends of the poles were spread apart on the ground and loaded with the heavy lodge skins and the cooking pots. The women carried their babies in cradleboards lined with fur, but the young children, the old and the sick perched on top of the loaded travois.

Long before the camp had begun to move, the women and children had overcome their shyness at the presence of the strange white men, and they traveled with their usual chatter and noise.

Corporal Eddy rode between Sykes and the scout in the lead with the older men, but he looked back often, watching the way the others traveled.

"I don't see how they expect to surprise any game," he observed, grinning as he straightened in the saddle.

"They aren't hunting seriously right now," explained Ross. "There won't be any women or children around then, but they have to come with us to take care of the meat."

It was past the time for the evening meal when they reached a valley wide enough to hold all of the lodges and equipment. A stream of clear, pure water ran nearby a meadow large enough to graze the horses for a few days.

The three white men waited until they knew where the Indian lodges would be placed, and then rode outside the circle, climbed a dozen yards up the side of the valley and made their own camp. By the time it was dark they could look down on the completed circle of tepees.

"Flying Hawk will expect us to eat with him tonight," Ross informed his two companions, "especially since we gave them the rifles. What I can't figure out, though, is how to explain that they're just a loan. I don't think they have a word for it in their language. If they do, I don't know what it is."

Sykes and Eddy both stared sharply at the scout. "You didn't say anything about that before," complained Sykes. "You said if they promised ahead of time they would return them."

"I know, and they would. I just don't know how to get 'em to promise anything like that ahead of time."

"By God, Ross!" exploded Sykes.

"Well, nobody asked me if I could do it, and I figured they needed the guns."

"Mr. Ross," said the corporal, "I have to see that they return them. That's the main reason I'm here. I'll have to try to take them away from them."

"They'll expect you to give them something in exchange then."

"Wait a minute," said the corporal suspiciously, reaching out to the scout's arm. "Is this something the two of you had planned?"

"No," answered Sykes, "it isn't. Ross, those guns are on loan from the army, that's all. You find the words you need to make that clear, or I'm with the kid. I made a deal."

"All right, all right! Looks like I'm not going to be friends with anyone this trip." He laughed to himself as the three of them started down to the Indian camp.

Passing between the lodges in the outer circle, Eddy saw two women fastening the bottom edge of a tepee to the ground. He strolled by, his eyes fastened on the younger one until they reached Flying Hawk's lodge. While they waited outside, they watched the activity in the camp. Fires already burned both inside and outside most of the lodges and the smell of food wafted through the air.

Without the wind of the lower plain, the air in the mountains was strangely still, and the cloud of smoke hanging over the camp seemed to close them in.

It was several minutes before the chief appeared at the opening of his lodge. He held the flap to one side as he looked at the white men. Then he motioned to Ross, and the three walked toward the chief.

"They got rules on how to act in there," whispered Sykes to the soldier. "He'll tell you where to sit. Don't walk in front of anybody getting to your seat and don't talk when anybody else is talking."

Sam Ross smiled at Sykes' back as the gunman stepped inside the opening and then stopped, his eyes on Flying Hawk.

Later that night Sykes spelled out the watches he

wanted them to take, and then turned to the scout. "What do you think about that, Ross?"

"Good idea," he approved.

"What? I thought you'd say we didn't need it."

"Probably don't, but there's always a chance."

"Ross, you're a puzzle to me. One minute you act like there's nothing you don't trust them with, and the next thing you act like you don't trust them at all."

"It seems that way because you don't know them, that's all. They don't think the same way about things. You think about everything in only one way, and even though some people might call you lawless, Sykes, you've got a code of conduct so narrow—hell, I know you well enough already to guess just about everything you're going to do before you do it. But it's not the same with them. For one thing, they're more religious. They go by what the spirits tell them to do. And they got lots of spirits. Everything has a spirit, as a matter of fact. Even the animals have powers at times. So if one of them has a dream tonight about going to war and he can talk some of the others into going with him, they'll go right in the middle of this hunt."

"And if he dreams they're to go after three white men?" asked Sykes, watching the scout's face.

Corporal Eddy sat bolt upright and looked around nervously.

"They might," conceded Ross. "You always got to be careful what dreams you provoke." As he spoke, he glanced in the corporal's direction. Although the young soldier's eyes were trying to penetrate the shadows around him, his jaw was firm and he appeared steady.

After a moment the scout chuckled softly. "That is, of course, until they accept you as a friend. Then they're the most loyal people I know. I've never seen a white man as could beat them at that."

Eddy turned slowly and looked at the scout. "Do they figure someone like me is a friend or an enemy?"

"That's kind of on an individual basis. They don't know you yet. You help them with those guns tomorrow, and you've got a chance."

Sykes did not sleep while Eddy took his turn at the watch, but during that time he saw nothing to make him think the corporal could not handle the duty. If anything, Eddy was more alert than Sykes felt himself, and he seemed as fearless as Sykes hoped he would be.

By morning a soft mist was rising from the stream. It formed into a streak across the side of the hill above them and filled the valley between the two peaks to the west of them. Except for the mist, the sky was still clear.

Ross shook himself awake and ambled to the fire Sykes had built inside a circle of rocks.

The agent looked up from the coffeepot as the scout approached. "Some of them left already," he remarked.

"Sure. They don't go out at night without a good reason, but they'll go at the first sign of light." He looked through the haze at the sky. "Looks like their prayers for good weather were answered," he said, unpacking a cup from his saddlebag and pouring some coffee. "It's going to be a good day."

Corporal Eddy joined the men at the fire. "Jesus," he whispered, looking around him. "What a place!"

"In what way, kid?" asked Ross.

"What a place for a hunt."

"You like to hunt, don't you?"

"There's nothing I'd rather do. And I want to try those rifles myself. I never had anything like that back home."

"Well, you'll have to wait a while longer. It'll be this evening probably, after you teach them about the guns, before we ought to go out there with them. We want to be sure they know what they're doing first."

Sam Ross was wrong about how long it would take the Indians to learn how to use the rifles. By noon Corporal Eddy could not see what else they needed to know, and he was surprised how little he had needed Ross to talk to them. At first the targets he set up for them were too easy, but he developed a realistic view of their abilities as the morning went by.

By the middle of the afternoon there was fresh meat in the camp. A herd of elk coming down from the higher mountains had been sighted, and with the new guns a dozen of them had been felled before the rest could bolt away.

Corporal Eddy was grinning as he rode up the hill from the Indian camp. "I haven't seen that many elk all at once for a long time. Seems like they could eat all winter just on that."

"It's a good start," agreed Ross.

After he took care of his horse, the soldier opened his saddlebags and took out a small metal hook attached to a long line. Then he poked around the edges of their camp, looking for something to use as bait. The agent walked up behind him.

"That looks like a fishhook," declared Sykes.

"It is. Didn't you see that stream down there? I could see the trout in it every time I went near it," he responded eagerly.

"You got another line?"

"Sure. You want to fish, too?"

"It's been a hell of a long time since I've tasted fresh trout."

"You want to go, too, Ross?" invited the corporal.

"No, I'll hold the fort here," Ross declined. "I'm not much of a fish eater."

"You don't know what you're missing," Sykes told him. "The kid's right. There's plenty of fish in that stream. You heat the frying pan. It won't take us long."

They returned in a half hour with three large trout. Although Ross had a fire blazing, Sykes had to get out a frying pan himself and put it over the flames. While it heated, he cut a slice of bacon for grease in which to cook the fish and Corporal Eddy cleaned their catch. As the fish sizzled in the pan, Sykes sat back on his heels and reached for his tobacco. He glanced at the scout and saw he was frowning in the direction of the Indian camp.

"You're damned silent, Ross," said the gunman. "What's on your mind?"

"Not much."

"What's wrong with these fish?"

Sam Ross sighed as he looked down at the frying pan. "They're taboo, if you want to know."

"They're what?"

"Taboo. The Blackfoot don't eat fish."

"Why the hell not? If they need food for the winter, there's nothing better. They can be dried and smoked just like meat."

Corporal Eddy gazed dreamily down at the Indian camp. He thought he could see Night Quail beside the fire in front of the lodge nearest them. While he watched, she turned as though she could smell the fish cooking and looked up through the trees.

"Well, I don't want to hurt their feelings," said the corporal. "There's lots of meat."

"What's the matter with fish?" asked Sykes, straightening up.

"They belong to the Under Water Persons, and if you make the Under Water Persons angry, they can cause a sudden storm."

Sykes looked around at the sky. "Well, there's no storm coming now." As he squatted on his heels beside the fire again, he stared at the one small cloud he could see above the mountains. It seemed to hover over the source of the stream. While he studied the cloud, it changed its shape and seemed to grow larger and darker.

He turned the fish over in the frying pan. "There's no storm coming, Ross," he repeated, emphasizing each word.

"I don't think I want any fish," Corporal Eddy decided.

"I know I don't," said Ross.

"Goddamn it!" cursed Sykes. "I suppose the two of you would be happy if I threw them back in the water."

"Might as well be on the safe side," replied Ross, watching the agent as he paced around the fire. "Wouldn't want to end this good weather."

"Christ!" The gunman grabbed the frying pan and stalked down the hill past the tepees to the edge of the stream. He flung the contents of the pan out into the middle of the water. Then he knelt beside the stream, scooped up a handful of sand and scraped the pan clean. When he was finished scouring it, he tilted the pan into the water until it had an inch of water in its bottom, and then he flipped the water and sand out into the center of the stream.

As he turned to go back past the lodges, he caught Many Arrows standing at the edge of the camp watching his every move.

Chapter 21

Lieutenant Barkley rode at the head of the wagons, watching for trouble, but with the wagons empty and the weather warm again it was an easy trip. The detail reached Fort Benton without incident, and then turned back to Fort Mason.

The lieutenant called a stop each day before the sun went down, and as soon as his tent was pitched he ensconced himself in it, away from the other men. He had his meals brought there, and he did not take part in the evening activities of the men.

They reached Fort Mason one afternoon when the sun was hanging low in the sky. He ordered the troops to step double time as they clattered into the fort, and insisted on an inspection in the middle of the parade ground before he dismissed the men. Afterward, as he trotted his horse to the headquarters, he glanced sideways in the direction of the colonel's house.

Colonel Forbes was still in his office when Barkley stopped in the doorway.

"Come in," invited the colonel. "What is your report?"

"No problems, sir. We encountered no difficulty whatsoever in the escort."

"Good. I didn't expect any, of course, with the

empty wagons. Seems like the savages know about things like that."

"Yes sir. I'm sure they do. We didn't see a sign of them."

"I've got another assignment for you, but it can wait until tomorrow."

"What is it, sir?"

"Sykes claims he's found a still up in the mountains southwest of here, and he says whoever's running it is selling whiskey to the Indians."

"That's not legal, is it?"

"No. At least, there's a law against bringing it into Indian territory. I assume the same applies to selling it to them."

"Why in the world is Sykes worried about that?"

"I know what you mean. However, he has reported it to me, so we'd better check it out. If it's true, I want you to break up the still, of course."

"I suppose this is the same mythical band of white outlaws."

"He thinks so."

Lieutenant Barkley watched the colonel's expression and he could see that they held the same opinion of Cole Sykes. His contempt played across his face. "I wonder how much longer we'll have to put up with him around here."

"Oh, I don't think too much longer." The colonel stood up, smiling to himself. "No hurry about checking that out tomorrow, Barkley. Give the men a good rest."

"Yes sir." The lieutenant turned briskly, then hesitated. He spun around toward the commanding officer. "If you don't mind, sir."

"Yes?"

"I was surprised when I didn't see Miss Ashley on the supply train."

Colonel Forbes grinned as he walked around the end of his desk. "And pleased also, I assume."

"Of course, sir."

"You might want to talk to her about why."

"Indeed?"

"She's used to military men, Barkley, and she actually seems to like it here. There aren't too many girls like that."

"I hope I'm hearing you correctly, sir."

"What other reason could she have for staying?"

"I don't know."

The colonel reached for the pipe on his desk. "Take your time tomorrow, Barkley."

Lieutenant Barkley rode up and down the line of mounted troopers. Their horses were curried and their harnesses gleamed from saddle soap. Each man carried a new Winchester in the saddle boot under his right leg, a revolver on his hip, one hundred rounds of ammunition and a week's rations in his saddlebag.

The lieutenant reined up in front of Sergeant Pearce's horse and looked over his shoulder down the line of men. Several of the horses were snorting and tossing their heads with the freshness of the early morning, and beyond the end of the fort the mist was rising from the river.

Before he gave the order to move out, Barkley looked toward the colonel's house. Tricia came to the door behind her uncle and stood in the opening as the colonel started for his office. Barkley could tell she was watching the scene on the parade ground.

He straightened even more in his saddle, and, in a clear, crisp voice, ordered the men to form into columns. As Pearce repeated the order, Barkley raised his hand in Tricia's direction. She waved back, and Barkley swung his horse around and cantered to the front of the men. As he led them out through the gate, he did not look back again.

Before they reached the bridge, the troops turned to the south and headed in the direction Sykes had indicated on the map he had left with the colonel. As they crossed the open plain the men stayed in formation, riding four abreast. At first there was only the creaking of saddles and leather straps, but as the morning wore on, the men relaxed and talked among themselves. As long as they were in the open, Barkley did not send scouts out ahead or to the sides, and the men seemed more interested in the pleasant change in the weather than any danger around them.

When they stopped for a noon break at the base of the hills, the men were still relaxed. Before they started moving higher into the trees, Sergeant Pearce sent two men ahead to scout the way.

The map that Sykes had drawn was in Lieutenant Barkley's pocket, but he left it there and led the way without consulting it.

They climbed steadily for most of the afternoon, heading into a canyon similar to the one on Sykes' map. As they turned the first corner, the lieutenant raised his hand and signaled a stop. Sergeant Pearce turned to the column and barked out the command.

The two scouts were galloping back down the canyon toward them. "This is a dead end, sir," said the lead trooper, pulling up to Barkley.

"It can't be," snapped Barkley, glaring at the man.

"We went as far as we could, sir. There was no way a horse could go any farther."

Sergeant Pearce glanced around him at the walls of the canyon, and looked back over the heads of the men. It wasn't a place he wanted to be. The canyon sides were steep and there was no possible way to ride up them, but there was good cover for dozens of Indians or outlaws in the rocks above them.

"I suggest we ride out of here at once, sir," he suggested.

Barkley turned his glare on the sergeant's face.

"What are you afraid of, Pearce? Do you think you see Indians?" the lieutenant smirked.

"I don't see anything, sir," the sergeant replied coldly, meeting the officer's stare.

A moment later Barkley jerked his horse around and trotted in silence down the canyon beside the men. His face was stony and his eyes were fixed straight ahead. He led them back to the entrance of the canyon and then into a different branch of it, still not consulting the map in his pocket, although he did spend a considerable amount of time studying the landmarks above him on the sides of the canyon.

"No," he ordered a few minutes later when the scouts started to ride past him again. "We're stopping here for the night."

It was not until after his tent was pitched and he was waiting for his evening meal that he took out the map and compared it to the route they had taken. When he was certain he knew the way from this spot, he called Sergeant Pearce in and explained it to him.

The weather held for three weeks, and during that time the hunting was good. There was fresh meat every day, and when the women were not cutting and preparing meat for drying they gathered the berries along the stream. After preparing and preserving the food they scraped the elk and deer hides and left them to dry. During the daylight hours while the men hunted, everyone worked except the young children.

On the last day of the three weeks, clouds began to build up over the hills and by dusk they had grown dark and menacing. That night it snowed. Early the next morning the women loaded everything onto their travois and horses and began the trek down out of the hills.

"There's no need for us to wait for them," decided Sykes as he kicked their fire apart and scraped snow over it with the side of his boot. "We might as well gather up those rifles and head out."

Ross rubbed his hand over the three-week stubble on his chin. "It's not going to be that easy," he warned.

"I told you to make it clear to them," Sykes said gruffly.

"And I did—then, but they've had the guns too long now, and they've never had a hunt like this before, not since the times when there were buffalo everywhere they turned."

"Damn it, Ross, just this once you're going to have to think about something besides the Indians. We've got to get those rifles back."

"But not now," protested Ross. "We don't need them right now. I'll think about the best way to do it on the way back. They need to get that meat down where they can work on it some more first, and they sure as hell don't need to get snowed in up here. Let 'em get down to the plains first. I'll take the responsibility."

"Well, you've sure got it." Sykes walked to his horse, which was saddled and ready.

After the first week with the Indians they had stopped posting a guard at night, and the three white men rode out of camp around the Indians without even looking behind them.

Although the band of Indians had drawn out of sight, they could hear them down the length of the valley. Corporal Eddy sighed.

Ross looked at the corporal.

"What's the matter?" he asked.

Eddy sighed again, and then grinned at the scout. "After I got over being scared of them, I never had such a good time. There isn't any hunting like that where I come from."

"Oh, I thought you might be sighing over Night Quail. Seemed like you kept pretty good track of where she was most of the time."

"She never left her mother's side when I was around. I didn't even talk to her."

"That's probably just as well. It could go hard on her if they thought there'd been anything going on. They don't just sneer at women they think might not be virtuous."

"What do they do?"

"I've seen 'em beat near to death, and I've seen 'em killed—by their own relatives usually."

"Jesus! No wonder she was so shy." Eddy looked shocked and then chuckled to himself.

"What's so funny?"

"Oh nothing." He laughed again. "She knew every time I was looking at her what I was thinking. It was like we could talk to each other, and I don't even know the language."

"Some things don't take words to say," agreed Ross.

The corporal glanced behind him. "I guess not," he grinned as he straightened in the saddle.

* * *

Sykes stayed in town while Eddy and Ross went on to the fort. He looked after his horse and then went to his hotel and cleaned up. At the agency building he sat at his desk for over an hour and wrote, covering several sheets of paper before he finished. Then he sat back, read what he had written, and penned in a couple of changes. Satisfied, he folded the letter in an envelope and addressed it.

He stood up and stretched, leaving the envelope on the desk. There was no post office in town, and he didn't feel like going to the fort that evening. What he felt like was a drink and some entertainment for a change. The corporal might like three weeks of hunting all day, every day, but Cole Sykes could think of better things to do.

He thought about Eddy as he went out and locked the door behind him. Sykes had killed several men by the time he was the corporal's age. Maybe if he had gone hunting for deer and elk instead, and made calf's eyes at a shy Indian girl in the evenings—hell, what difference did it make now? Now there was only one thing he had to do, and that was to take care of his job well enough to stay out of Rawlins until his sentence was up.

As he walked past the hotel to the saloon, he thought about how long a young man like Eddy would last in Rawlins. Why was he thinking about the kid all the time? He was a funny one, that Corporal Eddy. He acted as though he respected the Indian girl for her virtue. Well, there'd never been a place in Cole Sykes' life for women with virtue.

He pushed through the swinging doors with more force than he needed to, and stopped to peruse the room before he walked to the bar. A dozen men were lined up there, and the only space left was at the far end, near the table where a card game was going on.

As Sykes walked toward the back of the room he studied the men standing at the bar and then the men around the card table. A kerosene lantern swung over the table, but the faces of the men were shadowed by their hat brims. Across the table from Sykes, with his back to the wall, sat a big man. His shoulders were hunched over the table as he looked down at his cards, and his hat hid the upper part of his face. All that showed was the thick, black beard below the brim of his hat.

The man looked up as soon as Sykes turned to the bar and stared at the gunman's back.

The drink in his hand, Sykes turned partly away from the bar and took a sip. A moment later he shifted a few inches farther and, putting his drink down, reached for his tobacco. As he rolled a cigarette he moved again until he was facing the card players directly, watching their game without showing interest in it.

A rifle leaned against the wall beside the man with the beard, and if it wasn't the rifle Sykes had dropped at the outlaw camp, it was a twin to it. If he could see the sights on the gun, he'd know whether it was his or not. He'd worked them over until they were different from any others, but the rifle was too obscured by shadow to make them out.

When he could see that his glances at the rifle were getting too much attention from the card players, he turned part way back to the bar and looked around the rest of the room. There was a woman sitting on the arm of a chair by one of the tables, and as soon as he looked at her she rose and swayed toward him.

She wore a skirt that reached no farther than her

knees, and a dozen inches of black stocking peeked out between her skirts and the tops of her high-buttoned shoes. She walked languidly, one hand on her hip, swinging her body in an exaggerated motion with each step. Her other hand was holding an empty glass in front of the plunging neckline of her dress. While she walked she eyed Sykes, her chin tilted to one side, her lips parted in a smile. Even in the poor light, he could see the pallor of her skin under the garish paint on her face.

"How about a drink for a thirsty girl, mister?" she suggested, moving so close he could smell the stale perfume and sweat.

He moved his eyes down to the bulges of flesh above her waist before he turned and motioned to the bartender. When she set her glass on the bar, he shoved his empty glass over beside it. While the bartender filled the glasses, the woman slid her hand through Sykes's arm and leaned against it.

"You're that Cole Sykes, aren't you? I'd heard about you before you ever came up here. I'd heard great things about you—how brave you are, and all sorts of things like that." She gave his arm a squeeze before she reached for her glass.

As Sykes picked up his glass he heard a man clear his throat loudly behind him. He looked over his shoulder straight at Sam Ross, who stood there with his eyebrows raised in a question.

Sykes straightened away from the woman. "What do you want?" he asked.

"Talk," he replied in the Blackfoot language.

Sykes looked from the scout to the woman, and then pulled away from her and took a few steps from the bar. "What about?"

"Let me get a drink first." Ross took Sykes' place

at the bar long enough to get a drink and then joined the waiting agent.

"You want to go to the agency to talk?" asked Sykes.

"No, I haven't got that much to say. I just thought you might like to know before you go any further, the surgeon up at the fort says nearly all the men that come down to this place sooner or later get the disease."

Sykes glowered at the scout and tossed back his drink in one swallow. He glanced over his shoulder at the woman, but when she stared invitingly at him, he turned away. "That the only reason you came down here?"

"No, I came to tell you Forbes is hopping mad about those rifles, but you might not have to get them back."

"What's he going to do about it? He isn't going after them, is he?"

"Well, first off he threatened me with the guardhouse again, but all he ended up saying was he'd make you pay for them if it was the last thing he did."

Sykes edged toward the bar. "Good. Let him try. I already wrote to the commissioner telling him he'd have to give me replacements for them. I told him if the army wasn't able to get a supply train through to the Indians, they had to have something better to hunt with."

"How many did you ask for?"

"A hundred."

"Considering how that outfit works, you might get a third of that."

"It would more than replace Forbes' rifles, wouldn't it?"

"Sure."

"That's what I figured."

The woman looked put out as the men continued to talk. When she saw the change in Sykes' expression she strolled back to her chair and two men took her place at the bar.

A moment later Sykes repeated the Blackfoot word for talk, and at once Ross raised his head and stared at the bottles behind the bar as though he was thinking hard about something.

"Take a look at that rifle against the wall behind you," Sykes whispered.

Sam Ross pushed away from the bar with an exaggerated sigh and scratched at the back of his head. "It's getting late for me, Sykes," he announced in a loud voice as he turned and glanced around the room. "Think I'll turn in soon."

"It's not that late. You've got time for another drink."

"Well, I don't know," Ross hesitated, leaning on the bar again. When he was close to the gunman he spoke, his voice low. "What about it?"

"I think it's mine. The one I dropped up there."

"How do you know?"

"I don't for sure. I need to see the front sights."

"What about them?"

"I moved them a quarter of an inch and filed them sharper."

Ross raised his voice to its normal tone and then laughed.

"That reminds me of some more news I almost forgot to tell you."

"What?"

"You know what they were going to send Barkley to do?"

"Yes?"

"Well, according to him, there was no such place;

you just made up the story. But according to the men with him, he got lost up there."

"Hell, I drew a map."

Ross lowered his voice again while Sykes grinned at him. "Go on," he murmured. "I'll see if I can get a look at it after—" The scout stopped as the man with the beard pushed his chair back, picked up the rifle, and walked out.

Chapter 22

Andrew Madden sat in the chair he usually occupied in the commissioner's office, his eyes on Tarking's back. Did the man do anything anymore except stand at the window, staring at the dome? It was a good thing the election was next week. Then maybe—

Commissioner Tarking removed his cigar as he turned away from the window. He seemed surprised to see Madden in his office. "Oh!" he exclaimed. "Sorry Madden. To tell you the truth I was thinking about something else for a moment. Why did I send for you?"

"I don't know, sir." The chief clerk raised his eyebrows.

"Oh yes, now I remember," said Tarking. "Look at those two letters, Madden. See if you can figure out what's going on. It's beyond me." He laughed as he turned to the window and jammed the cigar in his mouth again.

Madden reached over the front of the desk and picked up the letters Tarking had indicated and then settled back in his chair to read them. At the sight of the first signature, he glanced quickly at the signature on the second letter.

The commissioner remained at the window while

Madden read both letters. Then the sound of the chief clerk's fingers drumming on the arm of his chair turned Tarking around. The commissioner's expression was one of disinterested humor.

"They can't both be right, can they?" he asked.

"Of course not."

"Who is, then? You've met them both."

"Forbes, of course. Taking army rifles is stealing, any way you look at it."

"Sykes says the colonel let him have them."

"But only as a loan."

"Sykes says they're still on loan. He intends to return them."

"I couldn't get a hundred rifles to him now if I wanted to. There'll be no more boats up the Missouri to Fort Benton until next spring."

"What about the railroad and the stage? I thought they had daily stage service to the mining towns from the railhead."

"They aren't going to haul a hundred rifles on a stage. That's freight, not baggage. Tarking, whose side are you on, anyway?"

The commissioner studied the half inch of ash on the end of his cigar and then tapped it into a clay dish that had been found in the ancient Hopi ruins in New Mexico. "If the President saw fit to appoint Cole Sykes as the acting superintendent for the Blackfoot, you don't think I would go against that, do you?"

Andrew Madden rose slowly to his feet, fighting to keep composure as he placed the letters back on the commissioner's desk.

"No, keep the letters, Madden," the commissioner directed. "Write some kind of an answer to Forbes and then send somebody out there on the stage with a dozen rifles to replace the ones Sykes—ah—borrowed."

Madden knew that the commissioner was grinning at his back as he walked out of the office, but he did not give Tarking the satisfaction of appearing disturbed.

As soon as he was in his own office, Madden read the letters through one more time and then tossed them on his desk in disgust. A moment later he stood up and strode to his window, staring out with the same disgruntled expression until he suddenly realized how dark it had gotten. He pulled out his watch and studied it. How could it be so late? If he didn't hurry now, he'd be late for dinner, the dinner he had promised Tarking he would give in support of Tarking's appointment to the Cabinet.

As soon as Madden thought about the election, his mind went back to the letters and he picked them up and put them in his pocket. Lifting his hat from the coat rack, he set it squarely on his head and went out the door.

On the way home he leaned back in his carriage, his arms folded over his chest, his unseeing eyes fastened on the flickering street lamps as he passed. It was dark by the time he reached Georgetown, and he could see little of the expanse of lawn and gardens in front of his house. He would not have paid attention to them anyway. It seemed as though there was a light in every room in the house, and already a carriage stood in front of the doorway. He was late as he had feared. Well, Mrs. Woods had always understood before. The thought of his quiet, competent housekeeper was a welcome relief from the problems on his mind. Everything would be taken care of, and she would no doubt have arranged time for him to have a few words with his son.

He thought about his son as he walked through the door. After a day like today, he was going to make certain that Percival would not work for the Office of Indian Affairs.

Mrs. Woods bustled into the hallway as soon as the front door opened. "I'll take your coat and hat, Mr. Madden. Percival is in the parlor with Senator Nevin and his wife."

"He is?"

"Yes."

"How did you do that?"

"He's thirteen, Mr. Madden. There's no reason why he can't represent the family now. I explained to the Senator how you had been . . . delayed."

"Thank you, Mrs. Woods. I was delayed, indeed, although I'm afraid I rely on you more and more to take care of things like this. Well, imagine Percival—"

"One more thing, Mr. Madden. A letter came today. I think it might be business of some kind. It's from a Fort Mason."

"Here? It came here? Addressed to me?"

"Yes."

"Was there a return address? Could you tell who it was from?"

"Yes, I did happen to notice. I wasn't prying though," she hastened to add.

"Where is the letter?"

"Right here." She pointed to the silver tray on the hall table.

Madden picked up the envelope. He could see at once that it was from a woman, and the return address was indeed Fort Mason. Well, it wouldn't hurt Percival to act as host a few minutes longer. Ashley, Miss Patricia Ashley. Where had he heard that name before? He tore the envelope open and started to read the letter as quickly as he could.

* * *

Dear Mr. Madden,

Please do not consider me presumptuous in writing to you like this. I do hope you can remember the time that I was fortunate enough to visit your lovely home. Little did I realize when I was there and you showed us all of your fascinating collection of Indian artifacts that I would ever have the opportunity I now have to observe real Indians in their native lands. I am now visiting with my uncle, Colonel John Forbes, commander of Fort Mason. As his hostess—I'm the only one he has here—I wish to extend to you a very special invitation to visit us. I've heard that you often travel to the many reservations under your jurisdiction, and while I am here it would seem so appropriate to return your hospitality in this place.

The Blackfoot are certainly fortunate in the agent you have provided for them. Although Mr. Sykes is new here, everything he does shows that his first consideration is for the Blackfoot people—

Andrew Madden looked up from the page and stared down the hall until Mrs. Woods emerged from the kitchen. He folded the piece of paper and put it in the pocket with the other two letters before he turned to enter the parlor.

Chapter 23

A foot of snow covered the ground when Tricia woke up, and the wind had howled outside her window all night. She could still hear it when she lowered the covers enough to look in that direction. As soon as she felt the cold in the room she pulled the covers high again and looked away from the window, wondering if her uncle could wait for his breakfast that morning. Surely he wouldn't go out in weather like this.

She lay there for a few more minutes, luxuriating in the warmth. Then she sighed, rolled over again, and in one motion threw back the covers, sat up, slid her feet into her slippers and reached for her dressing gown. She was shivering as she fastened it around her, and she drew the quilt from the top of her bed and wrapped it around her before she started for the kitchen.

The fire had been laid the night before, and she lit it, holding the quilt with her other hand. She thought about the warm robes she had at home as she filled the coffeepot with water. Of course, at home they also had servants to get up and light the fires.

By the time her uncle came down for breakfast, the kitchen was warming up. They had been eating breakfast in the kitchen since it had turned cold.

There was a heating stove in her uncle's bedroom, and when he came to the table he was fully dressed and ready for work.

"How long is this going to last?" she asked as he sat down at the table.

"You're feeling sorry you decided to stay now, are you?"

"No, but I certainly didn't bring the right clothes for this kind of weather. When I think of the things I have at home that I could use now." She laughed as she poured coffee for him and then filled her own cup.

"You do seem to keep your spirits up, Tricia. And I must say, it brightens my day to see you so cheerful every morning."

"Thank you, Uncle John. But why do you have to go to headquarters when it's like this?"

"The men are expected to carry out their duties no matter what the weather. I could do no less, now could I?"

"No, and I wouldn't expect you to either, I guess. The thought just crossed my mind when it was time to get out of bed." She laughed again, and then gazed out the window for a moment. "It seems more like two weeks 'til Christmas than 'til Thanksgiving."

"The weather can change. We might get a warm wind and then the snow will melt in a few days, or we may not see the grass again until spring."

"If that's the choice, I think I favor the warm wind, if you don't mind."

"It's an interesting bit of weather to experience. However, no matter what the weather, we need to do something special to celebrate Thanksgiving. You should be thinking about that."

"I have been."

"Good. What have you decided? We missed that going-away party. We could do something like that."

"Since this is the only time I've been near real Indians—well, I thought maybe we could have a Thanksgiving like the very first one."

"You mean invite the Indians to dinner?" The colonel gulped and held his fork poised in midair.

"Yes."

"My God," he exclaimed, "there are hundreds of them."

"I hadn't thought about how many."

"It is a fascinating idea, my dear, but we usually just have the officers and their families, so you had better limit it to a chief or two and their families."

"You mean I can invite them?"

"Why, I think it's a fine notion. You should see them all dressed up in their beads and feathers. They'll add a great deal of color to the whole event. Quite decorative, in fact. You always have had a way of planning interesting parties, Tricia. You can go ahead and tell Ross to invite them."

"I'll write the invitations today," she declared.

"You don't need to bother to write one for them," laughed the colonel. "They can't read."

Despite what her uncle said, Tricia wrote invitations for the Indians. Finishing them at last, she went to the front window and looked out. While she stood there, thinking about walking through the snow to the officers' quarters, she saw Cole Sykes ride through the gate and head for the barracks building. She smiled as soon as she saw him and then looked down at the envelopes still in her hand. She hadn't said anything about it to her uncle, but the envelope on top had the agent's name on it.

She gazed out the window again. Tracks led here and there where people had walked, but no clear pathway extended from one end of the fort to the other, although men were shoveling in front of some of the buildings. She hurried to the front door and out onto the porch covered with several inches of snow. She waved her arm as soon as Sykes turned in her direction, beckoning to him.

The agent watched her for a moment and then loped toward the house. She waited for him, shivering in the open doorway.

"Please come in, Cole," she called. Then she stepped back inside the door and crossed her arms over each other, rubbing her hands up and down them.

"What for?" he shouted.

"I have something for you. Can't you hurry?" She smiled back at his frown and took another step back. He finally swung out of the saddle and walked through the open door.

"The door was open so long it's cooled off this whole room. Let's go into the kitchen. Would you like some hot coffee?"

"I can't stay. I only came here to see if Ross wanted to ride out to the Indian camp with me and check on how they made it through the storm."

"Are you really going out there today? Good. I have something for them, too. Well, for some of them, anyway."

"You couldn't have anything for them."

"Yes, I could." She took the top envelope out of her hand and held it out to him. "There, I'll give you yours first. See what you think of that."

While he opened the envelope and read the invitation, she stood in front of him, still rubbing her arms and shivering slightly. "Do you have to scowl like that?" she asked. "Before you say anything let's go where it's warmer."

He followed her into the kitchen. "I don't see Colonel Forbes' name on this," commented Sykes, looking over the piece of paper in his hand.

"No," she laughed as she lifted the pot from the stove and carried it to the cupboard to get a cup. "It's my surprise for him."

"You know I won't be welcome."

"But this is to replace my going-away party, and I said I'd invite you to that."

"Why?"

"You should be here, that's why. You're the superintendent for a whole Indian reservation. It's almost half of the territory, isn't it?"

"Why do something that would upset your uncle? We have a hard enough time getting along as it is."

"Cole, you don't get along with Uncle John at all, so how can it be worse?" She set a cup of coffee on the table in front of him. They looked steadily at each other.

"I want you here," she insisted. "Isn't that a good enough reason?" She could feel her cheeks growing pink, but she sat down at the table and began sorting through the stack of envelopes. After a moment Sykes took off his coat and hat and sat down.

"As long as you're going to see Sam today, would you mind giving this to him?" she asked as she set another envelope beside the gunman's cup. "And here are the ones for Flying Hawk and Many Arrows and their families." She watched the astonished expression on Sykes' face as she placed the second and third envelopes on top of the one for Sam Ross.

"What are you trying to do?" he asked, his eyes glued to the invitations on the table.

"Don't you remember the first Thanksgiving? I've decided that since I'm where there are Indians, I would like to have a replica of that Thanksgiving. You should know, Cole, that where I come from I'm known for the parties I give. Although you don't seem very excited about this one, invitations to my parties are, well, sought after."

"You want the Indians to decorate your party, is that it?"

"Uncle John said they are quite colorful."

Cole Sykes picked up the envelopes addressed to the chiefs and walked to the stove. He lifted the heavy lid over the firebox and dropped the invitations inside.

"What are you doing?" cried Tricia, jumping up and running to the stove. She shoved his arm aside and looked down at the envelopes curling into ashes. "What did you do that for?" she demanded. Her face twisted as she looked up at him.

"They aren't decorations," he told her calmly. "They're people."

"You—" Tricia stopped herself and stared uncomprehendingly at him for a moment. Then her shoulders sagged and she turned slowly back to her chair. With one elbow on the table and her chin in her hand, she stared, unblinking, at the tablecloth. Sykes took a sip of coffee and reached for his coat.

"Oh, sit down," she said without looking up. "Don't go yet. You're right, of course. I admit it."

"Why would you send them written invitations that you know they can't read?" Sykes sat down across from her.

"It's the only way I know how to do it. Cole, I do want them to come. Will you invite them for me, please? Whichever way would be proper."

"No, I'm not going to make a spectacle of them for your amusement."

"I promise I won't do anything like that. I'll treat them any way you say."

"They're people, you know."

"Oh, God, Cole, I know that. But I've never been near a single Indian in my whole life! Uncle John always makes me stay in the house when they're here."

"You'd better get to know them before you start sending them invitations. What if Many Arrows brought a lance with a scalp hanging on the end of it? One with—" He reached playfully across the table and touched a lock of her hair. "One with hair this color?"

Her eyes widened as she pulled her hair out of his hand. "Has he got one?"

"I don't know." He smiled at her and took another swallow of coffee. "You want to ride out and see? It looks like the clouds are going to break up, and the sun might come out. Flying Hawk's band is only about five miles away right now, and they're not very warlike this time of year. Be a nice day for a ride in the snow."

The offer was tempting. But she only continued to stare at him. He laughed. "You're not afraid, are you?"

Tricia could hear her heart pounding with excitement, and a certain pleasure at the thought of defying her uncle surged up in her. "Of course I'm afraid!" she exclaimed, "But I'm going anyway."

"I wasn't serious," Sykes confessed, backing off. "I wouldn't take you out there."

"Oh, yes you will, Cole! You've invited me, and I accept your invitation. And I shall invite them to Thanksgiving dinner in whatever way Sam Ross says is right."

"No, Miss Ashley, absolutely not."

"I wonder what I can wear that will be warm enough." She laughed at him as he stood up. He was studying her face as though seeing it for the first time.

"There's no road," he persisted, still trying to dissuade her. "Can you ride a horse?" he added, thinking that would put a stop to this.

"Yes. I've ridden all my life."

"In a skirt?"

"You can't get out of it, Cole. Captain Olin's wife said I could borrow her sidesaddle whenever I wanted it."

Her warmest outfit was the blue suit she had worn on her journey out. The jacket and skirt were both made of a wool and trimmed with bands of deep blue velvet. The jacket fit snugly around the waist and then spread out over the fullness of the skirt. Under the jacket she wore a white shirtwaist with ruffles of lace at the collar and all down the front. Under her skirt, for warmth, she wore as many petticoats as she could get on. She put on the blue velvet hat that matched the suit and tied a veil over it to secure it tightly against the wind.

Standing in front of her mirror, she approved of the way she looked, except she wished she had her fur-lined cape to top off the outfit. But that was far away now. She sighed once, thinking about it.

As she turned away from the mirror she fingered the lock of hair that Sykes had fondled and pulled lower over her shoulder. Then she went into her uncle's room and took two of his army blankets. They would have to do for her outer wraps.

She left food on the kitchen table for her uncle's noon meal and a note saying she had gone riding.

By the time she was ready, Sykes was in front of the house with two horses. He helped her into the saddle, and then she arranged the blankets, one around her shoulders and the other over her lap. Although the sun was shining the temperature was still below freezing.

Sam Ross was waiting for them by the gate, and he rode to her side so that she was between them as they left the fort.

The snow was deep, but it was light and dry, and it only slowed the horses in the places where it had drifted higher. At first Tricia felt exhilarated in the cold air. Her horse was fresh and spirited enough to make the ride a pleasure, and it felt good to be out of the fort and moving through such a dazzlingly white world. But as they neared the Indians, she noticed that the men became more attentive to their surroundings. With a shiver she recalled what Sykes had said about the scalp on Many Arrows' lance. She was not sure whether the chill she felt was from the cold or the thought of the possible danger.

Suddenly her mind turned back to her childhood. She laughed softly. "You don't know how much this reminds me of when I was a child, Cole. I was forever taking dares. I couldn't pass one up, and then I'd have to do the most dreadful things."

Sykes moved his horse closer to hers until their knees nearly touched, while Ross held his mount a stride behind them.

"Like what?" asked Sykes, surveying the glistening landscape.

"I can remember climbing a tree until I couldn't bear to look down, and my father had to climb up to retrieve me." As she chatted, he unbuttoned his coat and flipped its tail behind his Colt.

"Cole, what are you afraid of?" her bright tone disappearing.

"We're almost there," he explained, avoiding her eyes. "When we get there don't go running up to the chief or anything. They have their own way of doing things, and the rules for women are different. If he invites us into his lodge, you'll have to sit on the women's side."

"Would he invite you and not me? You wouldn't leave me alone, would you?"

He turned for a moment and looked directly at her. "No, I won't leave you alone. But you wait until you know what to do." When she nodded he glanced back at the scout. "Ross, you take the lead now. You know what Miss Ashley wants to do. Let's do it and get out of there as fast as we can."

Ross pulled his horse to one side and rode around them. "She'll be the first white woman they've had in their camp. They'll be curious, that's all."

She knew that Sykes was studying her, and she turned to face him.

"You asked for this," he said, "but we can still turn back."

"No. Oh no, not now!" she answered firmly.

"Are you sure you can do it? I've seen Indian women look shy, but I've never seen them look scared."

"Do I look scared?"

"Yes, a little."

"Well," she breathed deeply, "I won't look frightened—unless you do." As she spoke, she straightened in the saddle, letting the blanket drop from her shoulders. She pulled it away and held it and the other blanket in Sykes' direction. "Here," she offered, "take these. I'll be warm enough for the next few minutes."

Then she arranged her skirts so that they were spread in a sweep over her legs, pulled her jacket into place, and fluffed up the ruffles at her neck. She glanced at Sykes as she positioned the curl of hair in full view on her shoulder. Grasping the reins in both hands, she sat as straight as she could in the saddle while continuing to move in harmony with the horse. She lifted her chin until her head was high, her eyes straight ahead of her, her lips curved in a half smile.

The first sound she heard was the barking of dogs, and then a shout, almost like a town crier. As they reached the top of the rise she could see the tepees. A huge circle of lodges lay before her, smoke rising from the center of each, some with colorful designs painted on their sides. At first, only a few Indians peered from their lodges, attracted by the frantic yelping of the dogs. By the time Sam Ross pulled up in front of her, Indians clustered around at the entrance of every tepee.

Tricia waited until Cole Sykes dismounted and stepped to the side of her horse. Putting her hands on his shoulders, she let him catch her as she slid from the horse. Once on the ground she could feel the cold seeping through her shoes almost at once. She took Sykes' arm, lifted her skirts above the snow, and walked erect at his side through the outer ring of tepees to the center of the camp.

Sam Ross walked ahead of them, greeting the people as he passed. As they walked by Many Arrows' lodge, the war chief stepped out and followed behind. When the three of them stopped in front of Flying Hawk, Tricia was surprised to hear Sykes speak a few words in their language. She did not look at the agent or change her expression, however. She fastened her eyes on Flying Hawk and composed her face into polite and proper lines. After a moment, while Ross spoke to the chief, she realized how tightly she was gripping Sykes' arm, and she loosened her hold. But she did not move away from him.

The scout and the chief exchanged comments, and then Flying Hawk turned and stepped inside his lodge.

"Oh." Tricia felt deflated. "I didn't have a chance—"

"Hush," whispered Sykes. "We're going inside. Wait in the doorway until he tells you where to sit. I'll be on his left and you'll be on his right. Don't walk in front of anybody. I have to go in first."

Sykes waited until Ross had moved out of the opening, and then pulled his arm away from her hand and ducked inside. He vanished into the lodge. She looked over her shoulder at Many Arrows. The Indian was standing only a few feet behind her, impassive, unmoving. He was as tall as Sykes and as strongly built, and his face had the same hard expression. Even his eyes, as black as she had ever seen, were not very different from Sykes' cold, blue ones. She turned her back to him again and though she was trembling, she somehow managed not to hunch her shoulders against the tug she imagined on her hair.

Sykes stepped out of the opening and beckoned her inside. She stood, watching the chief, and then lowered her head a few inches and clasped her hands in front of her. When Flying Hawk motioned to the women's side, she walked that way while the two women separated and made a place for her between them. Although there was hardly enough room for her skirts, she walked behind the woman closest to her. She saw that the women were sitting with both legs to the same side, although the men sat cross-legged. As she lowered herself into place, she held her skirts to one side and sat in the same position as the other women.

She glanced almost furtively at Sykes and saw something in his expression that was different. He met her eyes for a moment, and for the first time she saw open approval in his face. As she smiled back at him, the lodge suddenly became a warm and good place to be.

Tricia watched the ceremony intently. They all played their roles, and the ritual was not so different from many of the formal affairs she had attended in Boston. Everyone knew the rules and followed them instinctively.

From time to time she glanced at the other women. They did nothing to interrupt the men, and she sat as silently as they. As the time passed she could feel their eyes more and more, as they boldly stared at her. She was watching Sykes take a puff from the pipe when she felt the fingertips of the older woman touch the velvet trim of her skirt.

At once Tricia looked down and held her skirt out closer to the woman. With that, the woman on her other side touched her skirt, and Tricia turned and smiled at her. In response, the woman warily lifted Tricia's skirt a few inches and felt the lace at the edge of her petticoat.

Suddenly the lodge seemed very quiet, and she realized the men were all watching. She raised her eyes to glance at Sykes, and his expression was still one of approval. Looking down again to where the woman had touched her petticoat, she slowly pulled her skirt a few inches higher above the lace. Then she sat still and listened as Sam Ross spoke to the chief. They talked for several minutes, and she hoped he had finally gotten around to conveying her invitation.

Again when she glanced up, the men were all looking at her. This time she turned to the chief and tried to convey by the expression on her face that she wanted him to accept her invitation.

The chief's eyes rested on her briefly, and then the men resumed their talk. She looked down at the heavy buffalo robe in front of her. She thought about how warm and comfortable it was inside the lodge compared to the snow and cold outside. She reached down and stroked the fur.

She wished she could talk to the women beside her. What would they have to say? And while the sound of the men's voices droned on, she thought about how different their lives must be from hers.

As Cole Sykes helped her into the saddle, she shivered in the cold. They had been a long time in the warmth of the lodge, and the sun was already low in the sky.

"Did he agree to come?" she asked impatiently as Sykes walked to his horse.

"Yes."

"I'm glad. I want them to come now more than ever."

"Why?" As he rode to her side he held out the blankets.

"No. I don't want those yet," she said. "Wait until we're away from here." Although she had to fight to keep her teeth from chattering, she rode from the camp the way she had come in. As soon as they were over the first rise, she took the blankets and wrapped them tightly around her. She was chilled through and could not stop shivering.

"It's dropping cold fast," noticed Ross. "Going to be a bad one tonight." Then he reined his horse out ahead of the other two.

"You want to ride with me?" offered Sykes. "We can go faster that way."

She responded without hesitation. "Yes, I need you to hold on to me. I'm afraid I'll shake myself right off of here."

They stopped their horses for a moment side by side, and he lifted her into the saddle ahead of him and wrapped the blankets snugly around her. She nestled into place and he took the reins from her horse into the same hand that held his own and started ahead again. When a shiver shook her body, he wound his other arm around her and held her tight against him.

As the warmth gradually came back to her, Tricia became increasingly aware of the nearness of the agent. She noticed how she was perched on his lap and that his arms were around her. She became aware of the constant motion of the horse, moving them against each other. She had not the slightest inclination to move away from him, and when the lights of the town and the fort shone ahead of them, she sighed.

"What was that for?" he asked, breaking the silence of the ride.

"I don't know. It must be that I don't want this day to end."

"You liked it?"

"Didn't you?"

He was silent as the horses started through the town.

"Didn't you?" she repeated, straightening a little.

"Yes," he admitted. "I liked it."

"Good. And you will come to Thanksgiving dinner, won't you? You must."

He looked down at her as he answered. "I'll have to. Someone must see that you treat them right."

"I will treat them right, Cole, if you'll tell me how."

He let his horse slow and stop when they reached the livery stable at the far edge of town. "The way you rode into that camp—God, it was beautiful."

She lifted her eyes and, watching his lips, she moved her hand to his shoulder and pulled herself toward him.

As he lowered his head toward her, the roar of a gunshot shattered the silence, and Sykes' hat jerked on his head.

Chapter 24

Sykes jabbed his spurs into the stallion and bolted into the open doorway of the livery stable, pounding headlong down the aisle between the stalls until they were in the shadows at the back. Luckily the beams were high, or he and Tricia would have been dashed to the floor.

Sam Ross jerked his rifle out as he followed the agent in through the door. He slid from the saddle as soon as his horse cleared the doorway and ran back to the entrance to peer cautiously into the street.

"What the hell was that?" hollered Gaines as he burst through the door from the harness room.

"Stay back," called Ross urgently. "Somebody just shot at Sykes and Miss Ashley."

"Miss Ashley?" The blacksmith squinted into the back of the stable where he could hear Sykes' horse snorting and pawing, and then he reached behind him. Emerging from the harness room, he held a shotgun in his hand.

"Who's in town?" asked Ross.

"Nobody special that I know about, but I haven't been paying much attention."

"Any soldiers?"

"I saw a few ride through a while ago, but I don't think they stopped. Where did the shot come from?"

"I'm not sure. From behind Sykes someplace. Could have come from the hotel." The scout studied the upstairs windows of the building. "Sykes," he called out over his shoulder, "stay here while I check out a few things."

"What?" called the agent. "You see something?"

"No, but I want to see who's at the hotel and in the saloon."

As the scout eased out of the doorway, Sykes glanced down at Tricia. Even in the dark he could see the concern and fear in her face. "That was a damned fool thing," he growled. "Who the hell would shoot that close to a woman?"

"Cole, you—I saw your hat move. If you hadn't leaned forward—" she was close to tears.

"It was too near to you."

She rubbed her head into his shoulder and he tightened his arms around her.

It was a half-hour before Ross returned. He came in through the doorway without paying attention to what was behind him. "You better get her up there fast, Sykes," he advised. "Forbes has got the whole army out looking for her."

"Oh Lord," sighed Tricia, stirring in his arms. "I was afraid of that. I'm not surprised. Cole, you'd better help me get back on my own horse now. I'll have to make a proper entrance."

"What did you see besides the army?" asked Sykes.

"Go out the back way," Ross answered, ignoring his question. "I'll cover you up to the fort. Gaines, you watch from here."

"I can go with you if you want," offered the blacksmith.

While the men took their positions, Sykes lowered Patricia to the floor. Her horse was standing a few feet away, and as he helped her into the saddle, she touched his shoulder.

"What was it you were going to do before that shot?" she whispered softly.

When he said nothing, she slid her hand from his shoulder to behind his neck. "Don't I deserve something for today?"

The hand behind his neck applied steady pressure until he lowered his head so she could touch her lips to his. Then she let him lift her to the saddle. She laughed softly, a hint of mischief in her voice. "How worried Uncle John must be! Now, Cole, just drop me off, and don't come in the house. I'll do all the explaining."

"What are you going to tell him?"

"I don't know yet, but I'll know when I see him. What can he do now, anyway?" she asked disdainfully.

"You want to know something? You're sure a damned handful for a man."

"I am indeed?" Her tone betrayed her pleasure.

Part way up the hill they passed a detail of soldiers cantering from the town. When the men saw Tricia they turned and followed her into the fort. Sykes helped her down outside the colonel's house and she disappeared inside. Sykes followed the returning soldiers to the stables and sought out Ross at his stall, ignoring the troopers as he clattered down the aisle past them.

"What kind of a fool would have shot at me while she was right there?" Sykes asked as the scout began to unsaddle his horse.

"He shot high."

"Or he was a poor marksman. Who are you thinking?"

"I don't know. It could have been one of those horse thieves, or it could have been—" Ross paused and looked around him at the soldiers.

"Barkley?" Sykes finished for the scout. "Would he pull a trick like that? Jesus, she was right there!"

"He's jealous, Sykes, and now he has two failures to his record that he can blame on you. At least he takes every opportunity to tell people they were your mistakes."

"I suppose he figures he's a good shot, good enough to try a trick like that."

"Probably."

"The next time I see him—" There was no need for the agent to finish his threat. Ross looked away from the grim expression on Sykes' face.

He rode out of the stable moments later and headed for the gate at a lope. The temperature had stayed below freezing all day, and the snow was still dry and unpacked even where it had been trampled. The stallion was not slowed by it. When he reached the stable in town he went around to the back door and let himself in.

Pulling the door closed behind him, he listened for the metal clang in the blacksmith shop. No light had shone from the front as he rode into town. Suddenly he heard a shuffling sound and then thuds as if something was striking or falling against the wall where the rows of horseshoes hung. Then he heard the unmistakable sound of a fist driving into flesh.

In the next instant he hit the ground beside his horse and started at a run through the stable. Reaching for the door to the blacksmith shop, he grabbed his

Colt. When he jerked open the door, all he could see across the room was a dark, struggling mass of men straining against one another. Gaines was tall compared to the others, and a moment later Sykes could make him out fighting alone against two men.

When they did not notice him, Sykes pointed his gun at the ceiling and fired once. Before the men could respond, he jammed the gun into his holster and leaped on the back of the man nearest him.

As Sykes landed a blow on the side of the attacker's head, Gaines shouted out.

"Is that you, Sykes?" he bellowed. "Welcome to the . . ." He was interrupted by a stunning whack to his mouth, and his greeting faded into a grunt.

Dodging quickly, Sykes ducked a blow that grazed his cheek, and the outlaw lunged into him. He caught Sykes enough off balance to shove the agent away from the others. Sykes pounded both fists into the man's sides, but what he felt was hard and unyielding. Before Sykes could break free, the outlaw thrust his leg between the agent's knees, hooked his foot around one leg, and surged his weight forward.

Sykes lashed out at the man's head as he started to tumble backwards, and the two of them sprawled on the floor. Sykes twisted sharply as he fell, trying not to get pinned under the outlaw. But as his head snapped back, it hit something hard on the floor. He fought to remain conscious as the man pulled away from him.

"Let's go," the man yelled as he raced for the door. A moment later the other man tore past Sykes. The agent rolled over and gingerly felt the back of his head.

Hugh Gaines slammed both doors closed and barred them before he lit the lamp hanging near the anvil. As soon as he had a light in the room, the blacksmith turned and peered down at Sykes.

"So it was you," he gasped, still out of breath. "I thought so. You all right, Sykes?"

"Hell, no," returned the agent, one hand on the back of his head as he sat up. "What do you keep on your floor anyway?" He turned until he could see the sack of horseshoes behind him.

"That's what they were after," claimed the blacksmith. "I've had them stolen before. Figured tonight might be the night for it after that shot at you. That's why I was keeping an eye on the place after you left. I pretended to leave for the night, and then I came back and surprised them here."

"You should have surprised them at the end of a gun," said Sykes. "What was the idea of taking on two of them at once?"

"I only saw one of them at first. The second one was outside the back door, watching, I guess. Mostly, I can handle about anybody, one at a time." His tone was explanatory, not boastful, and Sykes did not doubt him. He'd seen Gaines' arms while he worked at the anvil.

Sykes stood up slowly, to keep his head clear.

"You want your horse put away?" asked the blacksmith. "I can do it while you take it easy for a few minutes."

"Go ahead." Sykes reached for his tobacco. "Thanks."

"I owe you the thanks, Sykes. I wasn't winning that one. You let me know when I can do something like that to help you out, and I sure will."

Chapter 25

Cole Sykes woke up early on Thanksgiving morning. He took extra care with his shaving and washing, and put on the last of his clean clothes. There was no barber in town, and he frowned in the mirror over his washstand at the length of his hair. There was no laundry either, and it was time to see if he could talk one of the laundresses at the fort into doing his wash again.

He ran his fingers through his hair and put on his hat. Picking up his coat, he carried it downstairs to the dining room.

He was sipping a final cup of coffee when Sam Ross came to the door.

"You all set?" asked Ross.

"Soon as I get my horse." Sykes stood up and walked out of the hotel with the scout at his side. There had been no new snow for over a week and what was left had mixed with the dirt, churning up a thick mud that froze into sharp ridges and grooves during the night.

"I'll be glad to get out of here for a while," remarked Sykes, looking along the street before he entered the stable.

"You hear anything about more supplies coming for the Indians?"

"Not a word so far."

"I went up to the camp yesterday," explained Ross. "They're going to be out of food soon." The scout waited outside the livery, picking a spot where the sun reflected off the wall. A few minutes later they rode out of town, heading toward the Indian encampment.

"They're farther up the river now," Ross offered. "They ran out of grass for the horses, and the women are trying to find bushes where there are still some berries."

Sykes dug his fist into his right thigh. "I don't like this party today. If they're hungry, they don't need to see all the food that's likely to be around."

"That's why I mentioned it," advised Ross.

"You think they'll try to steal from the fort?"

"Might be a good idea to talk about a hunt next week on the way down."

Sykes looked at the mountains on his left, mountains that were so high and rough the peaks still showed only traces of snow, even though the lower valleys were a solid blanket of white. "They can't get up there now."

"I know, but Many Arrows says he saw the tracks of some buffalo when he was out last week. If this weather holds, it wouldn't take that many buffalo to make a difference. But that's not the problem. They're out of ammunition, and they can't count on doing very well with nothing but arrows."

"We'll get some ammunition ready," Sykes decided. "You and I can see to that."

Ross laughed. "Guess I can enjoy that meal today, after all," he concluded as he kicked his horse into a gallop.

The dogs began barking when the Indians invited

to the fort emerged from their tepees. Flying Hawk and Many Arrows strode in the lead, the two women and First Moon following behind, wrapped in blankets that covered their clothes. But Flying Hawk and his son had on their brilliant bonnets of feathers.

The men had decorated their ponies' flanks with bright geometric designs, and when Many Arrows' horse tossed its head, Sykes could hear the tinkle of bells. The women's horses had wooden saddles, and Red Beads' pony wore a robe slung behind the saddle for First Moon to ride on.

They left the camp four abreast, but when the trail through the snow narrowed, Sykes dropped back to Many Arrows' side and left Ross to talk about a hunt with Flying Hawk. Many Arrows gave no sign that the agent was there, and Sykes did not try to force anything different. Instead he concentrated on the area around them. Neither Indian carried weapons, and there were none on their horses. In case there was trouble, he and Ross were the only ones armed.

Although Sykes was concentrating on their routes, he could make out enough of what the two ahead were saying to know the chief was agreeing to another hunt.

As the trail narrowed beside the river, the riders spread out in single file. The chief went down first and then Ross, but both Sykes and Many Arrows pulled up at the same time and eyed each other. It was the first time the Indian had looked directly at Sykes during the ride. The agent could see that the young chief had not accepted him.

Sykes touched the reins lightly, and the big bay danced backward. Then he motioned for the Indian to go ahead.

Many Arrows glanced quickly at the horse that had seemed to move without a signal from its rider and kneed his horse ahead down the bank. Sykes followed, watching over his shoulder to see that the women made it down without any trouble.

They rode two by two again until, reaching the river, Ross pulled aside and stopped. Sykes frowned and then realized why. Many Arrows rode ahead to the edge of the water, and the three men chanted in unison, their heads lowered toward the water.

Sykes remained in the rear until they entered muddy Main Street. He rode forward to Many Arrows' side, and the band passed through town four across, the white men on the outside, the women and First Moon behind.

A few people were already grouping on the sidewalk and more gathered as the riders moved ahead. "Don't hurry," warned Sykes in the Blackfoot language as he slowed his horse and straightened in the saddle.

Flying Hawk turned his head and looked at Sykes, and then he dropped his blanket from his shoulders until it hung over the back of his horse. Long, deep fringes dangled from the sleeves of his soft elk-skin shirt, and both shirt and leggings were heavily beaded, with quills sewn into the seams of the latter. Necklaces of beads and bear teeth hung from his neck, falling below the strips of ermine fur at the sides of his headdress.

Following Flying Hawk's example, the women loosened their blankets, and at once the sound of bells grew louder. Only Many Arrows continued to stare ahead, unmoving.

When Sykes heard the bells, he glanced back at the women, and he could see how Red Beads had gotten her name. Her dress was heavy with beads, all of them a brilliant crimson. Her face was without expression, like the men's, and she gazed straight ahead at her husband's back. Sykes could not help but admire the way she looked.

They rode into the fort and through the center of the parade ground, proud and assured, as they had ridden through the town. Tricia stepped out on the porch and, a moment later, Colonel Forbes, resplendent in full dress uniform, walked out and planted himself beside her.

"Well," exclaimed Ross, "looks like Forbes is going to do it right, too."

There was no place in front of the house to tie all the horses. But as they stopped, the colonel motioned behind him, and Corporal Eddy came out and walked toward them. "I'll take care of the horses." He was smiling broadly, and he greeted each of the Indians by name as he took their ponies' ropes. "Mr. Ross, you tell them I got orders to take these horses down to the officers' stables while you're having your dinner. Colonel Forbes said to give them a feed, too." Sam Ross translated quickly before the orderly started to lead the horses away.

Tricia stood on the porch and greeted each of them as they filed past her into the house. Cole Sykes waited behind the others. Red Beads and First Moon were the last to enter, and as Red Beads mounted the steps, Tricia put her hands out to her. Then she turned to the interpreter. "Sam, tell her—what a beautiful dress!"

While Ross spoke to Red Beads, Cole Sykes stepped up to the porch, his eyes on Tricia. She was wearing a dress that he had not seen before. It was one that was—well, beautiful described it, too, he thought. As she stood there, smiling at Red Beads, Sykes felt his throat tighten.

Red Beads lowered her head as Ross finished

speaking and murmured a few words, and then she followed the others into the house.

"She said thanks," Ross informed Tricia as he went in behind Red Beads.

Tricia's eyes strayed to Sykes, and when he stopped in front of her, she slowly raised her eyes until she could look into his. He didn't try to hide what he was thinking.

There seemed to be nothing to say after that, and she slid her hand through his arm and walked into the house at his side.

The furniture in the front room had been moved aside, and a long table extended from the front of the room through the archway and across into the dining room. The table was covered with white cloths and places were set along both sides. At three places along the table, large glass jars were filled with the dried plants and grasses of the prairie.

"Is it all right?" asked Tricia, appealing for Sykes' approval. "We have punch to serve," she pointed to a separate table with a large bowl and cups. On it was another, smaller jar bursting with dried flowers.

While she served the punch, Cole Sykes stood with the Indians. They had stopped inside the door to the front room, and as the officers and their wives came to meet them, Sykes spoke in the Blackfoot language, introducing them. He had to speak slowly and deliberately, thinking about each word before he said it. When Tricia brought Sykes a cup of the punch, she held it so that he had to touch her hand to take it. When he touched her hand, she did not let go at once.

There were a half dozen children in the house, and while their elders drank the punch that had too much sherry for the children, they looked at one another and grew restless. First Moon was no different from the rest. He held his head down, as he had been told to do, for as long as he could, and then he smiled when he saw a boy his own age squirm away from his mother's side and move closer to the table. Plates of sliced pickles were already out. The boy watched until no one was paying attention and then reached up and snatched a piece of pickle and shoved it into his mouth. As the boy walked away from the table, First Moon could see by his expression that the pickle must taste very good.

When First Moon looked up at his mother, she was listening intently as the agent tried to talk correctly in their language. First Moon suddenly turned away from her and sidled toward the plate of pickles. Before he could reach it, he bumped into a wall of soft skirts and a glass of punch poured down over him and the skirts.

"Oh," gasped Tricia as First Moon ran smack into her. Then she looked down in dismay at the splashes of liquid on both of them. Suddenly she heard the sharp sound of Red Beads' voice as she jerked the child back to her side.

"No," Tricia put her hand out toward Red Beads. "It's all right. It doesn't matter. Oh," she looked frantically around for someone who could say the words for her. But both Ross and Sykes were talking to someone else.

First Moon was clinging to his mother's skirts, and when Tricia saw the severity of the frown on his mother's face, she knelt down in front of the boy. "It's all right," she soothed, "everyone has accidents." Sensing someone close, she looked straight up at Many Arrows, standing over her and the boy. The expression on his face was more severe even than Red Beads. "No, no," she insisted, rising to her feet. "It's not important.

Please don't look like that! I don't want you to do anything!"

While she fumbled for words with Many Arrows, Sykes moved quietly to her side. "Cole, tell them it's all right, please."

"What happened?"

"First Moon bumped into me and my punch spilled—and it doesn't matter. Tell them it doesn't matter. I don't want him punished for it."

"It's going to take Ross to explain all that," admitted Sykes. "I don't know that many words."

"Then get him, please. I'll wait here." She was relieved that Many Arrows stalked off while she waited. When the scout came to her side, Red Beads listened for a moment, and then spoke quietly to First Moon, at the same time holding him firmly by the shoulder.

"Sam, ask her if she'd like to bring First Moon upstairs while I change my dress. He's as wet as I am, and she can wash him off." She glanced at Sykes as the scout began to translate for Red Beads and then smiled at his nod of approval.

Lieutenant Barkley was the last to arrive, and he opened the door for himself while Tricia was seating people around the table. Her uncle had agreed to placing the Indians in the positions of honor, and she accompanied them to their places.

She was standing by Many Arrows' chair when Barkley entered. She smiled and called to him. "Over there, William," she indicated his chair with her extended hand.

The lieutenant's face reddened, and he replied with exaggerated politeness. "Thank you so much, Miss Ashley." He approached the table, and as he pulled out his chair, he announced loudly, "You are indeed the perfect hostess."

His sarcasm was not lost on Tricia, but she lifted her head and moved to her own place at the far end of the table. As soon as she sat down, the door to the kitchen opened and the cooks from the officers' mess began to carry the platters of steaming food to the table.

During the meal Cole Sykes was seated where he could see Tricia, but not close enough to talk to her. After the meal, the colonel stood up and offered the men cigars and brandy in the front room, and Tricia stayed with the women and children in the dining room, serving the women more coffee and giving second pieces of pie to the children.

An hour later when the officers and their families started to leave, Tricia walked to the door to accept their thanks and say good-bye. While she stood there Lieutenant Barkley walked to her side and stood at her shoulder, commenting in loud whispers to the other officers as they departed.

After Captain Olin and his wife left, Sykes saw Barkley say something to Tricia and smirk as he turned and looked in the direction of the Indians.

Tricia gasped and stared in horror at Barkley. His obscene suggestion that she enjoyed the game of trying to seduce an Indian brave stunned her. Just as Barkley let out a loud guffaw at her consternation, Sykes was at her side.

Before the officer could utter another word, Ross moved to Flying Hawk. The agent said nothing as he stopped between the lieutenant and the Indians. But he moved his hands menacingly to his hips and glared at Barkley.

"No Cole," cried Tricia, as she hurried to intervene. She slid both hands through his arm and tried to pull it down to his side.

As soon as she touched Sykes, he could see the disdain in Barkley's eyes turn to anger. The agent held the stare while he lowered his arms and then placed one hand over Tricia's. "Isn't it time for you to go home, soldier boy?" he hissed, his voice low enough not to carry behind him but loud enough to mock the rage in Barkley's eyes.

"I've had all I'm going to take of you, Sykes," threatened Barkley. The lieutenant made no effort to keep his voice down. "Why don't you just say where and when? You've got a lesson coming I'd like to teach you."

"No!" cried Tricia. "Cole, don't listen to him!"

Sykes kept his eyes on the lieutenant's while he deliberately put his arm around her shoulders and held her against his side.

"Tomorrow afternoon, two o'clock, in the street in front of the Trapper's Last Chance," challenged Sykes.

For several seconds the only sound in the room was Sam Ross' voice, speaking quietly in the Blackfoot tongue.

"And the choice of weapons, Mr. Sykes?" asked Barkley, his voice clear and distinct in the silence that followed Ross' translation.

"Fists," Sykes decided.

"Ahh," exulted Barkley. "My choice exactly. I shall look forward to the time." He turned and slammed the door.

"Oh no!" wailed Tricia, looking up at Sykes. "You don't realize he was a champion, do you? No one could beat him at West Point. He's never been beaten."

Sykes slid his arm from her shoulders as he turned to face the others in the room.

"Cole, you mustn't," she implored, taking his arm with both hands again.

As he walked to Ross and the Indians, his eyes passed over the colonel's face. It was clear that Forbes did not think Lieutenant Barkley could be beaten either, and Sykes was certain the lieutenant would have no trouble being freed from his duties to make the appointed time.

"It's time to leave, isn't it, Ross?" asked Sykes.

"Any time," agreed the scout.

They rode to the camp with Flying Hawk and his family and then left immediately.

The camp was no more than a hundred yards behind them when Ross slapped his clenched fist on his thigh and started to laugh. When he had recovered himself enough to talk, he turned to Sykes. "Now," he joked, "I've got to figure out whether to put my money on the West Point Academy or the Rawlins Territorial Prison. What do you figure?" He continued to chuckle until the agent glanced at him.

"What do they learn at West Point?" asked Sykes.

"Oh, fancy stuff from what I've seen. A lot of tactics, move your feet a lot and jab around quick-like."

Sykes looked thoughtful. "It wasn't like that in Rawlins—or before."

"Didn't figure it was," Ross grinned. "So I think I'll put my money on Rawlins."

"What do you mean, put your money on it?"

"Come on, Sykes. You've given everybody time to make bets a dozen times over. You don't think there'll be a soldier, townsman, or Indian that'll miss betting on the fight now, do you?"

"Indian? I don't want them to start gambling."

Ross looked sharply at the agent to see if he was serious. When he saw that Sykes meant it, he said simply, "You're too late, Sykes, they've been gambling for several hundred years already."

The next morning Sykes went into Warner's store as soon as it opened and bought all the lead, powder, cartridge cases and primers Warner had that would fit any of the Indian rifles, and then he went to work at the bench in the agency, putting bullets together.

In the middle of the work, Ross rode up in front of the building and peered in. He hitched up his horse and went into the agency.

"I see you're at it," he observed as he walked in the door.

"If they shoot them off as fast as they did before, it'll take plenty of them."

"Not everybody has your kind of aim, Sykes. What else can they do?"

"You ready to help?" dared the gunman.

"You ready to fight? That's the big question today?"

"Pull up that other chair, Ross," invited the gunman, ignoring the question as he made room at the bench.

"No, I can't stay. I just brought a message from Miss Ashley."

"She hasn't got anything to say to me right now."

"Well, she thinks she has."

"You know what she's going to say. She already said it yesterday."

"I don't know what she has on her mind. She just asked me to tell you she wants to see you."

"Tell her I don't want to see her right now, I'm busy."

"It wouldn't hurt you to . . ."

"Jesus, Ross. I don't want to see her now. Tell her that."

"All right, I'll tell her. But she won't like it."

Sykes continued working on the bullets and when he had finished, he set aside enough for his own needs during the winter. He had left none in the store and, until supplies got through, he didn't intend to run out himself. Maybe the Indians would be more careful if they didn't have so many.

At noontime, he looked up from the bench and pushed his chair back. Halfway to his feet he stopped and stared out the window.

She was wearing her blue riding outfit, and she rode alone down the center of the street looking for the agency.

He went out to the sidewalk and stood until she halted her horse.

She smiled at him despite the expression on his face.

"What are you doing here?" he demanded.

"You know perfectly well. Will you help me down, please?"

"No, you turn that horse around and ride back right now. I'll watch to see that you make it."

"I don't think I can get down by myself in a way that would be considered ladylike."

"Tricia, you do what I say."

"Come here, Cole."

He shook his head as he walked toward her, but when he was standing beside her and she held her hands out to him and leaned in his direction, he reached up and took hold of her waist. As she slid down she rested her hands on his shoulders, and when she was on the ground, she stood looking up at him while her fingers tightened on his shoulders. Then she stepped up to the sidewalk, holding her skirts above the dirt.

Sykes led her horse to the front of the hotel and tied it to the rail, and then walked back along the sidewalk. Tricia was standing a few feet inside the agency office looking around when he stopped in the doorway.

"So this is your place?" she commented. She turned and faced him. "I've wanted to see it."

"Why?"

"So I can imagine where you are and what you are doing all day."

"What for?"

"Because it interests me, of course."

"How could it?"

"For heaven's sake!"

"What are you here for? You can't stop that fight."

"Of course, I can't stop the fight. Don't you think I know that much about men?"

"Well then, what the hell . . ."

"Come in and close the door, and then I'll tell you why I'm here."

He pushed the door shut behind him. She clasped her hands in front of her, and he could see her swallow and take a deep breath. Nothing inside the agency was painted and, against the background of dull browns and greys, the vivid blue of her dress and the fairness of her face and chestnut hair were framed as though she were in a picture.

"Well," she began, and then hesitated, as though what she had to say was very difficult. At the same time he could see the color in her cheeks deepen. "I know what men look like after they fight. Their faces are all swollen and bruised, and their lips are split and very sore, and I—well, you might not be able to kiss me for some time afterward, so I thought—"

Tricia took a step toward him and suddenly he was holding her against him, both arms tight around her, and her arms were around his neck, holding him close. When he kissed her he could feel the same emotion surging through her. And this time he didn't let himself think that it was wrong and useless and that he couldn't have her.

When he lifted his head moments later, he held her only a little less tightly. She laid her head on his shoulder, her forehead against the side of his neck.

"That was a good idea, wasn't it?" she asked, speaking softly as though short of breath.

Sykes caressed her back and her long hair and took a deep breath. "Just before you came I was going to get something to eat. You want to eat with me?" he invited.

She lifted her head gently and pulled his face down until she could meet his lips.

"Yes," she answered after she kissed him, "if you'll kiss me again afterward."

It was one o'clock by the time Sykes took Tricia to her horse and lifted her to its back. People were already gathering in the street. He walked beside her horse for a while and then watched her gallop away from him, across the bridge and up to the fort. He waited until she rode through the gate, out of his sight.

Turning back along the street, he saw Gaines walking toward him. The blacksmith was grinning as he fell into step beside the agent. "You got anything you want me to do?" he asked.

Cole Sykes reached to his pocket and pulled out his tobacco. "I could use someone to hold my coat, I guess," said Sykes as they stopped outside the agency office. "I haven't seen Ross since this morning."

"Could be he doesn't want to take sides against the army," suggested Gaines. "He works for them." The blacksmith pulled a tobacco sack out of his pocket and rolled a cigarette, while Sykes rolled one for himself. He snapped a match into a flame and held it out toward the agent's cigarette first.

Sykes leaned forward far enough to light his cigarette and then blew out a lungful of smoke around it. "I thought everyone up here smoked a pipe," he remarked, the cigarette bobbing up and down between his lips. "Or a cigar, if you've got enough brass on your coat."

Gaines grinned as he took the cigarette out of his mouth with the mannerism Sykes always used. "I did smoke a pipe before you got here," he drawled. "Then when I saw you—well, I got to wondering why you preferred this. Damn, but it took a lot of practice to get the tobacco to stay in the paper. It kept coming out at both ends. Guess that's why most people prefer to smoke a pipe. It's easy."

Sykes narrowed his eyes slightly to keep from smiling as he glanced past the blacksmith to a group of the men gathered on the sidewalk across from him. Then he looked down at the mud in the street. It had dried out so that it was not exactly mud, but it was still wet and heavy. As he watched the street in front of the saloon, a half dozen horses trotted down the center.

Gaines also noted the muddy street. "Looks like Barkley might get a little bit dirty if he falls down," he chuckled.

Sykes left the cigarette in his mouth as he bent over and took off his spurs. He threw them into the office behind him and pulled the door shut. "How about a drink?" he offered. "We can wait in the saloon as well as any place."

Chapter 26

The tumult in the street grew steadily louder while they stood at the bar. During that time Sykes drank one beer. He spoke little, and Gaines left him to his thoughts.

At five minutes to the hour, Sykes stepped back from the bar far enough to reach the buckle of his gunbelt. Before he unfastened the buckle he undid the thong around his thigh, and then he let the belt drop away from his hips, holding it next to the holster so his gun would not fall out. He put the belt and gun on the bar between him and the blacksmith. He hadn't worn his coat, but he took off his hat and vest and laid them on top of the gunbelt. When he was ready he took the last swallow of beer, turned, and walked to the swinging doors.

The blacksmith picked up the vest and hat and put the gunbelt over his shoulder before he followed behind.

As Sykes pushed through the doors, the level of noise in the street dropped to a murmur, and then a cheer went up as though it had been planned ahead of time. A ring of men had already formed in front of the saloon, but while he stood there a narrow aisle opened up for him to walk to the center of the street.

The gunman scowled over the heads of the crowd. Many Arrows and a dozen of his warriors sat on their horses behind the crowd. Sam Ross was beside the chief. They were half a dozen feet from the nearest group of men, and they sat in silent contrast to the noise around them.

Hearing a shout at the other side of the crowd, Sykes turned with everyone else and listened to the sound of horses, a lot of horses, crossing the bridge. A moment later, Lieutenant William Barkley, at the head of his entire platoon, rode into sight. Captain Olin was at the lieutenant's side.

Instead of a cheer for Barkley, the men in the street grew so silent that the creaking of the saddles and the jingling of their bridles were the only sounds Sykes could hear. Once off the bridge, even the footfall of the horses was muffled in the soft, wet dirt.

Lieutenant Barkley was in full uniform. The buttons of his coat gleamed on his chest. His hands were covered in leather gloves with cuffs so long they went halfway to his elbows. When he pulled up at the far side of the crowd, his men spread out in a double row behind him. As he swung out of his saddle, Corporal Eddy came forward and took his horse's rein. At the same time Sergeant Pearce swung down and walked over behind Barkley. Then the lieutenant stood arrogantly in front of his horse, staring at the crowd, until a pathway opened in front of him to the center of the ring.

As Barkley started through the crowd, Sergeant Pearce a pace behind him, Sykes stepped down in the street and elbowed through the crowd. He stopped inside the ring of men and faced the officer. He watched as Lieutenant Barkley removed his gloves and handed them to the sergeant. Then the officer unbuckled his sword and pulled off his coat, his hat, and finally his spurs.

Sykes stood, unmoving, his face set and expressionless, his eyes steady on the other man. When Barkley glanced at the agent from time to time during his methodical preparations, it was with a half-smile of contempt.

When the officer was ready, he dropped his hands to his sides and stepped slowly into the center of the street. At the same time Sykes lowered his hands and walked forward.

"Fists you said, Mr. Sykes?" Barkley reminded him as he brought his hands up in front of him and doubled them. He held his left hand extended, his right hand close to his face. As Sykes stepped forward, another cheer started to rise from the crowd, but it was choked off as Barkley's left hand shot out and snapped the agent's head back before Sykes had his hands all the way up.

Barkley landed three blows before Sykes could break through his defenses to merely graze the officer's cheek. Again Barkley's right jerked Sykes' head back.

The agent circled to his right, his fists high while he watched for an opening. When he thought he saw one, he reached out, but Barkley slammed his arm aside and struck with his other fist. Sykes tasted the salty blood in his mouth.

Before he could dodge away, Barkley's fist flashed again and a wild shout went up. "First blood!" The first round of bets had been decided, and they had gone to Barkley.

The officer tagged him again squarely in the mouth, almost as though he were playing with him, grinning at the same time. Sykes struck hard at Barkley's midsection. That time as he stepped back he felt satisfied with the blow. Barkley was soft where he should have been hard. Sykes already knew he couldn't beat Barkley's speed, but while Barkley had landed two or three blows to Sykes' one, none of them had done more than cut up the agent's face.

Sykes took another smashing right as he moved in close enough to wind his arm around Barkley's middle and then pound at his side. At the same time, Barkley tried to pull away and suddenly tripped. The two of them crashed to the ground. For a moment, as they flailed in the mud, locked together, neither of them could strike a blow.

"You said fists, Sykes," croaked Barkley, shoving with his forearm against the agent's chest.

Sykes pulled away then and jumped up while Barkley rolled over and got to his feet. Sykes no longer heard the screams of the crowd as he wiped his hands along the sides of his pants.

Barkley continued to move lightly on his feet, and he tapped at Sykes' face with his left as he closed in again. By then Sykes knew that Barkley's right was going to follow, and he rolled his head to one side as he smashed his fist into Barkley's midsection. But instead of the right, Barkley drove a left into Sykes that sent him reeling into the mud behind him.

"First knockdown!" the cry went up.

"All right, you bastard," muttered Sykes as he struggled to his feet. "Let's see what you can take in that soft middle of yours." He lunged at the officer and slammed both fists, one after the other into his middle, until Barkley toppled back and dropped his elbows lower, close together in front of him. Then Sykes hit him again, and when Barkley dropped his hands still lower, the agent slammed his fist into the side of Barkley's nose.

The lieutenant dodged back and circled to his left as though he needed to gain time. At that sign of weakness Sykes moved into him again. The agent took a blow to his cheek as he punched into Barkley's middle, but this time he could feel his knuckles hit metal, and at once the cry of "low blow" rose from the soldiers' side of the ring.

Barkley stepped back at the sound of the cry and lifted his head slightly from behind his hands. As soon as he did, Sykes struck at him again, and the officer staggered as he took another step back. Suddenly he rushed in and delivered two blows to Sykes' face before the agent could reach through and drive a fist into Barkley's middle one more time. The officer was still moving faster than Sykes, and he grinned from behind his fists.

After that Sykes made no attempt to fend off the precisely executed blows. Instead he waded into the man's sides, trying to stay inside the reach of Barkley's arms, slugging at him until finally the officer started to go down. Then Sykes stepped back and slammed a vicious right into Barkley's jaw.

The lieutenant twisted as he flopped backward, and he lay where he sprawled, the side of his face in the mud.

The agent gasped air into his lungs as he spread his legs apart to keep himself steady while he waited for Barkley to get up. It took him a moment to realize that the man was unconscious, and then he turned and staggered in the direction of the saloon.

At first he did not hear the cheering from the townspeople, but when he felt hands slapping him on the back as he stepped up to the sidewalk, he looked in the direction of the Indians. Except for Many Arrows, they were talking among themselves. Only the war chief sat unmoving, his eyes on Sykes, and there was something in the way Many Arrows met the agent's eyes that held a challenge.

He didn't need to look in the mirror when he got up the next morning. Tricia had been right. Lieutenant Barkley had done a thorough job of slicing up his face, and Sykes didn't think he wanted to show it for a while. The only satisfaction he had was that although Barkley probably looked better, he probably hurt every time he drew breath.

Sykes stayed in his room for most of the next two days, waiting until he felt like eating and talking to people, and then on Monday he decided it was time to take his laundry to the fort. Only a little of the swelling had gone down, but he could move his jaw easier now. He gathered up his laundry, collected his horse, and headed for the fort.

If the people up there weren't going to have anything to do with him, he might as well find out right away.

He knew the laundress in the first tent wouldn't help him, so he rode to the next one, where Sergeant Pearce's wife and two of his daughters had done his laundry before.

As he started to dismount outside their tent, a woman's voice called out to him.

"Oh, Mr. Sykes."

The voice issued from the tent he had just passed, and when he looked behind him the woman who had refused to do his laundry before was beckoning to him. He settled back into his saddle and rode over to her.

"Mr. Sykes," she repeated, tilting her head to one side as she looked up at him, her lips slightly pursed. "Is that laundry you have there?"

"Yes ma'am," he replied, leaning toward her far enough to rest one arm across his saddle horn.

"Surely you weren't going to ask anyone except me to do it. You do remember me, don't you, Libby Jones?"

"Now that's an interesting change of mind, Miss Jones."

"Well—you didn't say who you were when you came here before. How was a girl supposed to know?"

"And what do you know now that's any different?"

"Mr. Sykes! That's a silly question."

"I don't think it's a silly question. There aren't any more stripes on my arm than there were before."

"Well, I didn't know you were the new superintendent of the whole reservation. You didn't look anything like that. You looked like one of the—the kind of men that hang around down in the town."

"I am one of the men that hangs around down in the town." He straightened from the saddle horn and picked up his reins.

"Mr. Sykes, don't be like that. You get right down and bring your laundry with you." She turned partly away and put one hand on her hip, looking at him over her shoulder. "Come along, Mr. Sykes."

He swung down, dropped his reins over his horse's head and then untied the sack of laundry behind the saddle. She waited until he was ready to follow her into the tent, and then she walked ahead of him.

"Do you stay here all winter?" he asked, looking at the canvas walls of the tent.

"I have lots of blankets." She turned and put a hand suggestively on his arm. "And, of course, there are always—others who like to keep me warm. Important others, like you, Mr. Sykes. Do you mind if I call you Cole?" She slid her hand over his arm while she moved closer to him and peered up at him.

"My," she exclaimed. "That must have been a terrible fight. Just look at your face! Can I do anything to make it feel better? Can I do anything to make *you* feel better?"

When she moved close enough to brush against him, he looked past her, out the other side of the tent in the direction of the colonel's house. After a moment Libby glanced over her shoulder, and then she turned partly away. "Well, I don't believe this," she exclaimed. "What's she doing?"

Patricia Ashley was walking toward the row of laundry tents with a sack of clothes in her hands.

"What *is* she doing?" asked Libby again, an edge of anger creeping into her voice.

Sykes remained silent, watching Tricia as she approached.

"Wait until she gets here," she said tartly. "She won't know whether I should starch the collars or the shirt tails."

When Tricia was nearly to the tent, Libby stalked to the washtubs and reached into them. She was scrubbing a white shirt over the washboard when Tricia put down her bundle. "These are Colonel Forbes' things," announced Tricia, without looking at Sykes.

"How do you want me to do them?" asked Libby, grinning past Tricia at the gunman.

"You've been washing his clothes for a long time. Why do you ask?"

"Well, Miss Ashley, I just thought you might have special instructions. You've never come here. Why else would you walk all the way over here—now?" She continued to watch Sykes as she spoke, giving the last word emphasis.

"Oh." Tricia cried out when she looked at the agent. She gasped and put one hand up to her mouth, staring at his face.

The laundress laughed harshly. "What's the matter, Miss Ashley? Haven't you ever seen a man who's been in a fight before?"

Tricia turned and stared for a moment at the other woman, who walked over to Sykes' side and peered up at his face again. "I'm sure I can make that feel better, Cole," she whined, touching his arm. "I was just telling him that."

Tricia's eyes widened as she met the laundress' smile. She turned away abruptly and walked rapidly toward her house.

Sykes stood there, frowning at Tricia's back, until he felt Libby's hand tighten on his arm. Hearing her laugh, he looked down at the triumph in her eyes, staring at her as she swayed against him. He grasped her wrist roughly and removed her hand from his arm. He turned and went out of the tent to his horse.

He loped across the far end of the fort toward the gate, watching Tricia as she ran the last few steps to her house. She nearly tripped on her skirts as she flew up the steps, holding them with only one hand, the other hand covering her face as she pushed into the house without a glance behind her.

Sykes pulled up at the gate and sat quietly for several minutes. He rolled a cigarette, lit it and walked his horse along the inside of the fort where he would pass in front of the store and the building where the unmarried officers lived.

A couple of soldiers Sykes did not know were standing in front of the store, watching him silently as he rode by. When Sykes turned and looked directly at them, one reached up to the angle of his jaw and ran his hand along it as though he knew how Sykes' jaw must feel. They seemed neither friendly nor unfriendly, and the agent said nothing.

He saw no one outside the officers' quarters as he approached, but just as he reached the building, Captain Olin came out and walked to the edge of the porch. The agent reined in.

"Good fight," Olin remarked, his expression neutral like the others.

"How's Barkley?" asked Sykes.

"Hurting as you'd expect, but it hit hardest on his pride, I'm afraid."

"I never could have beat him if he hadn't let himself get soft in the middle. You're not hard enough on your men, Captain."

"I didn't see that blow he's talking about. How low was it?"

Sykes put his cigarette to his lips with his right hand so that the officer could see the scrape across his knuckles. "I hit the top of his belt buckle."

The captain's face relaxed as he studied the knuckles. "Those suspenders he wears keep his pants pretty high. Barkley will have to take it as a fair fight and get over it. Nobody can win every fight." He raised his hand in a half-salute as he turned away.

So Barkley was claiming an unfair fight. Well, that wasn't surprising, but it probably meant more trouble. He continued at a walk until he reached the colonel's house where he swung down and ground-reined his horse. He dropped his cigarette in front of him and stepped on it, blowing out the last of the smoke as he walked toward the house.

There was no answer to Sykes' knock, even though he waited and then knocked a second time. He opened the door and stepped inside.

"Miss Ashley," he called. When there was no response he called again. "Tricia!" In the silence that followed, he could hear what sounded like bedsprings shifting under a person's weight.

He waited long enough for her to come out of her room if she was going to, and when there was only silence he started up the stairs. The door to her room was open, and he stopped in it, nearly filling it as he stood there staring at her.

She was lying face down on her bed, her head turned away from him, and she did not move to look at him.

"Are you jealous?" he asked.

"No," she blurted out, her voice betraying her tears.

"My God, Tricia," he said as he walked over and sat down on the edge of the bed.

She kept her head buried in the pillow. "Go away," she moaned. "I don't want to see you."

"Well, I'm here."

"Go away, I said." She turned to face him then and propped herself up on her elbows. "You can't be in here. What if Uncle John comes home?"

He smiled as much as his swollen lips would allow as he studied her face. Her eyes were red and her face was flushed and shining with tears. "Right now you don't look a lot better than I do," he observed.

"Oh!" She flung herself face down on her arms. "Get out of here!"

He stood up and suddenly reached down and pulled her from the bed to her feet. "What happened to all of those kisses you had for me the other day?"

"I don't want to see you," she cried, standing quietly in his grasp, her head still turned away from him.

"Tricia, you didn't want to see me with the laundress, that's what you didn't want to see, isn't it?"

"My uncle has let me know what kind of person she is."

"Well, I hope Forbes has let you know what kind of a person I am, too."

"He's certainly tried."

"And he's right."

"I suppose—those awful women from the town, too?"

He could feel her shake with sobs, and he wanted to take her in his arms. Instead he dropped his hands to his sides. "I've got nothing I can offer you." He spoke seriously, yet sincerely. "You know that. The way things are going around here, I've got a damned good chance of spending the next five years in prison, and I'm not likely to come out of there the way I go in. There aren't many that do."

She covered her face with both hands. "I thought the way you kissed me the other day that you might—love me."

He had to clench his fists to keep from reaching for her. "I wouldn't know anything about that, and if I did, what would be the use?"

"I'd wait for you, Cole, if you had to go back."

"You'd what?" he asked in astonishment.

She lifted her face. "I'll wait for you, if you have to go."

"Oh God, didn't you hear what I said, Tricia?"

"Yes, but you're tough—and if you knew I was waiting, maybe that would help somehow."

His throat filled and blocked the words he wanted to say. He could only fold her in his arms. She put her arms around him and her head on his shoulder, carefully as though she thought he might hurt there, too.

They held each other until she stopped crying.

Her voice was muffled against his coat when she spoke. "Cole, when your laundry is finished, I'll get it for you."

He smiled. "All right."

Chapter 27

As Sykes started down the hill to the bridge, he could see riders coming across the snow from the south, driving a herd of horses ahead of them. While he continued down to the bridge, they stopped the herd. Two men broke off and rode at a fast pace toward the fort.

Sykes crossed the bridge, glanced at the riders again, and then stopped to watch. When the two men were inside the fort, he turned his horse and headed back. Not many white men herded horses in the winter around here. He could only think of some that might, and one of the men riding into the fort had a dark, bushy beard.

As soon as Sykes entered the gate, he looked around for Sam Ross, but neither the scout nor the two riders were in sight. He checked the barracks, but Ross was not there either. Two horses were tied outside the headquarters building that hadn't been there before, and Sykes rode in that direction.

As he approached the horses, he could see rifles on both of them, and he slowed as he rode by. He reined in beside the second horse, reached for the rifle and pulled it far enough out of its scabbard to see the sights. When he was sure it was the rifle he had dropped at the outlaw camp, he pulled it all the way out and held it while he swung down and tied his horse. He walked into the headquarters building and along the hall to Forbes' office, the rifle tucked under his arm.

He stopped short in the doorway. Two men were sitting opposite the colonel, and Sykes recognized the one with the black beard. Sam Ross sat in the chair at the side of the room where he had been the day that Sykes had arrived at the fort, and Corporal Eddy was the orderly of the day.

Forbes looked up as soon as Sykes stepped into the doorway. "I'm busy, Sykes. You'll have to come back later if you want to see me."

"I don't want to see you. I just stopped by to thank these gents here for returning my rifle."

The two horse herders twisted in their chairs, watching the doorway. Although Sykes saw their faces harden at his comment, neither moved.

"What do you mean?" demanded the colonel. "You're out of order barging in here like this."

Sykes watched the bearded man. "This is the rifle I dropped where I found the stolen Indian horses."

"What are you trying to say?" The bearded man leaped to his feet and faced Sykes squarely. The outlaw's right hand strayed to his gun.

"Sykes, get out of here," ordered Forbes, rising to his feet. "This is Blacky duBois and his foreman. They're horse ranchers from Grass Valley. We've been buying horses from them for years because they know how to train them for the cavalry. Now if you'll just leave—"

"Ross," Sykes interrupted the colonel's speech. "You figure Many Arrows can tell his horses when he sees them, even with shoes on them?"

"I reckon," replied Ross.

"Corporal Eddy," barked Forbes, turning to the orderly. "Get a detail of men to put Sykes out of here."

The corporal hurried to obey the order, and Sykes leaned one shoulder against the doorway. "What if Many Arrows can identify his horses?" he persisted.

"You don't think I'd take the word of an Indian against a white man, do you?"

"I see," noted Sykes. He stared at duBois. "Thanks again for returning my gun. Watch for me the next time you're in town."

As he walked down the hall he listened for the sound of footsteps, but when no one followed him, he went to his horse. As he rode toward the gate, his rifle upright in his hand, stock on his thigh, he saw half a dozen soldiers running on the double toward the headquarters building.

Corporal Eddy halted the men as soon as he saw Sykes and walked into the road at an angle to meet the agent. When he raised his hand, Sykes stopped in front of him.

"One of the horses that was stolen from here comes when I whistle," he informed Sykes. "I trained it myself."

"Is that right?" Sykes mused. "Let me know if it's with that bunch, will you?"

"Yes, sir. I certainly will." He turned and waved the rest of the men back to the barracks before he faced the headquarters building again.

It was afternoon when Sam Ross finally came down to the agency, and he was frowning as he walked in the door. "You sure as hell have a way of getting under Forbes' skin. Now he won't let me go with you on the hunt."

"Why not?"

"He'd rather see the Indians starve than help you with anything. You couldn't just call him 'sir' once or anything, could you?"

"No."

"I didn't think so." The scout turned a chair around, and, straddling it, leaned his arms across the back and put his chin on his arm. "I hate to miss that hunt. I haven't run buffalo in a long time, but maybe it's worth it, seeing somebody stand up to the big boss. It's good for him. Seems like being the top man too long kind of goes to a person's head."

"I wouldn't know," said Sykes. "Did he buy the horses?"

"Yep. And after what you said, he didn't even send anybody out to look at them first. Just closed the deal like he knew what fine, honest men they were." The scout rubbed his chin on his arms. "By the way, Corporal Eddy said to tell you one of the horses knows him."

"I'm going after those horse thieves as soon as I get back from this hunt," decided Sykes. "You can bet it's the same outfit that's selling them whiskey, and I wouldn't be surprised if they were the ones that killed Silvers. I might as well take care of it all at once."

"One of you against a dozen of them? Those were Silvers' odds. Of course, that was a little different."

"How was it different?"

"I'm only guessing."

"Your guesses are good enough for me."

"I'm pretty sure Silvers brought the first of that bunch in here. Blacky came along later."

"And horned in?"

"That's what I'm guessing."

"So he probably killed Silvers?"

"You ever notice the heels of his boots? They're higher than yours even, and narrower."

"You saw tracks around the body?"

"Yep, so you better wait until Forbes lets me go with you."

"And until he lets me have a platoon or two? That might be a while. Why didn't you tell me this before?"

Ross laughed. "Takes a while to get to know somebody like you." Then he lifted his head and stared out of the window. "But as long as I'm here," he said, getting slowly to his feet, "I'll back you."

When Sykes looked out, he saw half a dozen men loping down the center of the street, Blacky duBois in the middle of them. The outlaws stared at the agency building as they went by, but they did not stop until they were in front of the Trapper's Last Chance. They dismounted and went inside.

"Two against six, Sykes. That's better odds than I thought you'd have," the scout pointed out as he set the chair back where he had found it.

"We can make it three," offered Sykes.

"How?"

"They get their horseshoes at night from Gaines' stable."

"You want me to get him?"

"Yes."

The agent drew his Colt and checked the loads while Ross walked across the street to the blacksmith shop. Then he waited for the two men outside on the sidewalk. Neither of the others wore handguns, but the blacksmith was carrying his shotgun, and Ross got his rifle from his horse. He also unfastened the flap over the bowie knife hanging at his side.

Cole Sykes checked the position of his revolver

one more time as the three of them started along the sidewalk. Reaching the saloon, Sykes pushed through the swinging doors first and then stepped to one side while the other two men came in behind him and spread apart, one on either side of the agent.

As Blacky duBois turned slowly away from the bar, he put both elbows on it behind him and stared at the agent, his lips forming a smile. The five men with him turned at the same time until they all faced Sykes. They all wore revolvers, and they looked ready to use them.

"You're a fool, Sykes," called duBois. "A goddamned, Indian-loving fool."

"Silvers was the fool, Blacky, for turning his back on you. Wouldn't he give you a big enough cut?"

"What do you mean?" The outlaw pushed away from the bar and dropped his hands to his sides.

"You killed Silvers, duBois. You better learn more about Indians before you try to imitate them."

"What are you accusing me of, you—" Still talking, the outlaw grabbed for his gun, but it was only half out of his holster when Sykes' bullet slammed him in the chest. He fell back against the bar and crumpled on the floor.

Sykes crouched lower and continued to fire. All around guns were blasting. He felt a bullet burn across his shoulder as the blacksmith and Ross dropped down. When his own gun was empty and he reached for the scout's rifle, Ross shot once more from the floor. The back door of the saloon slammed, and the firing stopped abruptly. Two of the outlaws had escaped, but four of them lay sprawled in front of the bar.

When he was sure that Ross was still in control of his gun, Sykes pulled bullets from his belt and reloaded. At the same time he kept his eyes on the bodies of the outlaws. "How bad you hit, Ross?" he asked.

"I'm not," the scout assured Sykes, standing up. "I was just getting out of the line of fire. How's Gaines?"

The blacksmith groaned when the scout pronounced his name and tried to roll over, but his leg was bent at an unnatural angle and blood was seeping from a wound at the side of his head where a bullet had grazed him. After the first attempt to get up, Gaines lay still.

"Looks like that leg's broken," Sykes observed, glancing at the wounded man.

"And what's that on your shoulder?" asked Ross.

"What do you think?"

"How bad?"

"Not bad." Sykes shifted his shoulder. It hurt to move it against his clothes, but he could tell the bullet had only broken the skin. He finished reloading and moved forward to check the outlaws lying across the room.

As the agent walked toward the bodies, the bartender poked his head from behind it. "Now who the hell's going to pay for this mess?" he asked.

"You are," said Sykes, still watching the bodies on the floor. "It'll teach you to be careful who you serve drinks to."

Many Arrows and his warriors, their faces painted for the hunt, their weapons and horses ready, waited for the agent. Two young boys were with them, holding several extra horses. Sykes spoke haltingly to them until Many Arrows nodded that he understood no one else was coming. Then the agent divided the cartridges he had brought and told them he had no more, that they would have to make do with the ones he had been able to get ready.

It was not as much ammunition as Many Arrows wanted, but he showed no sign of disappointment. He ordered the others to get more arrows for their bows and to bring their lances. He went to his own lodge and gathered up all his arrows.

"Didn't he bring bullets?" asked Red Beads.

"Some. Not enough."

"Why not?"

"I do not know. He has not provided for us even as much as the other one. He does not fulfill the treaty any better."

"He is not at all like the other one," agreed Red Beads. "But you were the one who traded the soldiers' ponies to Blackbeard—"

"Be still, woman."

"I'm sorry," she murmured, lowering her eyes.

Many Arrows stopped in the opening to his lodge and looked at his wife. His voice softened. "I will bring you food and good skins to prepare."

She raised her head and looked at him. "And I will bring you your next child, perhaps before you return. Grabs Thorns has almost finished the cradleboard."

He looked down at the thickness of her body and then at her face. "I will bring the soft hide of a calf," he whispered. Then he turned and strode to his horse.

Flakes of snow swirled in the air, floating down in the breeze. Many Arrows looked at the sky above. In the past, he would not have ridden out in the winter when the sky was so low, but that was when they had stores of dried meat and berries and could wait for better weather. Now when they believed that the white man would feed them, they were hungry.

Although the white man rode beside him in the lead, Many Arrows did not speak to him on the ride to the place where he had seen the buffalo tracks. During that time the snow fell heavily until the way ahead of them became difficult to see. When he could tell that the tracks would soon be covered by the snowfall, he urged his horse ahead faster.

As soon as they reached the place where he had seen the buffalo sign, he turned and followed the tracks. Half an hour later they came across the fresh sign of the buffalo. Shortly after that, they sighted a dark mass against the snow ahead of them.

When he saw them, Many Arrows felt disappointment. The herd was small. Before the white man had come there would have been thousands of them. Not even a hundred remained in the herd. He turned to the agent.

"There aren't many," cautioned Sykes. "We need to be careful to get all we can."

"Yes," agreed Many Arrows, "but we have few bullets."

"Shoot only when you're sure of a hit."

"We must shoot many times to be sure of a kill."

"Hell, I know that," Sykes spoke to himself. Then, in the Blackfoot language, he told Many Arrows, "This horse that was yours will know what to do. I will bring down as many as I can."

"We must circle that way," declared Many Arrows, pointing upwind. When the white man nodded, he turned and motioned to the other hunters, already spreading out and approaching the herd slowly so as not to startle them until they were close enough.

The white man dropped behind to the middle of

the group of warriors as Many Arrows led the way around the herd. When Many Arrows motioned for the Indians to split into two groups, one on either side of the herd, Sykes rode with the group that galloped to the left, and Many Arrows continued at the head of the group to the right.

They moved forward as close to the herd as they could get before the outlying beasts began to swing their heads nervously, sniffing at the wind. Suddenly the Indians rushed forward.

Many Arrows rode close to the side of the animal nearest to him before he shot, and the buffalo crashed to the ground. As he rode on, the snow stung his face, but he pushed into the wind until he had emptied his gun. He pulled aside and looked back to see how well they had done while he reloaded. There were six or seven buffalo on the ground, stretched out behind him, and he could still hear shooting where the herd had thundered off.

As soon as his rifle was ready again, he dashed after the others. When he caught up to the herd, he looked for the calf he had promised Red Beads and shot it first. When his rifle was empty again he reloaded, using the last of his ammunition. By the time he had fired the final rounds, he could hear only an occasional shot. Soon, there was no more firing.

Despite the short supply of ammunition, it had been a good hunt. As he rode back, he counted more buffalo than they could carry home on their pack horses.

He called out, and then studied the sky until the others had joined him.

"There is more meat than we can take to the camp before the storm stops us. The women must come here. Kills Bear, ride to tell them. The rest of us will remain."

"No, Many Arrows," interrupted Sykes. "You can't bring them here. This is off the reservation."

The war chief pointed in the direction of the camp. "Go, Kills Bear. They must be here before dark, or it will be too late. Already there is too much snow, and the wind is still rising."

Many Arrows looked straight ahead as Sykes leaned toward him. After a moment the agent straightened in his saddle without saying anything more.

As the agent picked up his reins and laid them on the side of the horse's neck, Many Arrows turned to him. "You will not go to the fort for the bluejackets," he ordered. "You will stay here."

Sykes met Many Arrows' stare for several moments before he lowered the hand holding his reins.

The wind had dropped by the end of the second day, and all of the meat had been brought into camp. Many Arrows looked around before he went into his tepee. "Where is First Moon?" he asked as he sat down at the far side of the fire. "It is too cold for him to be outside, and it is nearly dark."

Before Red Beads could answer there was a cry outside, and then a whimper as the child ran in through the opening.

"What is it?" asked Red Beads. "Why did you cry out?"

"Nothing," the child replied, holding one finger in his mouth as he looked away from his parents.

"What is it?" asked Many Arrows.

"I saw a light."

"A light? What kind of light? There are many campfires."

"Sometimes it was blue, and then it was white."

"Where was it?"

"By the horses."

"What were you doing by the horses? You are too small to be around the horses by yourself. We have told you that before."

"I couldn't go to them past the light."

"Was the light on the ground?"

"Yes."

Many Arrows stood up. "Was it between you and the horses?"

"Yes. What are you going to do? I won't go near the horses again." First Moon backed away as his father walked toward him. But Many Arrows went out of the tepee without looking at the child.

He strode through the camp toward the horses. It was late, and only the yellow of the campfires behind him broke the darkness. When he was beside the horses, he stood for a long time watching them without seeing anything. As he turned away he moved his eyes over the hillside beyond the snowy field. At the top of the hill he could see a blue-white pinpoint of light. When he looked around the sky, it did not seem clear enough to see the stars, and the light was where the clouds were unbroken. While he watched it, the light seemed to grow larger and then it shrank back to the size of a star again. He stood with his eyes on the light, and seven times it seemed to swell and then shrink again until he could see it no more.

He slept restlessly that night. His sleep was without dreams until an hour before dawn, when he dreamed of the light. He was standing again, beside the horses, and the light came down the side of the hill. It passed under the horses, dancing from under one horse's belly to another, and then it leaped to the back of Many Arrows' horse, the one he had taken from the white man, Cole Sykes. The light circled the horse, making a web of lines around it. Then the light circled seven times around the war chief before it stopped on the ground in front of him. As soon as the light became still, it began to swell until it was the size of a man, and Many Arrows could see an old person in the middle.

"Napi!" he cried aloud in his sleep. Red Beads stirred at his side even though Many Arrows did not wake up.

"Napi," he cried again.

The old man reached out and pointed his finger at Many Arrows. "There will be war," he intoned. "Only those who prepare will be saved. Tell your young men to paint their faces and their horses and pray. There will be war!" As soon as the old man finished speaking he disappeared, leaving only the bluish-white light, which shrank smaller and smaller.

"Napi!" called Many Arrows, bolting upright in the robe, fully awake. He repeated the name softly again, three more times until he had spoken it seven times. At the end of the seventh repetition, he threw his head back and gave the wolf howl.

He could hear voices murmuring and calling from the other tepees, but he did not answer. He did not speak to Red Beads when she lifted herself beside him. For the rest of the night he sat staring into the coals of the fire.

Chapter 28

Lieutenant Barkley tried to avoid meeting his eyes in the mirror while he shaved. He knew his face showed little signs of the fight, and he tried to take satisfaction in that. He'd seen Sykes ride by, and the gunman had certainly looked like the loser.

Barkley drew in his breath slowly and straightened in front of the mirror. If he didn't let it show, no one could tell how it felt where Sykes had pounded his midsection. Of course, he didn't mind talking about that damned low blow. If there had been a referee, as at West Point where he had never been beaten, Sykes wouldn't have gotten away with that. At least his men understood what had happened, and who the hell else mattered? A low blow is what you have to expect when you fight with someone less than a gentleman.

He finished dressing late in the afternoon. Colonel Forbes had given him a few days to rest. Now he was a man who understood honor. *He* wouldn't hit anyone below the belt.

The lieutenant walked to his window and looked in the direction of the colonel's house for a few minutes. Then he walked downstairs and entered into the officers' dining room. He held himself carefully, trying to move without making his sides hurt worse, at the same time trying not to show any pain.

No one mentioned the fight during the meal, and afterward he decided to go for a walk outside the buildings. A few flakes of snow filled the air, and he could see that the clouds hung heavy with more snow.

His stroll took him past the colonel's house, where he was careful not to stare or appear interested. When no one called to him to stop, he moved on down the far side of the parade ground. The only light ahead of him came from one of the laundry tents and, as he approached it, he could make out the silhouette of a woman against the canvas side. She was lifting part of her clothing over her head, and the lieutenant quickened his step as he neared the tent.

Without speaking, he opened the flap of the tent and walked in. "Libby," he whispered hoarsely, "I see you're getting ready for me."

"Oh!" she exclaimed as she turned, startled. Standing there in only her camisole and petticoat, her face relaxed when she recognized him. "So, you're up and about again?"

"I had a few days off. That's why you haven't seen me around. That bastard couldn't knock me off my feet."

"I see. Why are you here, Lieutenant?"

He walked toward her. "You know why I'm here." He reached past her and turned down the light.

There was no friendliness in Barkley's eyes as he looked at Sam Ross, seated at the side of Forbes' office. "I don't see what I'll need an interpreter for," he complained. "If they're off the reservation, I'll know all I need to know."

"You better take him," warned Forbes testily.

"You never know what will turn up, and it's time he did something for the army for a change, considering we're paying his wages."

"How do I know he won't take part in shooting down some more of our friends?" asked Barkley.

Ross stood up and, with one foot on the chair and his arm across his upraised knee, he leaned toward the lieutenant. "They may have been your friends," he said, "but Corporal Eddy has already identified one of the horses they sold as his."

"That will be enough, men," ordered Forbes, standing up. "Since more than half of the ranchers are now dead, I don't think we'll ever know the truth about that matter. I can't imagine the rest of them will be back this way soon. However, we can all look forward to spring, when I'm sure the Office of Indian Affairs will be wise enough—at my suggestion—to replace that coldblooded killer agent. I have that much faith in Washington, at least."

Ross walked to the spittoon by the door and loosed a stream of tobacco juice. When Barkley turned to leave, the scout followed a few feet behind him.

Barkley ordered his entire platoon into the saddle, including a bugler and a muleskinner, with mules loaded for several days' campaign. The snow had stopped by the time they rode out of the gate, but the clouds were dark and low, threatening another storm.

Sam Ross rode beside Sergeant Pearce, directly behind the lieutenant, and the rest followed, four abreast, where there was room. The horses had been a long time in the stable, and they were fresh and willing, although the snow was the heaviest and deepest it had been that winter.

They followed along the southern boundary of the reservation, looking for the place the woodcutting detail had described, a place where an Indian camp had gone over the boundary and headed south. It was the middle of the afternoon before the snow ahead of them showed where the Indians had traveled. There was a thirty-foot-wide trail where they had passed, and the tracks of the travois poles were clear, even though they had been partially covered with snow.

At once Barkley ordered the detachment to the south, following the trail, and an hour later they could see smoke ahead of them over the next ridge. Beside them, a quarter-mile away, Ross could see what was left of the carcasses of several buffalo. At least they had some luck.

"What's that over there?" he called out, pointing to the shapes on the snow.

The lieutenant turned in the direction of the carcasses and then looked over his shoulder at Ross. "You're the scout. Go and see," he snapped.

Ross rode toward the mounds, but as soon as he reached the first depression that put him out of Barkley's sight, he turned south and rode along the bottom of the low area in the direction of the Indian camp. He could hear the crack of a rifle firing in the distance, far enough away to be on the far side of the encampment.

He grimaced at the sound of it. There was no telling what Barkley had in mind and, by the sound of the shot, Sykes was still with the young men, out on the hunt, and the camp was unguarded.

Many Arrows sat on the cliff where he had seen the light the night before. His face and hands were painted for war, and he wore his long eagle headdress. His horse was decorated and ready, and he held his tomahawk and lance in one hand. His other hand grasped the reins of his horse. There was no use for an empty rifle.

He had prepared as Napi had told him, but he was alone. The others had said they believed him, but they had chosen to follow the buffalo instead of their war chief. He stared above the white plain below him until he heard a rifle fire. So the white man still had bullets he had not shared with them.

Many Arrows glanced down in the direction he knew the hunters had gone, and then he turned his head and gazed at the column of soldiers approaching the camp. At once he kicked at his horse's sides until it plunged down the steep hillside in front of him, sliding and slipping as it went.

Barkley continued nearly to the top of the ridge between the soldiers and the camp before he signaled a stop. When the men had pulled up behind him, he motioned for Sergeant Pearce to ride forward.

"It's time to teach these savages a lesson," he said.

"What, sir?"

"We're going to surround them and wipe them out."

"But, sir—"

"They're off the reservation, aren't they?"

"But there must be mostly women and children down there. It sounds like the men are hunting beyond the camp."

"Don't worry. We can take care of them later. And Pearce, there are no women and children down there—just Indians."

The sergeant swallowed as he faced the lieutenant, but he said no more.

Barkley stared at the top of the rise, his eyes

bright with an anticipation he didn't try to hide as he gave Sergeant Pearce his orders. "Take the bugler with you and surround the camp. When the men are in position, have him sound the attack. And make sure all the men understand—no survivors! It's time the redskins learned who's in charge out here."

Sergeant Pearce clenched his jaw as he rode down the back of the hill. He gave the orders, and two lines of men and horses moved off until only Corporal Eddy was left, standing still and staring in the direction of the camp.

The sergeant hardened his voice. "You came out here to fight—didn't you, corporal? You aren't going to fold now, are you?"

"I fought in the war, sir," responded the corporal. "And I did my part. But nobody ever asked me to kill women and children before." Corporal Eddy could not hide the horror in his eyes.

"You should never have gone hunting with them." Pearce jerked his horse away with unnecessary force.

The corporal picked up his reins and rode to close the circle at the back of the hill. He drew his revolver from its holster.

At the sound of the bugle he dashed up the hill with the others, but before he even reached the top the shooting began. The troops on the far side must have been closer to the camp. A moment later he tore through the circle of lodges and he raised his revolver as a young boy ran out of the tepee, pointed a bow and arrow at him. He fired and the child crumpled.

Right behind the boy, a young woman fled into the snow. It was Night Quail. Eddy pointed his revolver at her until tears stung his eyes. He cursed as he rode closer to her, his voice choked with sobs.

While he held his fire, another soldier rode up on

his flank and aimed at the girl. Eddy lunged his horse into the path of the soldier. As the trooper's horse veered to one side, Eddy faced Night Quail again and, throwing down his revolver, he reached out as his horse galloped by her side.

He pulled her into the saddle ahead of him and turned and spurred his horse out of the camp. At the same time he heard Barkley's voice, ordering him to stop, but he kept going. A bullet plowed into his shoulder, but he only held Night Quail closer and clenched his hand on the reins. Another bullet dug into his leg before he reached the brush beyond the camp and could swerve his horse to one side.

Sam Ross was beyond the camp, halfway to the hunting party, before the sound of the bugle chilled his very soul. As he rode past the first buffalo lying in the snow, he saw Sykes coming toward him. He shouted to the agent in the instant before the firing broke out behind him.

The Indians were already riding hard behind Sykes, and they raced on past the two white men as soon as they understood what Ross told them.

"Barkley's in the lead," explained Ross, turning with Sykes to follow the warriors.

"Who are they shooting at?"

"I saw them circling the camp. Sounds like they're planning a massacre."

Sykes wanted to curse and shout and scream like the Indians, but he only dug in his spurs and leaned out over the bay's neck, giving the stallion his head as he ran toward the camp beside Ross.

Before Sykes reached the edge of the camp, he saw movement on the riverside, and then Red Beads, with First Moon in her arms, broke out of the bushes and ran toward the encampment.

"You get the kid," yelled Sykes. "I'll get her. Go in front of her."

"Got it," called Ross. He galloped past Red Beads, snatching the boy from her arms. At the same time, Sykes lifted Red Beads and held her across his saddle. Then the agent wheeled and headed back into the brush.

As he stormed into the bushes, Sykes looked back and saw Many Arrows racing his horse into the camp. The war chief rode with his tomahawk raised, his mouth open in a shriek.

"Let me go!" cried Red Beads. "He will die, and I will die with him."

"No," argued Sykes. "I will go back for him."

"He called to me."

"You stay with Ross, you hear?" Sykes lowered Red Beads to the ground as the scout swung down. "You keep her here, Ross," urged Sykes.

"You can't do anything back there except get yourself killed," warned Ross.

Before the scout finished speaking, Corporal Eddy broke through the brush. He was still holding Night Quail across his saddle, but his face was ashen with the effort to stay on his horse. Blood covered his chest and leg.

"Night Quail," cried Red Beads, reaching out to the horse.

Eddy slid Night Quail to the ground as Red Beads ran to her side.

Sykes turned and rode back the way he had come.

Grabs Thorns followed Flying Hawk to the opening of the tepee, but before she could see outside, she heard a shot and the chief slumped to the snow. Seeing that he still lived, she looked frantically around her for a weapon. There was only the fire. She seized a burning stick from it and ran to the doorway, thrusting it in front of the horse racing past her. The soldier had been aiming at Flying Hawk, but his shot went wild as his horse plunged to one side, away from the firebrand. Then he was gone and another soldier reared up before her.

As he rode up, fighting his shying horse, Sergeant Pearce pointed his revolver at the Indian woman bent over the fallen chief. But before he could pull the trigger, a picture of his own wife standing over his body flashed into his mind. He cursed as he held his horse to the firebrand and then brought the revolver down over the woman's head. She dropped unconscious on top of her husband. In that instant, he heard Lieutenant Barkley's voice, yelling orders above the rest of the din, but he did not look in his direction.

Cole Sykes pulled up outside the edge of the encampment. It was already clear what kind of slaughter Barkley had ordered. He pulled his rifle as he dropped from the saddle. There was one man, and only one man, he wanted in his sights now, and he knelt on one knee behind a log, waiting for his chance.

With bows and arrows against the army guns, few of the warriors made it through the camp more than once. Only Many Arrows seemed to ride as though no bullet could bring him down. When he reached the far side of the encampment, he turned and plowed through the middle of it where the fighting was the thickest, and again he came through it unharmed. When he had lost both his tomahawk and lance, buried deep in the bodies of bluejackets, he pulled his knife from the sheath at his waist and wheeled his horse on its hind feet. Only a few war cries could be heard now, and his voice was already hoarse from screaming, but he raised it again as he rode ahead.

He stabbed and slashed as he went, the blade of his knife red before he had gone a dozen feet. And as before, he rode through the camp unharmed.

He wheeled his horse one more time, and then he saw the white man, Cole Sykes, the man that had taken his wife captive, kneeling like a coward behind a log. Many Arrows raised his knife high as he swerved his horse toward the agent.

As soon as Cole Sykes had the man he wanted in his sights, he followed him with his rifle, making sure of the shot. In the instant before he squeezed the trigger, a weight thudded across his back and an arm circled his neck. He could not move enough to get his hands to the arm strangling him, and he tightened the cords of his neck, trying to get enough air to keep from blacking out.

"Turn, white man, and face your death!" It was Many Arrows' voice, and the chief spoke in near-perfect English.

Sykes could not do anything until the arm around his neck loosened enough for him to fill his lungs with air and then he twisted, slamming his fist behind him as he tried to roll under the weight of the warrior. Hitting the side of the Indian was like hitting a solid wall, but Sykes did not notice. He'd seen Many Arrows' last ride through the camp, and he had to know where that knife was.

As soon as he saw the blade, Sykes put both hands on the warrior's wrist and tried to break the momentum of the downward thrust, but he could not stop it before its point stabbed into his chest.

Chapter 29

"Can you keep these women here?" asked Ross, as he helped Eddy sit down and brace his back against a small tree.

"Yes, if you can get them down on either side of me."

Ross spoke to the women and they nodded. Night Quail moved to Eddy's side, so close that the soldier could put his arm around her shoulders.

"I told her you took her as a captive because you want her for a wife," said Ross. "She'll probably stay easy enough."

The young man looked at Night Quail's bowed head. "Well, I do," he confessed. "If I pull through this—goddamn it, Ross, I do."

"Night Quail," Ross spoke to the Indian girl. "You take care of him so he will live and you'll have many children." Then he turned to Red Beads, and spoke to her until she too sat down beside the soldier, holding First Moon close.

"You're going to have to keep her here," Ross changed to English. "Take hold of her arm. She's pretending to agree, but she's determined to die with Many Arrows."

The corporal reached out and grabbed Red

Beads' wrist, holding it on the ground between them. His face was white, but he still looked determined when he peered up at the scout again. "You tell Night Quail what I'm doing," he smiled. "I don't want her to get jealous."

Ross translated the message as quickly as he could, and turned and leaped on his horse.

There was no way to save the Indians if Barkley had ordered a massacre. From the methodical sound of the shooting, it must be nearly over. He hoped that Lieutenant William Barkley was still alive and was going to stay alive long enough to know who killed him.

As soon as he saw the uniform he was searching for, he started around the outside of the camp, trying to get as close as he could without being hit first. When Ross was near enough, he slid his horse to a stop, raised his rifle to his shoulder, and pulled the trigger.

There was no explosion. The bullet had misfired and, when he tried to get it out, it was jammed in the chamber. He threw the gun to the ground as the lieutenant wheeled his horse, turned and pointed his revolver at something on the ground behind a log.

The lieutenant fired as Ross rode forward.

The scout stopped as soon as he could see Many Arrows and Cole Sykes struggling together on the ground behind the log, the knife in Many Arrows' hand poised over Sykes' chest.

Ross could not tell whether Barkley had hit either of them, but as the lieutenant rode closer and took a second, careful aim, the scout leaped to the ground. The only weapon in sight was a bow lying beside a fallen warrior. He grabbed it and then searched around for an arrow. The only one he could see was lying in the body of a soldier. The bluejacket was sprawled face up, staring at the sky, his hands wrapped around the shaft poking from his chest. Ross grabbed the arrow and slapped the shaft to the bow string as he turned toward the lieutenant.

"Barkley, you bastard!" he screamed, as he stretched the rawhide as far as it would go. At the same time he heard a horse coming up fast behind him, but he did not turn. He waited until he could see the startled look of recognition on William Barkley's face, and then he let go of the string. He saw Barkley clutch at his chest and heave backward out of his saddle, and then he whirled to face the rider behind him.

Sergeant Pearce was half a dozen feet behind the scout, and his revolver was raised and aimed, but his eyes were not on Ross. They were on the falling commander. The sergeant watched fixedly Barkley's body hit the ground and lay still.

"You're in command, Pearce," yelled Ross. "Call it off!"

At once the sergeant wheeled his horse and shouted orders to the men. A moment later the bugle sounded.

Cole Sykes felt the burning in his chest, but he heard and saw nothing except the Indian on top of him. He strained against the arm holding the knife with both hands, twisting until he finally managed to get out from under it. As he moved to one side, Many Arrows raised the knife again. The blow Sykes struck to the Indian's face made little difference.

The agent kept his eyes on the knife. That was one thing he'd learned at Rawlins. For a moment he got a straight-arm hold on the Indian's wrist, and he drove his fist into Many Arrows' side. At the same time the Indian dropped flat on Sykes' body, circling his neck with his arm while he wrapped his leg over

Sykes, so that the agent could not lift his knee to brace himself.

Sykes gripped the warrior's wrist with his left hand as he fought to get his right hand up between them. When he finally reached the Indian's chin, he put the heel of his hand under it and shoved upward, thrusting Many Arrows' head backwards. At the same time, he could feel his strength ebbing while the Indian seemed fiercer than ever.

In what he knew was his last effort, he let himself go suddenly limp, and then as the chief started downward, he rolled his head to one side and brought his shoulder up into Many Arrows' chest, trying to knock the wind out of him. For an instant the Indian rolled to one side and, in that second, Sykes shoved out from under him and scrambled to his feet, pulling his Colt.

He leveled the gun at Many Arrows as he stood up, facing him, his knife raised to strike again.

"By God, Many Arrows, I'm not your enemy! What are you doing?"

"Stop it, both of you," bellowed Ross from behind Sykes. "Didn't you hear that bugle? It's over."

Many Arrows stared at the two of them for several seconds before he slowly lowered his hand and then looked past the white men to where his people were lying dead.

Sykes lowered his Colt and put it away. He too looked around him, staring in silence. No oaths were strong enough for what he could see.

Barkley's body was lying where it had fallen, face up. As soon as he saw it, Sykes stepped over the log and walked to the lieutenant's side. While he stood looking down, he pulled out the skinning knife hanging from his belt and put his foot on the side of Barkley's head. He bent over and seized the top of his hair.

* * *

Corporal Eddy fought off the dizziness as long as he could, blood seeped from both his wounds. He could still hear the sounds of the battle when his back slipped from the trunk of the tree.

As soon as he fell unconscious, Red Beads stood up and spoke to the other woman. Night Quail looked at the soldier for a moment before she stood up and walked away from him at Red Beads' side. While they were pushing through the brush, the bugle sounded ahead of them.

Sergeant Pearce stayed with the soldiers on the side of the hill overlooking the camp until the wounded and dead had been taken from the camp. There were not many casualties compared to those of the Indians. He could see only a few Indians moving about, most of them women and children. The only man he could see was Many Arrows, walking through the camp between Sam Ross and Cole Sykes. He watched the three of them approach Flying Hawk's lodge and carry the chief's body inside.

A moment later Many Arrows appeared again, calling out in the direction of the brush until Red Beads and another woman and a child ran from the bushes into the camp.

As he turned to order the detachment to leave, he saw a cavalry horse walk out of the bushes the two Indian women had been hiding in, and he sent a half dozen men down to search in that area.

Many Arrows sat behind the fire in his father's tepee while Sam Ross and Cole Sykes bent over the wounded chief. When it was clear they could not stop the bleeding and his father would not live long, Many

Arrows motioned the white men away. As he spoke, ordering them out of the camp, his father put up his hand.

"No, my son," he whispered.

"I will avenge this," vowed Many Arrows. "The Blackfoot will kill every white person on these plains." He turned to face Sykes. "Run, white man, while you have the chance. In the spring I will gather all of the bands together. It was meant to be! Last night I was told in my dream to paint and prepare for war. And was not the Spirit with me the whole time? I alone of all the warriors live. And I live for vengeance!"

Flying Hawk raised his hand a few inches. "Bring me my medicine bundle and then prop me up that I may speak better."

"Let's go," suggested Ross.

"No," Sykes disagreed. "I have to argue on the chief's side."

"Let's go, I said. If he wants to open his bundle, we don't belong in here."

Cole Sykes stared at the scout, and then he stood up and followed him out.

"There is little time," gasped Flying Hawk when the white men left. "I will speak first, and then we will have the ceremony. Sit beside me, and hear what I tell you."

As soon as Many Arrows sat down, Flying Hawk spoke without stopping.

"You have proven yourself in battle again. You have proven that your Spirit is strong in you. You will be a great leader of our people. I believe you will take my place as the chief of all the bands of the Blackfoot nation. But you must lead them forward, though it cost you more than you think you can stand. The white man is too strong. He has no end to his bullets, and food always comes to him so that he can make war in the winter as well as the summer. The way of our people must be the way of peace on the land they have left us. We hunted away from those lands after we had promised to stay. Leave those of us here that were chosen to die here. Take those that were saved back to the lands that are still theirs. Lead them well for their benefit and not for your own—and your Spirit will not leave you. And now I will transfer the medicine bundle of the Hawk to you. Sing with me the first of the seven songs—all of you—"

As Cole Sykes rode away he heard the chanting begin in the lodge behind him and then, a moment later, the wail of death took its place.

Chapter 30

The water Ross used to wash the wound on Sykes' chest was ice cold. There were flakes of snow in the air again, but Sykes sat on the rock at the edge of the stream, feeling neither the cold nor the frigid water.

"You'll live," commented Ross as he studied the wound with the blood rinsed away from it. "Many Arrows keeps his knife good and sharp. It's a clean cut." Then he laughed to himself as he stepped back. "What did you do with that scalp?"

Cole Sykes stood up, reached into his coat pocket and held it up. "I thought Forbes might like it. Let's get up there while it'll still mess up the polish on that big, fancy desk of his."

"I don't think that's such a good idea," scowled Ross at the trophy. "And it won't do you any good, will it?"

"It'll feel damned good. I know where I'm headed after today, and I'm going to need some memories like that to see me through."

"You don't understand the army very well, do you? Hell, they won today. They aren't going to hold it against you. If anybody noticed you beside Barkley, all they could have seen you do was fight an Indian. Just keep your mouth shut, and you'll probably be congratulated. I'm in a worse spot than you. Sergeant Pearce saw me put that arrow into Barkley."

"You did that?"

The scout grinned. "Put on your shirt, Sykes, and give me that scalp. I'll get it cured properly for you and hang it on a lance all decorated with fancy things so you can put it in your office. Just you and me and the Indians'll need to know whose it is."

"What's Forbes going to do to you when Pearce tells him?" wondered Sykes as he handed the scalp to Ross and picked up his shirt.

"How do I know? Maybe Pearce won't tell him. He sure called it off fast enough after Barkley fell, but I'm not figuring on hanging around the fort until I find out. Taking care of this scalp is more important, anyway. I'm going back to see what I can do to help."

"Why do you figure Pearce might not say anything?"

"The way he sat watching me do it, with a gun pointed at me all along."

"I'll be damned," Sykes shook his head in disbelief. "Don't go too far away until I've had a talk with the sergeant."

Sykes went to his room in the hotel and took off his blood-soaked clothes. When he saw that the wound was still bleeding, he got some cloth that he kept for bandages out of his saddlebags. He folded a piece over the wound and then tied a long strip of it around his chest to hold the bandage in place. After that he put on clean clothes and a heavy woolen coat and left the hotel.

He went to the Trapper's Last Chance and had a beer before he rode up to the fort.

Passing through the gate, he could see an unusual

amount of activity, even though there was enough snow in the air to nearly obscure the far end of the fort.

He rode to the front of the barracks, looking for the sergeant. When he did not find Pearce, he asked a soldier standing on the porch if he had seen him.

"He was going to report to the colonel, sir, and then see to the wounded men."

Sykes turned his horse. It was probably too late, but he might as well find out. He loped along the side of the fort until he could see that the headquarters building was dark inside, and then he turned back and went instead to the barracks where the wounded men would be.

Before Sykes could swing down at the hitching rail, Sergeant Pearce came out the door, hesitated for a moment when he saw Sykes, and then walked toward the agent.

"Looks like that Indian didn't get the best of you," he noted, studying the agent with a level face.

"No," agreed Sykes. "Ross called him off in time."

"Sam Ross?"

"Yes."

"Good man in a fight," approved the sergeant, his eyes still fixed on Sykes.

"Best that's ever sided me." Sykes took a deep breath and then let his approval show in his eyes.

The sergeant turned away. "We found Corporal Eddy in the brush," he said. "He was badly injured, and there were signs around him that he'd been left there by the Indians to die, but I think he has a chance of pulling through."

"One of the lucky ones today, then," remarked Sykes, picking up his reins.

"Yes," concurred the sergeant. The officer walked away.

It was still dark in the headquarters building when Sykes passed it on the way to the colonel's house. The agent's eyes were hard and cold as he went up the steps. At the sight of the colonel and Tricia sitting at the dining room table, he pulled his hat lower over his eyes. Although the colonel seemed to be eating with his usual appetite, Tricia sat back in her chair with her head down and her hands in her lap. As soon as Sykes knocked, she straightened and stared at the window while the colonel stood up and started for the door.

When Sykes moved far enough into the light from the window so that she could see him, she jumped up and ran past her uncle to the door and flung it open. Eagerly, she reached both hands out to him.

"Oh, Cole! Are you all right?" She threw her arms around his waist and held him tightly.

"Tricia, what is the meaning of this?" demanded Colonel Forbes.

"Cole, Cole!" she sobbed, her voice muffled against his coat. Then she looked up and put her hand to his hat. "Take off your hat and coat. I have to see that you're all right."

She pulled off his hat while he fumbled with the buttons on his coat.

"Tricia," Sykes halted her. "I have business with your uncle."

"I know," she admitted, her voice broken as she watched him.

When Colonel Forbes took his eyes off Sykes for a moment and stared at Tricia's back, the agent slid out of his coat. Instantly Tricia put both arms around him and held him again. "Oh, you are all right!" she cried. He put his arm around her shoulders and held her, feeling the sobs shake through her.

"Did your uncle tell you Barkley's men practically wiped out Flying Hawk's band?"

"No! Oh no! He only said there'd been a fight. All of them—Red Beads? and—and First Moon? Oh, my God!"

He held her close and he swallowed before he spoke. She hadn't asked what had happened to Barkley. "No," he told her. "They're all right, and so is Grabs Thorns, but Flying Hawk is dead."

"Many Arrows?"

"No."

She put her head on his shoulder. "What about William?"

"He's dead."

"Oh." She became quiet, but she did not loosen her hold around his waist.

Colonel Forbes cleared his throat as he strode back to the dining room table. "That will be enough of that," he stormed. "Sykes, you can't come barging into my home whenever you feel like it. If you have business with me, you'll conduct it at headquarters like everyone else. Good night, sir!"

Cole Sykes slid his arm away from Tricia's shoulders and stepped in the direction of the officer. "I'm here to find out where Barkley got his orders to—"

"Cole! Uncle John! Stop it! Hasn't there been enough fighting and hatred?" As she spoke she reached out to Sykes' arm and pulled him back. He looked down at her.

She met his eyes steadily until he took a deep breath. He let it out slowly and faced the colonel again.

"Colonel Forbes, I'll be at headquarters first thing in the morning." He frowned at Tricia, his eyes questioning.

"Thank you," she whispered.

Chapter 31

Andrew Madden waited impatiently for the stagecoach to unload. This was one shipment he was going to oversee himself. He stood on the sidewalk while they hoisted the box with the rifles down from the top of the stage. When it was on the ground he walked over to it.

Then he put one foot on it and took the last letter he had received from Sykes from his pocket. Folded inside of it was a brief note from Patricia Ashley telling of her intention to persuade Cole Sykes to marry her and inviting Madden to the wedding. He shook his head as he looked from the one piece of paper, with its grim, terse account of the massacre, to the other note. The rifles weren't the only thing he wanted to see about.

While the two letters fluttered in the cold December wind, he stared for several minutes in the direction of the Blackfoot country. The troops from Fort Mason had not yet arrived and he wasn't going anyplace until they did, but he wished they'd hurry.

Tricia smiled openly at the lean, greying man sitting at her right, in the place where Cole Sykes had sat the first time he had come to the house. "Mr. Madden," she said, "I haven't had a chance to tell you how good it was of you to make certain the rifles got here. I suppose everyone else has already said it, but I want to say thanks, too."

"Well, thank you, Miss Ashley. I must say your repeated invitation to visit here had something to do with it."

"Oh, but I know your reputation for caring about your work. I've heard you talk about the problems of the Indians before, and you sound more like Cole . . ." she glanced down the long table and then back at the guest, ". . . than most of the other men I hear talking about them."

"I've never heard Sykes say anything that sounded like he cared about anyone."

Surprised, she looked at Madden and then she leaned closer to him. "No one cares more about the Blackfoot, unless it's Mr. Ross. But you'll never know how Cole feels by talking to him. I hope you'll be able to see past that—that rough exterior to what he's truly like."

Andrew Madden smiled, and then he glanced down the table toward the agent. "All I hope now is that he doesn't get jealous of the way you're talking to me."

Tricia straightened and then gazed at Sykes until their eyes met. Madden looked from one to the other. When Tricia looked back at the chief clerk, her smile was even broader. "Mr. Sykes knows very well there is no one he needs to be jealous of."

Andrew Madden shook his head. "You can see something I don't."

"You haven't been around him enough, that's all. Sam Ross and almost all the other men I know see the good in him." She laughed shortly. "Only Uncle John can't bend enough to see it, but I've told him he has to be polite, at least, for my sake—"

"Does your uncle know your—ah—personal plans for Sykes?"

"Hush," Tricia laughed again. "Cole's still afraid he's going back to prison, and I haven't been able to force him to propose." She leaned confidentially toward the chief clerk again. "Mr. Madden, I know perfectly well how much influence you have in Washington. There is no reason why you can't get Cole a pardon, or at least a parole."

"And appoint you as the parole officer, I suppose."

"What an excellent idea!"

The clerk cleared his throat and looked at Sykes again. The agent's face was set in the same taut lines that Madden had first seen when Sykes walked out of the cell block at Rawlins. Except for the one exchange of glances with Patricia, Madden had never seen it any other way. "I don't know, Miss Ashley," he pondered. "I guess I'll have to judge the wisdom of that for myself. First I'd like to know what the Indians think of him."

"But there aren't any near here right now. Many Arrows took the rest of his people and went north to join Lone Medicine's band for the winter."

"How far away are they?"

"I don't know, but Cole is thinking of going to see them soon."

"He is?"

"Yes, the Indians don't like to travel in the winter, and they had quite a bit of meat from the hunt that ended . . . that awful day, so they aren't likely to come here."

"It's not going to be any easier for him to travel than it is them."

"You said you wanted to know Cole, Mr. Madden. Well, you should go with him, and I've just decided that I'm going, too. I want to see Red Beads again. She should have her new baby by now."

"Who?"

"Red Beads. She's Many Arrows' wife. Thank God, Cole was able to save her and First Moon."

"You know, Miss Ashley, Indian agents don't make a lot of money. How are you going to manage to live on it?"

Tricia smiled at Sykes as she answered, "Very well, thank you."

Sergeant Pearce included Corporal Eddy in the detail to escort the chief clerk to the Indian camp, even though the young soldier still limped on his wounded leg. When Pearce saw the number of articles the soldier was stuffing into his bedroll, he continued to watch him without appearing to do so. Corporal Eddy left nothing of value in the barracks.

It was just as well, thought the sergeant. The army could stand another deserter. Anyone who runs from shooting women and children, hell, what good was he in the army, anyway? Sergeant Pearce thought of his wife and children while he stared at his own blanket, but he did not load more of his own belongings into it than he needed for the trip.

The clouds broke on the afternoon of the first day away from the fort, and they traveled the rest of the way in the sun. It would have been a short trip in the summer, but breaking a trail through the snow was arduous, and it took three days to reach the Indian camp.

As soon as they arrived, Corporal Eddy asked to go with the others into the camp, and Sergeant Pearce agreed.

Many Arrows invited him along with the others into his tepee. When Eddy stepped inside, Night Quail was sitting at the end of the women's side nearest the opening. The chief motioned the corporal to the lowest place on the men's side, across the opening from the girl.

As he sat down Corporal Eddy faced her directly, and when she finally looked up at him, he smiled openly. She smiled slightly, mostly with her eyes, before she looked down again. After that, Corporal Eddy heard nothing of the others' talk.

Night Quail knew that he had come for her.

When the first pipe was finished, Sykes turned to the clerk. "Madden, I have to tell you something. Watch out for Many Arrows. He understands everything you say, and he can speak English, too, when he wants to make sure you know what's happening." Cole Sykes laughed as he looked at the Indian's expression. "You know, Many Arrows, ever since I found out, I've been trying to think of all the things I've said in front of you."

"Sam Ross warned you that we understood more than you think," replied Many Arrows. "He taught me along with his own children so that I did not know at times which language I spoke."

While the others stared at the chief, Ross chuckled. "It was funny at times, Sykes, but Many Arrows always wanted me to keep it a secret."

"Cole Sykes," intoned Many Arrows, "I have heard you speak much. I have seen much that you have done. I have felt your strength. You speak with a single tongue. You are a brave warrior."

Tricia leaned forward slightly and studied Andrew Madden's expression while Many Arrows raked a coal from the fire and put a handful of sweetgrass on it.

Then Many Arrows reached behind him, and when he straightened again, he held a long lance, its point high above the smudge from the burning grass. He passed the head of the lance through the smudge seven times, repeating a chant that Sam Ross joined him in saying. Then he handed the lance to Cole Sykes.

Sykes held it high so that the top of the lance and the objects dangling from it were in the shadows.

"Thank you, Many Arrows," he said. "I'll keep this mounted on the wall at the agency so your people can see it whenever they come there."

Andrew Madden looked intently up at the head of the lance for several seconds. "We have quite a collection of Indian art objects at the house," he said, while he continued to study the lance. He looked at Cole Sykes, glanced past him for a moment at Ross, and then looked back at Sykes.

"Barkley?" He made no sound as he moved his lips.

Sykes' nod was perceptible only to the chief clerk.

Madden glanced at Tricia and then stared into the smudge above the sweetgrass for several minutes. He did not seem to hear or see anything else in the lodge until the next pipe was passed to him.